SUBMARINER SINCLAIR

Submariner Sinclair Series
Book One

John Wingate

SAPERE
BOOKS

SUBMARINER SINCLAIR

Published by Sapere Books.

20 Windermere Drive, Leeds, England, LS17 7UZ,
United Kingdom

saperebooks.com

ISBN: 978-1-80055-209-8

Written for those who follow after, this book is dedicated to the Officers and Ratings of The Fighting Tenth who did not return.

THE SHIP'S COMPANY OF HIS MAJESTY'S SUBMARINE *RUGGED*

Lieutenant James Croxton, R.N., Commanding Officer

Lieutenant John Easton, D.S.C., R.N., First Lieutenant

Lieutenant Andrew Hickey, R.N., Navigating Officer

Sub-Lieutenant Peter Sinclair, R.N., Third Hand

C.P.O. George Withers, Coxswain

C.E.R.A. Reginald Potts, Chief E.R.A.

Acting P.O. Jack Weston, Second Coxswain

Acting P.O. Rodney Slater, Torpedo Instructor

E.R.A. Joseph Saunders, Outside E.R.A.

Leading Seaman David Elliott, Higher S/M Detector

Acting Leading Seaman Michael Flint , Leading Torpedoman

Signalman Alec Goddard, Signalman

Able Seaman George Stack, Gunlayer and 'chef'

Ordinary Seaman Tom O'Riley, Ward Room Flunkey

Able Seaman William Hawkins, Seaman

Able Seaman Alexander Davis, Seaman and Trainer

Able Seaman Henry Bowles, Seaman and Trainer

Ordinary Seaman John Smith, T.I.'s Mate

Stoker Patrick O'Connor, Stoker

S.P.O. George Hicks, Stoker Petty Officer

Ordinary Seaman Henry Keating, Telegraphsman and Telephone Operator

COMMANDOS

Captain Jan Widdecombe, Captain i/c

Commando Graves

Commando Jarvis

Commando Jock Macdonald

CHAPTER 1

First Command — The Narrow Seas

"Let go!"

As the little ship swung to her anchor in the tideway one mile off Ramsgate, the young Captain glanced at his watch.

Just in time for a quick supper before the convoy comes round North Foreland from Southend, he thought.

Wearily he unslung his binoculars and hitched them over the brass voicepipe. He clattered down the steel ladder but halted on the middle rung.

Looks nice enough, but it's all too quiet! he mused as his eyes scanned the peaceful scene.

Half a mile to the north-east, the massive cliffs rose from the grey deep. The first fingers of the setting sun stole across the sea and the rose-tinted cliffs were reflected on the placid surface of the water. Only the gentle hiss of the tide, as it raced across the swinging anchor-cable, betrayed the danger of these treacherous waters.

Peter Sinclair, Sub-Lieutenant, Royal Navy, Commanding Officer of Chaser 25, continued to enjoy the peace of the evening. He turned his head to the east, once again noting the ship's position. He was anchored in the Downs, off the quicksands of the Goodwins, now known as 'The Graveyard'. Some two dozen rusty sticks jutted out of the sea and Peter instinctively counted them again.

"Twenty-four," he muttered.

They were the masts of the wrecks now littering these dangerous waters — wrecks of the obstinate colliers and merchant ships sunk by the enemy, only nineteen miles distant. Shelled by the gunfire from German gun-emplacements on Cap Gris Nez, torpedoed by lurking E-boats, blasted by mines, and caught by the shifting sands, these grim reminders poked their rust-scarred masts skywards. But, undaunted, the convoys kept on coming — one westerly from Southend to Portsmouth, and one easterly; once a week, undeterred by the enemy's fury, they still passed through the Narrow Seas, for coal and food were the lifeblood of the Island. These sad, skeleton-like masts emphasised the sacrifice which the merchant sailors were making.

"Blast the Germans!" Peter growled, as he walked aft to the Ward Room. He reached the hatch and turned to give one last look to the north-eastward, but the convoy was not yet in sight. He was descending the ladder when he heard the spluttering of an aircraft. Peter turned his head and his grey eyes took in the outline of a single-seater fighter that swept three hundred feet above him.

The Spitfire crackled, coughed, and gusts of black smoke belched from its engine and he heard the whine of the wind as it hissed along the shapely wings.

She'll never clear the cliffs! Peter thought as he stood mesmerised by the tragedy of the returning fighter. She hit the sea half a mile away, in a large plume of spray.

Sickened by the sight, Peter began to turn away, but at that moment his heart leaped as a tiny white mushroom floated like thistledown above the subsiding foam to billow gently upon the sea.

"He's baled out," Peter yelled. "Action stations, Number One!"

The tousled head of Peter's First Lieutenant appeared through the Ward Room hatch. "Aye, aye, sir," shouted Sub-

Lieutenant James McDonald, as he rushed for'd to call the hands from the mess decks. "Action stations, action stations!"

The seamen poured out from below, and the little ship gathered speed and was soon alongside the crumpled silk parachute, which had now become sodden in the water.

The pilot lay on his back, his yellow Mae West a bright spot of colour.

"Well, that's sure dinkum of you, Cobbers!" a broad Australian voice twanged from the water as a tanned face grinned up at them.

Two seamen went over the side and hauled him to the scrambling net, and then the pilot slipped from his harness, whilst helping hands bundled him over the guard rails.

"Come and have supper!" Peter greeted him.

"Thanks, Cobber, I will."

Pools of water flooded the coconut matting on the deck as the dripping man padded forward to Peter's cabin below the bridge. The cook handed him a mug of hot tea as he went by the galley.

"Thanks a lot, chum."

"That's all right, sir," the burly cook grinned, "plenty more where that came from."

After a hot meal, Peter and Jamie McDonald took their temporary guest on deck. The sun was sinking below the horizon, and from Ramsgate's breakwater a white bow wave grew larger every moment.

"Bit late, that rescue launch!" the pilot observed.

The launch was soon alongside, its throaty exhaust coughing and spluttering in the swell.

"So long!" Peter said as he shook hands. "Good hunting!"

"Thanks — and the same to you."

The eyes of the two young men met. Their two lives were to go different ways. Peter's, to join up with the convoy now three miles distant and swinging down upon the tide. The pilot's, to give his life over the New Guinea jungles, and to win a posthumous Victoria Cross.

The launch was soon lost to view and already the green, red and white lights of the buoys could be seen winking in the gathering dusk. Ten minutes later, the black outline of the first ship slid by Chaser 25. It was the leading destroyer, shepherding her flock through the intricate swept channel of the Downs. Silhouette after black silhouette lumbered after her, until Peter had counted fourteen. Close on either side, diminutive M.L.s fussed around their charges, hustling them into their two columns.

They were now entering the dangerous area, for off the south-western buoy the German guns would inevitably start shelling from Cap Gris Nez. The shaded blue lights of signalling lanterns winked in the darkness, urging the ships to make all possible speed. Streamers of black smoke trailed from the squat funnels. The tide was under them, as they slid past the black outline of Dover Castle.

As 'tail-end Charlie', Chaser 25 was stationed at the rear of the convoy. Her duty was to keep the laggards closed up, and, in the event of disaster, to pick up survivors.

"There she flashes!" Peter murmured to Jamie, who was enjoying the night air on the bridge with his young Captain. It was futile to turn in until they were past the shelling area and far better to be blown to bits in the open than caught below in a steel coffin.

Sure enough, fine on the port bow of the convoy, the white light of the south-west Folkestone buoy winked its impatient warning as both young officers looked southwards towards the

French coast, which was now invisible in the enveloping darkness.

A vivid white light suddenly flickered along the southern horizon and the young Captain reached for his steel helmet, put it squarely on his head and tapped its crown for luck. Methodically he adjusted the strap so that it only reached the tip of his chin for he had once seen a man's neck broken by the shock of the helmet flying back against the blast, when the strap had been fastened beneath his chin.

At the head of the convoy, an orange flame burst and a sharp crack reverberated against the cliffs as the first shells exploded on the water. Spouts of foam cascaded upwards and golden plumes of spray showered gently downwards, lit by the fierce explosions of the next salvoes.

Peter tried to hide his eyes from the blinding flashes. The light dazzled him, so that he was blind for minutes afterwards.

"We're entering the area now," he said to the steel-helmeted lookouts, crouched by their Lewis guns in the wings of the bridge.

"So I can flippin' well see," the port lookout muttered to himself and his teeth gleamed as he grinned in the darkness.

"Start counting seventy-five," muttered Peter to his Number One, as the French coast danced into light again.

Both men glanced at their watches and waited with a sinking void in their stomachs. "Seventy-two, seventy-three, seventy…" Jamie counted. An ear-splitting crack interrupted his counting, and bright orange flashes lit up the bridge. Peter's sharply-drawn features turned towards the explosions but his eyes were shut to prevent dazzling.

"All right, Number One, pass the word, 'Normal Shelling Routine'."

Jamie moved to the brass voicepipe and shouted down it, "Normal Shelling Routine!" and from the wheelhouse below them, the Quartermaster repeated the order, his voice hollow and distant in the thick darkness.

Jamie went to the drawer of the chart table and fumbled for the large whistle which he hung around his neck as a long and distant rumbling, like midsummer thunder, reverberated along the French coast.

"There goes the sound of the guns! Strange, isn't it, after the arrival of the bricks?" said Jamie, half to himself. Once again the French coast lit up as he glanced at his watch. Just over a minute later, he put the silver whistle to his lips, took an enormous breath, and a long whistle-blast added its contribution to the cacophony.

"Down, all of you!" Peter shouted.

The men on the upper deck threw themselves flat, covering their heads with their arms. Seconds later, four spouts hurtled upwards, two hundred yards from their port bow and close to the dark mass of the last ship in the seaward column. A fierce blue light split wide the night, which became a crescendo of sound.

The men in the Chaser climbed to their feet again, but, as suddenly, the French coast flickered once more. Again the whistle blew.

Peter was at the voicepipe adjusting his course, but he threw himself to the deck and it was as well that he did so, for suddenly the night became as day in a holocaust of vivid flashes. Shells burst round them, one fifty yards short, and three over, in a perfect 'straddle'. A peculiar fluttering whined through the air and a sharp jar shook the little ship when the clang of metal upon metal rang from aft.

"We're hit, I think, Number One. Go and investigate." But already Jamie had bounded down the ladder and was back within the minute. "Only a splinter against one of the depth charges, sir. No damage."

"Better shooting than last week!"

"Yes, they are improving; and so they should, the perishing swine!"

"They get enough practice," muttered Peter as he moved to the voicepipe. "Port ten."

The little ship swung to port to follow the convoy which had altered to its new course for Dungeness. Astern of the Chaser, the south-west Folkestone buoy, now some three miles distant, still winked derisively and it slowly dawned on them that the shelling had stopped. Now a lull of eerie silence replaced the infernal racket.

"Well, another C.W. convoy safely through, Number One."

"Yes, sir, and nobody hit."

They removed their tin hats. Peter wiped his forehead, already sore from the weight of the steel helmet. "Better get some sleep, Number One. Send the hands to cruising stations."

"Aye, aye, sir. Good night."

"Good night, Number One."

Peter settled down to the loneliness of the night's vigil. He still kept the night watches, because his First Lieutenant was not yet experienced enough for them. The lookouts relaxed and started to sweep the horizon with their binoculars, their shadowy figures a blur in the wings of the bridge.

To the eastward the moon swung into the heavens, masked from the convoy by her gossamer veil of high cirrus. Night became as day, the pale luminosity spreading across the calm and glassy sea, grey and mysterious in its undulating serenity.

A grand night. I should raise Dungeness Light in an hour or so, Peter mused.

The wireless loudspeaker on the bridge crackled. Peter's head jerked to hear the message which was in code, but which he now knew by heart.

"From *Athelstan*. To all Convoy C.W.17: Suspicious vessels in sight, port bow. Am investigating."

"Confound it! That's the end of a peaceful night. E-boats, I'll bet," Peter muttered as he moved to the voicepipe. "Action stations!" he shouted down the voicepipe and, thirty seconds later, men stumbled from their hammocks to rush, half asleep, to their quarters on deck.

From the fo'c'sle just below him, Peter watched a small group of men clearing away the seventy-five for action. The clanking securing-chains dropped to the steel deck. The lean barrel swung to the port bow, the dangerous quarter. The steel tube shimmered in the pale moonlight.

Up ahead of him, the two columns of the rugged little coasters and colliers stretched to the horizon, but in the darkness to the westward, the column leaders were invisible. The Senior Officer of the Escort in the 'Hunt' class destroyer was out of sight.

Waiting was a cold and dreary business. Men huddled together for warmth, stamping their feet and swinging leaden arms in their heavy duffel coats. Repeatedly were they turned out for action, which only too regularly proved a false alarm.

"Same old story," muttered one of the gun's crew; "wish the perishin' Hun would let us 'ave a crack at 'im."

"You'll get your chance, matey, before this lot's over," the cook, who was the oldest member, retorted.

The loudspeaker on the bridge crackled again.

"Vessels identified. Am returning to my station."

"Fall out action stations!"

Peter sighed as he leaned over the bridge to give the order. This constant interruption of sleep made men irritable, but he was lucky in his ship's company. Not often was there serious grumbling.

Once again the convoy settled down to its journey westwards and trails of black smoke streamed from the jaunty funnels. Now the tide had turned and the convoy was only making four knots. By one o'clock in the morning, they still batted their way westwards, with Dungeness Light barely abeam. The occulting light sent its pencil ray streaking across the horizon, but for twenty minutes only while the convoy was in the vicinity. This was long enough, however, to betray it to the lurking enemy.

It's too bright for E-boats, anyway, Peter thought, *the western horizon's clear now, as bright as day. Reckon I can have a pipe in this visibility.* He turned to the lookouts. "Carry on smoking."

"Thank you, sir."

Gnarled hands fumbled for hidden 'roll-me-own's' and eager lips dragged at dank tobacco which was lit from the smouldering slow-match hanging by the chart table. Peter puffed contentedly at his favourite pipe and settled down on the hinged wooden seat fixed to the bridge-side. One arm over the 'splinter-mattresses' which festooned the bridge, he swept the horizon with his binoculars.

Nothing in sight! Might be a peacetime manoeuvre, he thought, *Royal Sovereign Lightship and Beachy Head next, and then we're nearly there.*

It really was a lovely sight. On either bow stretched two straight lines of merchant ships, the largest of which was only about 2,000 tons. To seaward of them, small dots of M.L.s chugged onwards, dipping and curvetting in the long swell. The unseen moon, screened by a film of fleecy cloud, cast her light upon a sea that ran like quicksilver.

Peter sighed contentedly. *Wish all these convoys were like this*, he thought, as he stretched his legs which were stiff with the inaction and the cold, even though he was wearing his sheepskin boots.

A prolonged roar rumbled from ahead, reverberating across the stillness, and Peter's head jerked upwards as he glued the binoculars to his eyes. A dull glow flickered from somewhere ahead. Then, as he peered, a shattering explosion from the head of the starboard column split the brooding silence. Another followed in quick succession. In the port column a huge spout of water leaped upwards.

"Mines! We've run into our own minefield," Peter gasped.

Men had already appeared from below and were manning their guns, but before Peter could press the Night Alarm buzzer, a shock hit the hull of the little Chaser as another ship blew up in the port column, only half a mile distant. A searing orange flame drenched the sky as Peter focused his glasses on the spot, but there was nothing to be seen; nothing but a frothing, heaving mass of water.

"My God!" he whispered. "How horrible!"

There was nothing left, nothing.

"Stop both engines!" Peter shouted down the voicepipe.

The little ship lost way and glided gently to a stop. Peter dashed to the chart table and ran his eye over the thin pencil line that represented his ship's position.

"We're in the swept channel," he argued, "… strange!"

The truth suddenly hit him. *Athelstan* had been hoodwinked. The ships which she had challenged had, in fact, been enemy mine-laying destroyers. They had laid their 'eggs' ahead of the convoy and had streaked, like sinister assassins, back to France.

Urgently the loudspeaker crackled again.

"All ships, repeat all ships, act independently, and proceed via swept channel to Portsmouth. Enemy have laid mines. Chaser 25 recover survivors. Acknowledge."

"Pretty obvious," Peter snapped, as he reached for the W/T transmitter. "Message received," he said.

The remaining ships of the convoy were already growing smaller as the distance widened, black smoke now pouring from their funnels as the convoy desperately forged ahead to clear the danger area. Then he noticed that the last ship in the starboard column had started to haul out of line to port.

She's trying to pick up survivors, thought Peter. He moved to the voicepipe.

"Full ahead both!"

The little ship tremored as she gathered way and the pulse from her diesels pounded in the Engine Room so that the ship shook.

This ought to trigger off any remaining mines, Peter thought anxiously. *I'm sitting on top of a minefield and they may be 'acoustics'. Not a pleasant thought this, as diesel ships were the most vulnerable.*

The Chaser closed the obstinate collier which was now two hundred yards on her starboard beam and Peter picked up the microphone of the loudhailer.

"Get back into position, please. Get back into station," he ordered.

"Blooming well get out of my way, I'm picking up survivors!" a Geordie voice yelled back across the water. Peter hesitated as he once more picked up the microphone but as he did so, an explosion like the crack of doom rent the air and a searing sheet of heat sent him reeling against the compass. His head spun as the shock struck the sides of the little Chaser, so that she listed suddenly from the impact.

A curtain of red and green flames leaped skywards, roaring into the night. Peter staggered and clutched the bridge-side, as into his consciousness was indelibly stencilled a sight he would never forget. The bows of the collier had disappeared and where they once had been a seething mass of debris and foam boiled and hissed. The ship's funnel leaned drunkenly for'd. Her stern was cocked out of the water, so that her propellers still threshed the air with slow beats, while the screams of dying men wailed through the night.

"Help me! For God's sake, save us!" came a desperate cry across the water from a stricken man in the port column as he flailed the water.

"Hard-a-port, full ahead together! Steer for that man in the water, Coxswain."

"Aye, aye, sir," the deep voice answered.

"Might as well save him, Number One, this other ship's a goner!" Peter yelled. "Stand by to pick him up, port side-to." As the Chaser closed on the pathetic figure struggling in the water, the desperate cries of other drowning men drifted across the waters from all sides.

"Stop both, stand by to recover!" but, as the Chaser went full astern to halt alongside the dark head bobbing in the oily sea, the man disappeared with only a ripple marking his grave.

Sickened, Peter turned away.

"Two men, starboard beam, sir," yelled the starboard lookout, pointing with outstretched arm.

"Hard-a-starboard, slow ahead together!" and the Chaser slid alongside another group of struggling men.

"Catch this line and come alongside the scrambling net," yelled a voice on the fo'c'sle. A heaving-line snaked through the air to plop across the struggling men who grabbed it, gasping and spluttering. Gently, slowly they were pulled alongside and strong hands snatched them from the hungry waters.

"Look at that, sir!" the starboard lookout yelled.

Peter's head jerked.

The stern of the doomed ship was barely a hundred yards away hanging poised between sky and water and looming some fifty feet in the air. She was settling fast, ready for her final plunge.

From the port quarter of the looming transom, a man hung head downwards, caught by his feet in the bight of a rope. He was swinging to and fro with the slow motion of the swell and trying frantically to clutch the rope and heave himself upwards to get back to the slanting deck. His body jerked like a marionette on a string. A terrifying silence gripped the scene, as men watched the pitiful struggles of the doomed man. Gasping sobs floated across the diminishing space of water that separated the two wallowing ships.

"I can't let this happen, even if she takes us with her," Peter whispered as he leapt for the voicepipe.

"Slow ahead port, hard-a-starboard!"

The Chaser slid in under the counter of the towering transom. The dark mass hung above the little ship's fo'c'sle, blacking out the sky. Slowly, foot by foot, the Chaser's bow edged nearer. Peter crouched low over the voicepipe, conning her with every ounce of skill and concentration he possessed.

"Midships, slow astern together."

So close were they, that he could hear the swishing gurgle of water as it lapped along the stern of the merchant ship and he could plainly see the rusty rudder jammed to port. The black mass hung and plunged in the swell fifteen, ten feet above the Chaser's bows.

"She's going, sir!" yelled a voice from the fo'c'sle.

"Grab him, go on, grab him! Cut the rope!" Peter shouted.

He could bear to look no longer but waited for the rending crash as the ship plunged down upon them.

Frantic hands grappled for the dangling body. Stretching over the guard rails, they clutched and reached again.

"Knife! No! Cut, cut!" was all Peter could hear from his helpless position on the bridge. A dull gleam glimmered on the fo'c'sle.

"Astern! Go astern, sir," screamed a man from the fo'c'sle.

Peter glanced over the bridge. A crumpled figure sprawled across the guard rails.

"Full astern together!" Peter yelled down the voicepipe. His knuckles showed white in the pale moonlight. The engines coughed into life. The huge mass plunged and slid downwards, towards the Chaser's fo'c'sle.

The Chaser quivered as she gathered sternway; faster, faster, she glided and pulled away. Metal screeched as it tore apart, but as suddenly the sickening sound ceased. The little ship shook herself and leapt astern as she came free, like a cork from a bottle.

"Stop both!"

The Chaser lost way, as her company watched the death throes of the collier. Already nothing but the counter remained. For a moment it hung there, her 'Red Duster' hanging limp but proud in the still night. Then, with a rush, she went. The water boiled for an instant, debris shooting to the surface, and she was gone.

The port lookout, a young seaman of eighteen, was vomiting over the side. It was all Peter could do not to keep him company, but, mercifully, more urgent problems demanded his immediate concentration.

Apart from the pathetic flotsam which marked the watery resting place of these brave ships, the silver ocean stretched before him. They were now alone, dependent upon themselves. They drifted upon the surface of the treacherous minefield and there would be little hope for them if they touched off a mine now.

Peter checked his doubtful position on the chart.

"Slow ahead together," he ordered.

The Chaser gingerly slid over the placid sea for another five miles. Not until Beachy Head was abeam to starboard, gleaming and white in the moonlight, did Peter relax and send the men below. Somehow, when floating on top of a gunpowder keg, it felt better to stay up on deck, because the cramped quarters of a mess deck were depressing and coffin-like.

It was now four o'clock in the morning and already the first steely light of dawn streaked the eastern horizon.

"Fall out action stations. Go to cruising stations, Number One."

"Aye, aye, sir. Orders for the morning?"

Peter shook his sleep-hungry head and suppressed a yawn.

"E.T.A. Portsmouth, 0730, Number One. We'll have breakfast off the Nab Tower, weather and Huns permitting. Good night, Number One, or rather, good morning!"

Jamie turned for the bridge ladder.

"… and, Number One…"

"Yes, sir?"

"I would like to see the man we took off. I'll see him later on."

"Yes, sir."

"… and, Number One…"

"Yes, sir?"

"Thank you, and well done."

"Good night, sir."

"Good morning!"

The Nab Tower jutted like a beckoning finger from the sea off Culver Cliff. The Chaser curved round and chugged up to Portsmouth Harbour. In the entrance she turned hard-a-port and glided up Haslar Creek, past the empty Submarine Base.

"Thank Heaven I don't serve in those things," Peter joked to his First Lieutenant.

Jamie was staring through his glasses.

"The ambulance is waiting, sir."

On the jetty at the end of the creek, the red-crossed ambulance stood waiting for its usual guests.

The Chaser came neatly alongside and the injured men were gently put ashore in stretchers. Peter looked down from the bridge. On the fo'c'sle his weary men waited to shove off.

"Cast off for'd!"

Ten minutes later the little ship moored inside the basin of the Submarine Base, the Chasers' operational headquarters.

As Peter reached the upper deck, he met his First Lieutenant who was looking extraordinarily embarrassed.

"Well, what is it, Number One? I am going below to get my head down," snapped Peter irritably, as waves of tiredness flowed over him. He was untoggling his duffel coat and peeling off his clothes and could not reach his bunk quickly enough.

"I am afraid I have made a frightful bog of it, sir. We have still got the man you took off on board," Jamie added nervously. "He requests to see you."

"Confound it, Number One, he should have gone ashore with the others. There's nothing the matter with him."

"That's the point, sir; he wants to stay with us."

"For crying out loud, Number One, it's time you woke up! I can't possibly see him. Send him ashore."

"Aye, aye, sir. Sorry, sir."

"All right."

Peter started for'd for his cabin hatch. He paused, scratching his head. "I've never refused to see a man yet," he murmured to himself. He took a pace backwards. "I'll see him now, Number One," he added wearily. "Send the Coxswain up with him."

On the quarterdeck of this little ship a strange scene was now enacted — one which Peter did not know was to affect the course of his whole life. A group of four men mustered around the depth charges as the Coxswain, an elderly man, started the proceedings by reading from a scrap of paper.

"Able Seaman Hawkins, sir. Requests to see the Captain privately."

The young Captain lifted his head to search the face of the requestman who stood before him. The seaman was not dressed as requestmen usually are. He had no cap. His blond hair was matted, covered with oil and grime, and he was unshaven. He was barefooted and he wore a dirty duffel coat. A man in his early thirties, his face was humorously lined, but it was not soft. Deep wrinkles creased the corners of his steady blue eyes which met fearlessly those of Sinclair.

"Well, what is it?" Peter snapped.

Able Seaman Hawkins was no orator. He shifted his feet and coughed, "Well, sir, it's like this 'ere, sir…"

The First Lieutenant grunted. He looked at his watch impatiently.

"Yes?" Peter asked.

"Well, sir — it's … well, sir."

"For Pete's sake, get on with it, man! What do you want to say?"

The man made an enormous effort and then the flood broke.

"It's not right for me, sir, to see you like this, I know, sir. But I'm bloomin' grateful for what you did, sir. You risked the ship an' all, sir, and…"

"Yes, yes, go on," said Peter, embarrassed.

"… I want to stay with you, sir, and join your perishin' little ship."

Peter coughed and tried to suppress a smile.

"There, sir, I've said it. Some'ow it's difficult to say these things. But I do want to stay with you, sir, if you'll 'ave me. You see, it's 'ard to explain, but I could be a good 'and to you, sir."

A lump had come into Peter's throat. He looked across the creek on this beautiful, crisp morning and then turned to his First Lieutenant.

"Are we down on seamen's rate in the complement, First Lieutenant?"

Number One hesitated warily, while he looked at the dishevelled seaman.

"Yes, sir, we are two short."

Peter paused.

"It's irregular, you know, Able Seaman Hawkins, and not catered for in King's Regulations and Admiralty Instructions."

"Yes, sir. I know, sir."

There was a long pause.

"But I will see what I can do. Stand over this request, Coxswain. Meanwhile, kit up this rating and let him go for'd."

"Aye, aye, sir. Stand over! About turn, double march!"

The traditional ceremony was over. The incongruous figure turned about and shuffled for'd in his bare feet, followed by a puzzled Coxswain.

Peter turned to his First Lieutenant.

"I'll keep this man, Number One. Fix it!"

"Yes, sir. I hope he turns out all right," Jamie replied doubtfully.

Peter looked at him.

"I have a hunch we shall see more of him. Thank you for making such a bog of it, after all, Number One. That's the way to get promotion!"

"Yes, sir," Jamie smiled ruefully.

Peter wearily strolled for'd to his cabin, a faint smile on his lips.

Able Seaman William Hawkins had joined the ship's company of Chaser 25.

CHAPTER 2

No Quarter!

The incident that was to alter two men's lives took place on the
following night. Chaser 25 returned to Portsmouth for a
night's leave, and at four-thirty that evening fifteen
unrecognisably smart men marched ashore in Gosport.

For those men left on board, there was to be no leave during
this spell in port because they had to man the guns and deal
with any possible damage. It was Peter's turn for shore-going,
as Jamie and he had made a rule between themselves that one
of them should always go ashore, because otherwise their
minds became stale with nothing to relax the tension. Even
wandering ashore during the blitzes afforded a change of
scene, for one could always meet a friend in Alverstoke and go
fire-fighting after the first incendiary raid. Peter left Jamie and
strolled ashore by himself, khaki gas mask slung over his left
shoulder.

As he strolled through the blackout, the sirens wailed to
announce the first wave of enemy bombers and, almost before
he could decide what to do, the first bombs were striking
Gosport and white flashes flickered along the dark outline of
the roofs. Steel-blue pencils of light swung into the night sky,
as the searchlights probed helplessly. Already the air was thick
with smoke and dust from the devastation of the first wave.
Over Portsmouth, the angry flames were reflected in the
clouds of billowing smoke, so that the whole horizon pulsed
crimson.

"Might as well go fire-fighting," Peter decided as he turned back towards Gosport. "Looks like being a busy night."

The empty streets narrowed as the dingy tenement houses huddled together, almost as if for comfort on such a wicked night and as he walked on, the second wave of bombers winged low over the streets. He heard the drone, looked upwards and saw three Heinkel 113's caught in a searchlight cone.

How wicked those black crosses look! Peter thought as he lengthened his stride.

Another formation followed closely on the tails of the first wave. Peter heard the 'whee-ee!' of the bombs and then the sticks exploded a few hundred yards ahead. A white glare gleamed before him, and then suddenly the remnants of the houses flickered into orange flames as the incendiaries danced into points of vivid light.

As Peter ran towards the stricken houses, the crackling of the flames formed a background to the screams of the trapped women and children. He vaulted the battered fence of the last house in the row.

One wall was sagging dangerously, and the roof toppled drunkenly outwards. From the windows of the top floor a yellow glow flickered. The curtains were strips of fire and, from above, Peter heard the cries of a child, lonely and afraid. He charged the front door which gave to the weight of his strong shoulders. A wall of smoke and heat hit him as he staggered inwards, so that he choked and gasped for air. He dashed blindly forward until his feet stumbled against the wooden stairs.

The second stick of bombs fell as he groped his way upwards, the stairway crumbling beneath his feet as he did so. A black chasm yawned in front of him and a red mist swam before his eyes as he clutched the collapsing banister. There was a deafening roar, and the crimson world spun into widening spirals of nothingness, spinning, spinning wildly into whorls of dancing light until he fell and knew no more.

The sailors too had gone ashore to stretch their legs. They also had been caught in the raid, and one of them, Able Seaman Bill Hawkins, was strolling by himself down a deserted street. He looked up as the second wave of bombers lumbered over him.

"Nearly as 'ot as Lunnon!" he growled.

He stopped in his tracks, fists thrust deep into the flaps of his bell-bottoms. This scene of enemy savagery always hurt him. It was the smell that did it, the acrid smell of burning that brought back the agony of his first leave.

Yes, that was it, the sour rankness of smouldering wood, drenched by water from playing hoses. This smell brought it all back. The shambles that had once been the street in which he had lived and loved since he was a child. The urgent ringing of the ambulance bell, the scream of tyres as the vehicle had lurched to avoid him. "Stand back, Jack, there's a perishin' landmine in that there 'ouse!"

The terrible explosion that had blown him backwards, shattering the night, as he tried to burst through the cordon of restraining arms! The kind hands that had tried to comfort him, while he sank on to a pile of rubble, his head in his hands, his eyes glazed and staring before him. "Janet, Janet! Oh, my God, the kids!" was all he had whispered. The pub-keeper who had taken him in for the night, who could not understand him when he went without breakfast after the nightmare night. "I'm going back to the ship," was all that he had said, as he had walked out into the bleak dawn.

Yes, it was the bitter smell that reminded him so vividly of something he wanted to forget.

"The perishin' swine," he whispered as he ran towards the flaming houses. The nearest was ablaze and one end was about to collapse. An old man stood coatless in the road, a thin arm pointing frantically at the burning house.

"Get them out. For Gawd's sake get them out!" he shrieked.

Bill hesitated. To enter this shambles might mean certain death, for the doomed building was already cracking and creaking.

"There's an orficer inside as well, Jack!" the old man screeched.

"Orficer?"

"There, look Jack, there's 'is blinkin' 'at!"

Outside what was once a door, a naval officer's dusty cap lay, like a signpost on a deserted moor. Bill snatched up the battered object. There was only one like it, the cap which the young Captain of Chaser 25 always wore — a battered wreck of a thing, which he always called his 'joss' cap.

Hawkins hesitated no longer but charged in through the open doorway. Protected from the sagging ceiling by a smouldering beam, a huddled figure in dark uniform lay crumpled amongst the burning wreckage. To the right of the staircase and past human help, a woman lay twisted, her child whimpering in her stiff arms.

Bill grabbed the child, dashed outside and bundled it into the old man's hands, and then bounded back into the furnace. His feverish fingers tore at the bricks, his huge shoulders heaved and strained against the beam. Masonry clattered around his head and flames licked, crackling wickedly along the floor.

He pulled the limp figure out by the legs and through the doorway as falling debris crashed around him. The building collapsed as he reached the open road, the limp body of his young Captain trailing after him.

Bill had not noticed the crash. He propped up the limp head in his lap and rolled back the closed eyelids. The eyes rolled, the body twitched as Bill tore off Peter's black tie and collar and gently slapped the white face. The body stiffened, twitched, and jerked into consciousness.

"C'mon, sir, c'mon! You're all right, sir, c'mon," Bill pleaded.

Peter blinked and shook his head.

"You're all right," were the first words he heard, kind words from a hoarse voice he knew. Across his consciousness there drifted the faint sobbing of a child.

"Try standing up, sir, then we'll get back to the ship."

Peter's groggy knees took his weight. He shook his reeling head, and passed a hand across his face.

"Where the dickens am I? Oh, it's you, Hawkins?"

"Yes, sir, it's me."

"Good. Let's get back to the ship."

"Come on, sir, lean on me."

"Thank you, Hawkins. I reckon we're quits now."

"I reckon so, sir. Let's get going."

The old man stared after them. In his arms a child lay sobbing. Tears trickled down his lined face as he wagged his old head in bewilderment.

The ship's company of Chaser 25 knew little of this incident and the debt Able Seaman Bill Hawkins had repaid to his Captain. It was as Hawkins had wished, for he had asked Peter not to mention what had happened. Nevertheless, it was from this moment that the mutual respect of the two men for each other matured into comradeship.

They were utterly different in their temperaments. Hawkins was some ten years older than Peter. Of an impetuous nature, Bill Hawkins found it impossible to keep out of trouble. He always spoke his mind which made things less easy for him, particularly when irritated by those ashore who were dodging the war. The memories of his personal tragedy were yet too raw to allow for toleration.

Bill was not tall, barely five foot two in his socks, but his huge barrel of a chest gave him enormous strength, and for a man of his build he was light on his feet. His arms were long for his body which accounted for his success in the boxing ring. He had become the welterweight champion of the Mediterranean Fleet before the war, but he seldom referred to it. When roused, his blue eyes would dance with points of light and he would lean forward, poised on the balls of his feet.

Perhaps it was his intense hatred of the Germans which bound him to Peter. They were both on the bridge some three weeks later when the Chaser was returning from Weymouth with a small tanker. They had hugged the coast and were rounding up for St. Alban's Head, a sharp bluff on the horizon.

As often happens in small ships, the last dog watch, from six to eight in the evening, was a time for relaxation and confidences. The tanker was giving no trouble, and Peter had strolled over to the starboard wing of the bridge where Bill Hawkins was keeping his lookout.

Neither knew how it had started, but for the first time in his life, Bill Hawkins haltingly told of the tragedy of his wife and children. Peter said little, but even though he was the younger man, he sensed the grief of the sailor and his silence gave comfort. When Bill's flood of words came to a faltering halt, Peter felt a bond grow between them, knitting them together in a strange companionship. They should both have felt embarrassed, but it was not so. Peter gave the broad back a gentle thump and returned to the compass while the sailor scanned the grey horizon, his jaw jutting with grim purpose.

Peter had to admit that they were all desperately tired. He had only to look at Hawkins there, gripping the rail of the bucketing bridge with one hand, to realise that no one was really tuned to this business yet and how long would this dreary war drag on? They had only experienced six months of this, and the news of disaster grew daily worse. Invasion was imminent with the Germans massing in the Channel ports.

But I suppose we'll all get used to it, he thought. *After all, we've only been operating for six months and*, he grinned to himself, *we're still afloat.*

He already looked older than his years, as he propped himself against a folding seat on the starboard side of the bridge. One arm across the binnacle for support, Peter gazed through salt-encrusted eyelids at the red-splotched coaster, wallowing in the broken seas.

It's odd, he mused to himself, *here am I, in command of a ship at the age of twenty-one, and responsible for the safe passage of that little 'widget' of a ship on my port quarter. I'm lucky. Some people never get this chance all their lives, but this is better than a C.W. convoy, any day!* — and he pushed back his battered cap to scratch the side of his head, where even now there were a few grey flecks. He was not as tall as he looked, for his lean and wiry frame gave a deceptive appearance of height.

"It's getting worse, sir."

Peter looked up. The small figure of Jamie, his First Lieutenant, was hauling itself up to the heaving bridge. A small and wiry Scot from Glasgow, Jamie was always cheerful, but good spirits did not compensate for the limited experience that even Peter possessed. Peter found himself on the bridge continuously, whilst Jamie learned as much as he could during the full days that slipped by so quickly. Swathed in a steaming duffel coat, his diminutive figure was always poring over the chart table, anxious to learn all he could in between bouts of dreadful seasickness. Thrown from side to side and swaying to the violent motion of the ship, Jamie looked up from the chart table.

"It's coming on to blow, sir," he shouted across to Peter against the soughing of the wind now screaming in the rigging.

"Yes, Number One, and we ought to feel it as we go through St. Alban's Race, just ahead there," shouted Peter in reply as he pointed with outstretched arm to the broken water that lay ahead, where the small tanker was heaving and wallowing in the trough of the short swell, her upper deck completely awash as she plunged through the green seas.

"There's too much wind for enemy aircraft, so we needn't worry about them; but I don't like this poor visibility," Peter continued. By the time they had smashed their way through the broken waters of the Race, snarling and jumping in angry seas, the visibility had shut down like a smothering blanket. The flying clouds swept low over the tiny ships, pitching and yawing within a stone's throw of each other.

Peter was anxious. Only another hour's daylight remained in which to make the hazardous passage of the Needles, an opening barely half a mile wide. In these conditions and with this bad visibility, he would need luck on his side to pick up those jagged rocks, so aptly named. Peter hated them at this moment.

Jamie went to snatch a meal in the Ward Room aft, and once more Peter was left alone with his problems. The two huddled figures of the lookouts tried to peer through smeary binoculars for signs of the cruel rocks that stood sentinel for the Isle of Wight.

These perishing Needles, thought Peter, *if I don't sight them soon, either the Shingles Bank will get us or I'll be late for my rendezvous with Chaser 27. We're both out on patrol tonight.* "Keep a sharp lookout, right ahead," he shouted to the lookouts.

"Aye, aye, sir!" came their gruff replies, as they strained their red-rimmed eyes into the biting wind.

"There she is!" yelled Peter.

Sure enough, fine on the starboard bow, he momentarily caught sight of the black top of a leaping buoy which instantly disappeared in a smother of foam.

Peter sighed with relief and steadied his ship on the black jack-in-a-box of a buoy. Wearily he picked up the Aldis signalling lamp, lined it up on the bridge of the wallowing tanker and flashed, "Follow me."

"Thank you," the courteous reply came blinking back haltingly from the pitching bridge of the rusty coaster.

Peter shouted down the voicepipe and felt his ship vibrate to her increased speed, as she plunged and butted into the vicious seas now running through the entrance of the channel.

Yes, I am lucky to be Captain of this little hooker, he thought as his eye roved affectionately over the small French Submarine Chaser, known by her unromantic and prosaic name, Chaser 25. She had been rushed over from Dunkirk, her plates merely bolted together in the haste to deny her to the Germans. Six months ago, he had proudly taken her out of the Southampton shipyard, where she had been patched up and given two 0.303 French Hotchkiss machine-guns.

Only a small ship, of low freeboard, with a turtle-backed upper deck, she was one hundred and twenty feet long. Built for the Mediterranean, this wild English Channel weather was not for her, for she was very wet in bad weather.

He leaned over the side of the bridge to watch the red-splotched anti-fouling of her fore-foot, rearing out of the seething water. Her bows lifted high, paused, and came crashing down again into the swirling seas. Peter ducked as she took it green and turned his back to the solid curtain of water that spurted upwards to smother the bridge. Faintly he heard the dripping wetness swilling around the deck as it drained away in the scuppers.

He pulled a sodden towel closer around his neck and felt a cold dribble trickling down to his stomach and then stood up and instinctively took in the scene again.

Already he was drawing ahead of the little tanker, but the dark shapes of the jagged rocks, cruel and menacing, seemed very close. The breaking white seas unleashed their fury against them, leaping high in spouts of foam and driving spume.

I'd better round up now, he thought, *though there's not much sea-room with the Shingles Shoal a quarter of a mile to port. I think we're through.*

In the haze to port, he could see the white foam breaking wildly over the shifting shoals that formed the western limit of the channel.

He fumbled for his tobacco pouch as he leaned thankfully over the fore-end of the bridge, and allowed his tired eyes to drift across the lowering clouds which swept down upon the threshing waters.

Two black smoke puffs, that was all…

Two black cotton-wool puffs, which were already losing shape and trailing in the wind just below the cloud.

For an instant Peter was transfixed. Growing larger with every second that passed, the yellow snouts of two Messerschmitt 109's hurtled down upon them.

Peter lunged at the alarm buzzer and its urgent summons sent men scrambling on deck. They clawed blindly along the heaving, greasy decks to the few machine-guns which were their only defence. One man slipped, half down on his knees, and his tin hat fell off to wobble gently over the side.

But it was much too late.

Below each Messerschmitt a black puff of exhaust squirted as they cut in their motors. The staccato roar of their engines, interrupted by the ruthless chatter of spitting guns, drowned even the howling of the wind. The fighters swooped down upon the small ship, raking her from stem to stern as they swung overhead at masthead height. Armour-piercing and incendiary bullets tore through her sides and rigging, twanging in an inferno of sound.

Whok-whok … whok, whok-whok!

The whine of the spattering lead made a strange background accompaniment to this devil's opera.

"Get down!" Peter yelled desperately to the two lookouts, standing goggle-eyed in the wings of the bridge. Hurling himself at the unmanned Hotchkiss, he spun it round in a vain attempt to bring the sights to bear on the two black fighters now already overhead. He stared at the grinning face of the helmeted pilot in the leading plane, and saw him relax after jerking the bomb release.

Wheee, wheee … wheee, wheee!

The small bombs dropped, egg-like, from the black bellies streaking overhead. They were so close that Peter saw them distinctly, his eyes fascinated by the toppling, globular horrors. He held his breath and braced himself for the shock. The sea jumped up to meet him as the ship jarred and shuddered. Two bombs fell short and two between Chaser 25 and her small tanker. They plumped into the heaving seas, racking the ships in sharp spasms. The aircraft shuddered and climbed hard to port for the refuge of low cloud and disappeared in the murk.

Peter felt a warm sensation in the seat of his overalls. Instinctively his hand felt for wet blood, but to his relief and amusement found only a smouldering hole.

"All over!" yelled Peter to the men now standing by their guns, fingers itching to loose off a round. Angry eyes that stung with shame at being caught unprepared, peered skywards.

"Never mind! That won't happen again, Number One, will it?" laughed Peter, a trifle breathless, to his First Lieutenant who had arrived panting up the bridge ladder.

"No blooming fear, it won't, sir!" growled Hawkins, now glued to his gun. "Those so-and-so's 'ave got it coming to 'em" — and with that he smoothed down the ruffled hair on his blond head.

The signalling lamp from the tanker now ahead of them blinked anxiously.

"Thanks. Are you all right?"

Peter sent Jamie round the ship before replying and it seemed an eternity before he returned.

"By a miracle, sir, no one even scratched," and he continued, grinning, "but the cook is livid. The cat has had kittens in the galley!"

"No casualties," signalled Peter, "except to the cat, which has produced kittens. Proceed to Portsmouth independently."

Another routine trip was over. In the dusk, the tanker waddled her way up the western Solent and disappeared into the November twilight from which the small smudge of another Chaser now appeared. She was Chaser 27, bound for the night's patrol with the weary Chaser 25.

"Ah well!" sighed Peter, turning his ship round so that she faced seawards again. "I suppose another night's patrol won't do us any harm."

Out loud he gave his orders, "Fall out action stations; cruising stations, Number One."

"Aye, aye, sir," replied the First Lieutenant, an impish light glinting in his Celtic eyes.

"Cruising stations, Coxswain!"

This imperturbable man, old enough to be the father of both his officers, shook his head and grinned.

"Only six months, sir, and we've had more than you get in ten years of peacetime Navy. I wonder how long this war is going on?" And, with that observation, he clattered off the bridge.

Chaser 27 joined up and led the way out of the Needles channel, now growing indistinct in the gathering dusk. With its own idea of humour, the wind had now started to moderate and already the sea had dropped, leaving a long, oily swell lumping across the entrance to the channel.

Wearily Peter dragged himself over to the chart table to make sure of his night's position, but, as he was doing so, the signalman started to pick up his Aldis lamp, giving 'T's in acknowledgment to a light that blinked astern.

"… from Chaser 17 … to Chaser 25 … return to Yarmouth Roads … I am relieving you tonight … all right for some."

"Hard-a-port," ordered Peter. "It's 'home James' for us."

The tired little ship swung round out of line, leaving Chaser 27 to wait for her new consort.

"Good night," signalled Peter. "I don't wish I was coming with you. Good luck."

Increasing speed, Peter went ahead and moored to the large buoy outside the snug harbour of Yarmouth. As he did so, Chaser 17, the Senior Officer, slipped quickly down on the tide, outward bound on her first patrol.

"Good luck and thank you," signalled Peter.

The white bow wave sheened clearly as she swept by, hands waving from her bridge.

I wish she had been able to have more time to work up, thought Peter to himself; *it's not so easy as you think out there.*

It was the last time that he was to see her.

As the twinkling stars glittered brightly above the little ship, swinging gently at her buoy, a small cluster of men gathered on her steel quarterdeck. Bareheaded, they stood in a semicircle around their young Captain who, with an unaccustomed Admiralty prayer book in his hand, was giving thanks to Almighty God for deliverance from their enemies. The quiet murmur of their thanks to Him hardly broke the silence of the night which gathered slowly about them.

"O Almighty God, who art a strong tower of defence unto Thy servants against their enemies; we yield Thee praise and thanksgiving for our deliverance from those great and apparent dangers wherewith we were encompassed: we acknowledge it Thy goodness that we were not delivered over as a prey unto them; beseeching Thee still to continue Thy mercies towards us, that all the world may know that Thou art our Saviour and Mighty Deliverer; through Jesus Christ, Our Lord."

"Amen," came the low voices in thankfulness, their responses floating across the water like a deep sigh.

Three hours later, two lean, black shapes slid silently across the patrol line off the south-eastern corner of the Isle of Wight. Undetected by the patrolling trawlers, the two MAAS-class German destroyers closed to within three miles of the signal station which was perched atop the massive bluff of Culver cliff.

On the bridge of the leading enemy destroyer, the German Captain turned and spoke curtly to the young signals officer at his side.

"You have everything ready, Herr Leutnant?"

"*Ja, mein Kapitan,*" the eager voice replied.

"These English pig-dogs are about to regret the day you were at Exeter University, are they not? Perhaps you will in your boat be sailing again here, as you did in the Solent three years ago?" A guffaw of guttural Teutonic laughter obsequiously greeted this heavy Hunnish humour.

"*Gott strafe England!* Then make der signal," ordered the Captain.

"*Ja, mein Kapitan. Heil Hitler!*"

Both officers exchanged a perfunctory music hall raising of their right hands and the young officer clicked his heels, then turned about to man the signal lamp in the port wings of the bridge.

Click-click-clack … clack-click-clack-clack … click-clack-click: the shutter of the lamp clattered. A thin pencil of blue light stabbed the darkness and urgently summoned the signal station ashore.

After a few seconds, high up on the cliff, an answering light replied with the coded challenge, '…A K … A K.'

"Ha! *Das ist gut!*" snarled the German Captain. "Go on, Herr Leutnant, and jumble your reply."

The young Ober-Leutnant flicked away on the shutter, his forearm working swiftly in time with the clatter. He made two indistinct 'BD's' following it up quickly with, "Do you know that we are here? May we enter harbour, please?"

The signal station replied after a short pause, "Proceed up harbour. Your berth will be signalled later."

Both destroyers had lain stopped, pointed towards the light. Now that their acknowledgment had been signalled, they turned hard-a-starboard and steamed off into the darkness at high speed. Having thrown the shore authorities into confusion, they were now in search of their prey and had not long to wait.

The lone, armed trawler, steaming up and down her appointed patrol line off St. Catherine's Point, did not even see her killers until it was too late. Using flashless cordite, they blew her out of the water, not waiting to pick up the doomed survivors who were left to drown in the swirling waters.

Sweeping round St. Catherine's, the two darkened destroyers, concealed by the blackness of the moonless night, streaked westwards, some twelve miles off the Needles.

"*Achtung!*"

The warning rang across the bridge from the excited voice of a young German sailor. His arm pointed to two small black shapes steaming slowly in line ahead, fine on the destroyer's port bow.

"*Donner und blitzen!*" the German Captain swore. "Herr Leutnant, make them a signal, 'Close me'."

"*Jawohl, mein Kapitan.*" Once again the blue light blinked.

The young Captains of Chasers 17 and 27 read the winking blue light which beckoned them in the pitch darkness.

"Close me. I have message for you."

The leading Chaser hesitated, unused to the guile and ruthlessness of this Channel war. She turned towards the winking light, her consort following in her wake. Both ships were at action stations. Huddled groups of seamen manned their 75mm guns on the clammy fo'c'sles, one round in each breech. The gunlayers' fingers itched on their triggers. The darkened silhouette of two destroyers, bows towards them, slid into the crosswires of their sights.

"Stand by!"

But the British guns never spoke…

As the German destroyers' sights came on, a merciless broadside tore into the two Chasers, splitting them asunder.

Safe now from retribution, the leading destroyer nosed into the wreckage-strewn water, intent on taking prisoners. In the swirling waters, the pathetic remains of two ships' companies struggled. Several burned and shocked men clung desperately to floating debris. A destroyer drifted down upon them, the water poppling along her sides, from which jumping ladders and scrambling nets dangled, offering them their lives.

Their young Captain's shock of red hair, matted by the black oil fuel, bobbed up and down in the oily scum. Exhorting his men to save themselves, he swam towards the destroyer, a flashing gleam of defiance in his battle-crazed eyes. Nearing the ship's side, he shouted at the top of his voice in a victorious yell of anguish, all reserve gone and all barriers down.

"God save the King! God bless England!"

In his exulting pride, he half heaved himself out of the water, while a jeering group of German sailors clustered on the upper deck, peering down inquisitively at him. One spat contemptuously over the side.

For an instant, the contorted face of this gallant young Briton dipped beneath the swirling debris. He reappeared a few seconds later and hove himself half out of the water, yelling defiantly, "God save England!" His arm swung above his head and a small round object lobbed unseen through the air to land amongst the jeering crowd of Huns gathered by the torpedo tubes.

As the grenade landed, bouncing and rolling along the steel plating, an orange flash stabbed the darkness. For an instant there was a shocked silence, then the screams of stricken and dying men rent the night.

Instantly the propellers of the destroyer went ahead, churning their murderous way like a scythe through the struggling swimmers, and staining the waters horribly.

From the starboard wings of the lower bridge a machine-gun spat, the green tracer lashing the water into spouts of boiling foam.

The destroyer pulled away and slowly circled. Not until the last defiant voice was silenced did the ruthless guns cease their butchery. The sudden silence shocked even the watching Germans as from the darkness, a choking voice hauntingly pursued them.

"… England … England!"

Once again the gun chattered.

The brave voice ceased suddenly, leaving only the swish of the water to disturb the silence of the cruel night. The enemy destroyers wheeled to the westward and disappeared into the darkness to sink yet another trawler off Portland, before returning to their Normandy base.

Off Yarmouth, gateway to the Isle of Wight, a little ship took her rest, swinging to the turn of the tide. Her young Captain turned restlessly over in his bunk, shouting to himself in his sleep, whilst, from across the mudflats of the river Yar, the plaintive cries of the curlew faintly called.

To the eastward, over the sweeping line of English hills which stood blackly against the line of the night sky, the first silver streaks heralded a cold dawn. The curtain was slowly falling on yet another night in the Narrow Seas.

CHAPTER 3

To the Enemy's Doorstep

"Sub-Lieutenant P. Sinclair, Royal Navy, is appointed to *H.M.S. Seahorse* for Submarine course." Peter Sinclair's eyes were riveted to the signal-pad which was held before him by his signalman.

"Thank you, Signalman. I'll show it to the First Lieutenant."

"Aye, aye, sir." The signalman hesitated.

"Well, what is it?" demanded his Captain.

The signalman looked his Captain in the eyes before replying.

"I am sorry, sir. I just wanted to say that we'll miss you."

From the first day, he had shared the boredom and excitements on the bridge with his Captain and this signal meant the ending of an understanding between the two men which had grown out of hardship and mutual respect.

"Thank you, Park. I shall hate leaving such a good ship's company. Good night."

"Good night, sir."

Alone in his small panelled cabin, Peter allowed his eyes to wander around the small tin box in which he had lived for the past months. On the bulkhead was his favourite painting, a bright watercolour of London Pool; from the top of his chest of drawers, the photograph of his mother smiled down at him, her serene face giving him the tranquillity he always felt whenever he looked at it. He needed her understanding now, for this news would worry her much more than it would trouble him. To her, it would mean weeks of waiting for news that never came. Weeks of strain bottled up in a heart to be racked and hurt every time the terse routine B.B.C. announcement came over the wireless: "The Admiralty regrets to announce the loss of His Majesty's Submarine — which has not returned from patrol and must be presumed lost. Next of kin have been informed." The knock on the door that might be the telegraph boy, ruddy-faced and panting from his long ride to the moors, the buff telegram envelope held in a reluctant hand.

No, Peter did not relish the idea much but it was a job of which to be proud, a real job. The more efficient he made himself at it, the more likely he was to survive.

Since the loss of his friends in Chasers 27 and 17, Peter's hatred of the Germans had intensified. Now he was glad, happy even, at the thought of being able to attack the enemy on his doorstep, for in submarines he would be able to revenge his friends and help, in his small way, to bring the ghastly business to an end.

Peter said goodbye to his ship's company on the quarterdeck. Slowly he walked down the two ranks of waiting men.

"Goodbye, Coxswain, thank you."

"Good luck, sir."

"Thank you, Chief, for the 'revs.' from the Engine Room."

"That's all right, sir. Good luck."

Finally he reached the last man in the rear rank.

"Goodbye, Hawkins."

"Goodbye, sir." A huge hand grasped Peter's.

"Good luck and thank you, Hawkins."

The two men gazed at each other for an instant.

"It's *au revoir*, sir," Hawkins croaked. "I've put in for submarines too, sir."

Jamie, who was standing alongside, smiled. "I have a hunch you two will be seeing more of each other, sir."

Peter coughed.

"Keep in touch, Hawkins."

"I will, sir."

The men were dismissed. Peter parted from Jamie in the Ward Room that they had shared for so long and then quickly clattered up the ladder, and with the cheers of his ship's company still ringing in his ears he clambered ashore. He did not look back at the grey ship lying alongside the jetty, but tried instead to think of the long train journey to Northumberland which lay ahead of him.

The training course had taken only seven weeks.

Twenty-four men found themselves being addressed by the Commander, a quiet, upstanding man, greying at the temples.

"As you all know, we are hard pressed. We have suffered very severe losses recently and most of our trained and experienced men have given their lives. That is why we have called upon you to make good the loss and to carry on where they left off. You may all have a choice of appointment, starting in order of examination results. The following appointments need filling," he continued, clearing his throat:

"Tenth flotilla at Malta — four officers. Fourth at Alexandria — six. Eighth at Gibraltar — four. Sixth at Rothesay — two.

"Well done, all of you. Let me have your choice by noon today. Thank you, good luck and good hunting!"

He turned on his heel and the young men silently dispersed.

So it was that Peter Sinclair chose for himself the Fighting Tenth at Malta; but he had still to reach the beleaguered island.

Gibraltar was the halfway house, and Peter reached the lonely fortress in a Catalina flying boat.

The Rock had not changed since he was last there in a Home Fleet destroyer. The main street still smelled the same; the 'Scorps', as the local inhabitants were affectionately called, still smiled their ingratiating smiles, and the jingling of jukeboxes and tinny pianos still chimed from the gloomy interiors of the cafés.

The 'gharries', pulled by flea-bitten little ponies, still picked their way through the thronging main street, cluttered up by scrambling children and squawking fowls. But as sunset shut down on the bustling street, the activities ceased as suddenly as a tap turned off. No longer did the twinkling lights spatter the Rock face like glow-worms on a midsummer's night. The rigidly enforced blackout threw the great Rock into massive relief against the purple night sky, its overpowering vastness like a huge backdrop to an immense stage. By night, Gibraltar seemed to be grimly at war, in strong contrast to its daylight gaiety. The dark alleyways, which led off from the only street, brooded sombrely down upon the town, the shutters of the overhanging houses clasping hands across the street to shut out the immensity of the heavens above.

Peter wandered back to the Submarine Depot Ship which was secured to the South Mole, with her small brood of submarines nestled against her towering side. At her forward end, the huge, blue shape of the ocean-going submarine *Tweed* lay stored and ready for sea. This was her last night in harbour, for, at dusk on the morrow, she was bound on yet another storing trip to the beleaguered island of Malta.

This huge and unwieldy submarine *Tweed* was for Malta, the last connecting link with freedom, for without her the besieged island could no longer hold out. To fight back she must have high octane aviation spirit for her few gallant fighter aircraft and *Tweed* carried the explosive stuff in her tanks. Malta needed food and the Tenth Submarine Flotilla needed engine spares and torpedoes; torpedoes, torpedoes and always more torpedoes. So desperate was the need for torpedoes to hit back at Rommel's supply lines, that the Flotilla Torpedo Officer was even diving down to retrieve them from bombed and sunken submarines in the dockyard: a horrible and gruesome task.

So *Tweed*'s passages were packed with gleaming blue torpedoes, while green smokescreen canisters cluttered up every corner and in this floating gunpowder barrel, Peter had his first taste of operational submarine warfare. *Tweed* was forbidden to attack the enemy under any circumstances. Her role was vital, for with her precious cargo she had to reach Malta quickly and safely. Nothing else mattered.

To Peter, the swift passage was like a dream. It was an unusual sensation to travel at one hundred and twenty feet below the surface, in an explosive machine, through enemy minefields, and three miles from the enemy's doorstep.

Looking at his messmates, he found it difficult to realise that they had been carrying out this unenviable run for many months.

Tweed surfaced at dawn off the tiny islet of Filfla, at the south-eastern corner of Malta. She broke surface astern of the minesweeper which waited to escort her up the swept channel of the protective minefield and into harbour. A wheeling Spitfire glistened above them, spiralling in the morning sun in a frenzy of delight.

It was a thrilling moment for Peter. For the first time, he absorbed the pleasure of sighting the besieged island from a submarine's bridge and was wonderstruck by the peace and serenity of the scene.

The sandstone of the island battlements and buildings was washed by the freshness of the new dawn, and, as each mile passed, the outline of the buildings sharpened. Against the blue sky the craggy battlements, ruggedly defying all assaults of the foe, stood clearly stencilled.

Here have we been for a thousand years, and here we mean to stay, their massive strength proclaimed. Blue seas broke into white cascades of falling spray as they crashed against the rocky bluffs.

Tweed was now within a mile of Grand Harbour, and the breakwaters were slowly opening to view. The mighty bastions of the ancient Knights of St. John glowered disdainfully down upon the clear aquamarine of Grand Harbour, shielded now by a black necklace of booms and nets. Slowly *Tweed* cleared the entrance to Grand Harbour and approached the smaller openings to Sliema Creek and Lazaretto Island. Breaking away from her escort she turned slowly to port, her casing lined by the seamen who were fallen in at Harbour Stations. The roar of her diesels died away, as she slid at last into her haven on her silent electric motors.

Peter turned his head towards the faint noise of children's voices. His eyes blurred at the sight of lines of women and children sprinkling the long breakwater like icing on a cake. Yelling and screaming, weeping and waving, they bellowed their little lungs out to welcome in yet another life-giving British submarine. They knew *Tweed*, as soon as she showed as a black dot on the distant horizon. To them she meant petrol, and petrol meant Spitfires to protect the skies above them. To these little knots of waving figures, the blue, whale-like creature wallowing in through the 'boom' spelled revenge in the shape of speeding torpedoes, bubbling their way mercilessly to their targets. To them, *Tweed* meant an earlier end to their hardships and miseries.

The great sanctuary opened up before them. Leaving Sliema Creek, the former peacetime destroyer anchorage, to starboard, *Tweed* slid in under the battlements of Malta, Lazaretto Island on her starboard bow. Already the blue shapes of the little submarines, lying like a shoal of sharks straining at their moorings, came into view. They were strung in a semicircle around the sandstone buildings called Lazaretto, the former leper colony which was built upon this barren Manoel Island.

Under the arches of the buildings, little groups of waiting figures, dressed in serviceable khaki shorts and shirts, stood ready to welcome once more the gallant maid-of-all-work, *Tweed*, who had again brought them more 'teeth', more smoke canisters, vital engineering spare parts, yes, and it must be confessed, just the odd and very precious bottle of refreshment!

But the old boat was not home yet, and turning slowly to starboard, she settled alongside a petrol lighter where some battered lorries awaited her. Hardly had she secured her wires, when the petrol hoses were connected. Within fifteen minutes, the hoses jumped and pulsated as the precious spirit poured into the hungry tankers, which then sped away in dusty, yellow clouds, bumping over the potholes, to take the priceless lifeblood to secret tanks at the edge of the airfields. Not until the last drop of petrol was emptied did *Tweed* relax, and then it was only to proceed halfway up Torpedo Creek to unload her precious torpedoes at the depot.

By nightfall, she was unloaded and her company went ashore, exhausted, dirty and hungry.

But Malta shook herself, took stock of her augmented arsenal, squared her shoulders and was refreshed.

CHAPTER 4

Baptism of Fire

The cold woke him. For some time he lay still, wondering where he was and enjoying the puzzle of his present whereabouts. If it was his beloved Dartmoor, where was the low murmur of the stream at the bottom of the cleave? The stars glittered like sparklers on Guy Fawkes night in a sky of indigo blue, but the Channel did not behave like this. With a contented grunt, he slowly turned over to switch on the lamp. His fingers found no switch but only groped softly against damp sandstone which exuded a musty moistness. While an eddy of wind rattled a corner of the corrugated iron sheet which gamely attempted to call itself a roof, he slowly gained consciousness.

Already the blue above him was lightening to a pale green, for the dawn was breaking fast. The tintinnabulation of church bells, chiming the hour of six, gently came to him from across the water. Now fully awake, he wandered out in his bare feet to stand beside his roofless and doorless room on the terrace which overlooked the green waters of the harbour. The cool flagstones felt soft to his feet and, looking down, Peter saw the rough sandstone steps which led down to the shower room.

The outer end of each step was decorated by a small, carved sandstone block. Discarding his pyjama jacket and grasping his towel and toilet gear, he slowly padded down the steps looking at each, and recalling the famous submarines whose names showed on the rough faces of the blocks of stone. Unobtrusively these talismen reminded those who now used the steps of the ideals and standards set by those who had gone before, but had not returned; who had, until very recently, trodden these same stone steps. Thoughtfully Peter made his way slowly down to the wash-places.

"Let go aft. Let go for'd."

At three-thirty two days later, His Majesty's Submarine *Rugged* slipped unostentatiously from her mooring-buoys off Lazaretto to nose her way out of the battered harbour. The little 600-ton submarine was sleekly, strangely beautiful in a sinister way. As she silently scythed her course through the green waters, which rapidly turned to a deeper blue on clearing the harbour entrance, her bows, pierced by the free-flood holes, grinned like the snout of a hungry shark.

To Peter, appointed as Third Hand to *Rugged* two days previously, this neat and tiny boat was a great contrast to *Tweed*. Immediately *Rugged* was clear of the boom, her diesels were started and she bumbled along at her maximum speed of ten knots. As she was diesel-electric, she had no clumsy clutches to operate when changing from the electric batteries to her diesel engines. This gave her speed in diving, an essential for these little boats operating on the enemy's doorstep.

But Peter had little time to notice what was going on around him, for he was concentrating on seeing that all was secured properly on the casing, the wires stowed and the gun greased. The duties of the Third Hand included that of Gunnery Officer, and Peter had been shinning up and down the conning tower with his weary gun's crew for the last two days, training them and himself for Gun Action, even though they were alongside in harbour.

Surprise was the essence of gun attack, and this could only be achieved if the gun's crew were swift and efficient. Peter's new Captain had insisted that his Third Hand should be perfect in his gun drill, and, on surfacing after the Trim Dive, he was going to exercise Gun Action. All went well. *Rugged* carried out her Trim Dive when clear of the swept channel south of Malta, and went to 'Patrol Routine', remaining on the surface all night.

So, for the first time, Peter was taking part in an offensive submarine patrol and carrying out the duties of one of the four officers in His Majesty's Submarine *Rugged*, one of the partners in the renowned Tenth Submarine Flotilla, affectionately known as 'The Fighting Tenth'.

Peter felt a surge of pride in the realisation that he had been chosen to serve here. In this little boat, his tubular steel home for months to come, he felt at home. Already he knew that his other three officers were keen for him to settle down and become part of the boat.

The Captain, Lieutenant Croxton, D.S.C., Royal Navy, had been a stern taskmaster to Peter, sparing no effort to ensure that he was as efficient as possible in the short time left to him before sailing. 'Joe', as the Captain was called, drove his officers and men hard, but withal, he had a mischievous sense of humour. His ship's company respected him, not because they liked him for his personal traits, but because he was an extremely efficient and successful submarine Commanding Officer. During an attack, when being counter-attacked and depth-charged by the infuriated enemy, he was as crafty and as cool as a Siamese cat. It was frustrating to a submarine's crew for their Captain to miss the target with his four torpedoes, after perhaps hours of tension during the run-in of the attack. To miss occasionally and to receive a hot depth-charging in return was part of the game, but to fail frequently and receive the same medicine was bad for morale, however pleasant a Captain might be.

But Joe Croxton did not miss. He was one of those born submariners blessed with what is known as a 'periscope eye'. Cool in action, his temper when he was roused seared flaming hot, shrivelling officers and men so that they wished they had never been born. But the storm was soon over and all was forgiven, providing the offender was repentant. Joe was no respecter of persons, as Peter well remembered when the First Lieutenant was the victim on one occasion.

Number One had put on a bad trim, and had broken surface for the second time, the back of his neck flushing with shame.

"What the devil is the matter, First Lieutenant? Can't you keep a proper trim?" the sarcastic voice of the Captain snarled, but for once in his life the First Lieutenant was unrepentant.

"I'm sorry, sir, but you didn't give me enough time to catch a trim on diving."

The First Lieutenant turned away from his Captain in a gesture of impatience and busied himself with the pump order instruments. The men in the Control Room sensed that a drama was about to be played, and a pin could have been heard to drop in the silence that followed.

"Very well, First Lieutenant, go to diving stations."

"Diving stations? Aye, aye, sir," replied Number One, a slight trace of resentment in his voice as he said, "diving stations!"

Tired men, wiping sleep away from their red-rimmed eyes, bundled their way into the Control Room.

"Eighty feet, First Lieutenant."

"Eighty feet, sir."

Slowly the First Lieutenant, hand on his left hip, legs astride, took the boat down to her ordered depth, but carelessly allowed her to slide past it to eighty-seven feet.

"I ordered eighty feet, not eighty-seven, First Lieutenant."

The First Lieutenant bit his lip but said nothing.

"Periscope depth," the Captain snapped.

"Periscope depth, sir."

Peter looked at Joe. His face was a hard, inscrutable mask, eyes glinting with anger. He stalked up and down the restricted space, a figure of suppressed fury. The Control Room crew dared not meet his eye and not even a wink passed between them.

The unfortunate First Lieutenant, in spite of desperate countermeasures, very nearly broke surface again, the boat porpoising about almost out of control and staying at twenty feet instead of the usual twenty-eight feet.

"What a performance! First Lieutenant, we shall remain at diving stations until you control this boat properly. Eighty feet!"

"Aye, aye, sir. Eighty feet, sir."

By now, the First Lieutenant was noticeably more restrained, and quieter in his speech, a sure sign of danger with him. But this time, he pumped out sufficient water, and settled nicely on the ordered depth.

"Periscope depth," the waiting figure of the Captain snapped.

"Periscope depth, sir."

Calmly the First Lieutenant unfolded his arms and took the boat upwards. A wicked point of light seemed to dance in the glowing eyes of the Captain.

How unlike they are, those two, thought Peter to himself, watching this drama being played out, *but Number One is on a sticky wicket!*

Once more the First Lieutenant felt that, longing to get back to their bunks as the men were, all eyes in the boat followed the pointers on the depth gauges, but he also knew that his ship's company would stay there until Kingdom Come before murmuring any disapproval.

And so this drawn-out exercise continued. Five more times did Number One take the boat up and down before Joe was satisfied. Number One had learned his lesson for all time, and in future attacks he was to bless Joe's apparent hardness. It was amazing to Peter that this incident seemed to weld the whole boat together and from then onwards, Joe and his First Lieutenant worked together in perfect combination. The others knew that nothing but the best would suffice, and that all was done in the name of efficiency. Efficiency meant survival.

No, Joe did not miss, so the 'troops' had confidence in him. He was angular and large-mouthed, with black eyes that burned in their deep sockets like a smouldering fire. In the summer, when dived by day on patrol, his uniform consisted merely of a coloured 'sarong' and sandals, a fashion and challenge to be taken up by the remainder of the crew, who vied with each other for the most alarming and gaudy pattern possible.

For the *haute couture* of this season, Joe bashfully entered the Control Room wearing for the first time a sarong brilliantly decorated with coloured butterflies; but this was soon outmoded and classed as 'too restrained' when the Outside E.R.A. appeared in one of his own design, purple tigers and green foliage predominating.

On Joe's shoulders rested the safety of the whole boat. By indecision or by one wrong decision during any second of the fourteen-day patrol, he could bring sudden and overwhelming disaster upon them all. All knew this, of course, and readily excused his frequent outbursts, nay, even loved him for them!

"Shift to night lighting! Lookouts in the tower!"

The orders were passed verbally through the length of the boat and the harsh electric lights were replaced by red bulbs, which threw an eerie crimson glow on all and sundry, plunging the boat into an atmosphere of sinister purpose. By this red light, eyes became accustomed to the darkness more quickly, lookouts having to remain in the darkness of the conning tower for only ten minutes, instead of the regulation twenty in normal light.

As a further precaution, a circular canvas 'skirt' known as 'the trunk' was fastened to the lip of the lower conning tower hatch and surrounded the ladder from the Control Room. An aperture, which formed a small doorway in the trunk, allowed a man to enter the canvas and climb the ladder into the darkness above him.

In the Control Room, the two lookouts, rustling in their weatherproof 'Ursula' suits, made ready to climb into the tower. Checking their binocular settings, cleaning the eyepieces and gathering enough periscope paper with which to clean them when once they reached the isolation of the bridge, the first two lookouts were important people. As far as the duties of lookouts were concerned, there were no differentials in rank or branch. Seaman or stoker, electrician or torpedoman, the best men had the job and considered it an honour. The duty lasted for an hour only, each alternate man being relieved half-hourly.

Special pills were taken daily to help their night vision, and the watches were organised in the most efficient manner possible in order to help the lookouts. After keeping an hour's trick as a lookout on a submarine's bridge, a man came below extremely tired. The watches were organised on a three-watch system: red, white, blue, each watch lasting two hours, although in surface ships, where the tension was not so great, their watches were four-hourly. But in a submarine the concentration of will and eyesight to maintain sixty minutes' worth of continuous, one-hundred-per-cent efficiency was enormous.

On the bridge, the Officer of the Watch kept two-hour watches, being responsible to his Captain for the safety of the submarine in all eventualities. He, therefore, kept an all-round lookout, whereas the two rating lookouts only swept the sector down their respective sides.

At night, Peter was always the first Officer of the Watch on the bridge. Following the signalman, named Goddard, who opened the upper conning tower hatch on surfacing, Peter would haul himself on to the bridge which still dripped with cascading water, dash straight to the voicepipe cock and open it. Down below, as Peter opened the valve above, the helmsman would be holding a bucket to catch the water which poured from the belled end of the copper voicepipe. Not until this was done, was the bridge in communication with the brain cell of the submarine, the Control Room. The Captain, following close on Peter's heels, would take charge, Peter and the signalman acting as lookouts. When the Captain was satisfied that all was well, he would order "Up lookouts", and from the depths of the conning tower, where they were waiting in the darkness, the two lookouts would emerge like some creatures of the night, with binoculars slung about their necks.

For this night of patrol, on passage from Malta to North Africa, the Captain remained on the bridge whilst Peter stood his watch from seven to nine, and again from eleven until one in the morning. During this time, he was made to dive the boat twice by himself, an ordeal which soon gave him self-confidence.

At nine o'clock, he was relieved by the Navigating Officer, a young Lieutenant by the name of Hickey whom Peter had known during Dartmouth days.

Hickey had pale blue eyes that peered out from beneath light, sandy-coloured eyebrows with faint bewilderment. He smiled but rarely, but then his whole face would light up with delight and he would lose his strained look. His eyes would crinkle at the corners and the dark brown mole in the corner of his right cheek would become lost in his infectious smile. Until Peter became used to it, he was fascinated by the disappearing trick of Hickey's mole.

Peter clambered down below, grinning to himself, and went into the Ward Room. He shed his sweater which he stowed in the locker formed by the settee on which he sat for meals, and which was his bunk by night. On the other side of the table, which was suspended at one end by a brass chain, sat the First Lieutenant, a faint smile playing at the corners of his mouth.

The high-sounding title of Ward Room was given to this tiny compartment, used by the Captain and officers. It was enclosed on three sides only, the boat's passageway running across the inboard and open end. The after-end was formed by the Control Room watertight bulkhead, the outer by the ship's curved side: the tiny galley formed the for'd wall, and from thence all food originated, 'cooked' by the boat's voluntary cook, the gunlayer.

The small table of the Ward Room, large enough to feed four officers, filled the entire space in the centre of the compartment. Around this table were two settees which did the duty of seats by day and bunks by night. Against the ship's-side end of the table was the First Lieutenant's bunk, directly under a maze of pipes along which crawled erratically the brown specks of friendly cockroaches.

By night, another bunk was outfolded above the after settee, so that, with no extra passengers, each officer had a bunk to himself, the Captain's being the foremost to allow him rapid egress to the Control Room.

In the eventuality of extra 'guests', however, the officers had to sleep 'hot bunks': the officer who came off watch had to use whichever bunk was empty. Not a very savoury custom but a warm one, nevertheless!

"Hullo, Sub! Enjoyed your first watch?" asked the First Lieutenant quietly. This unassuming manner of his was a quality which Peter was to admire so much in the days to come.

"Yes, thank you, Number One, but I've got such a heck of a lot to learn," sighed Peter, before he continued, "By the way, the Captain said he would be down for supper shortly."

"Good-o! I'm hungry. Would you mind telling the good news to O'Riley, the flunkey?"

At that identical moment, O'Riley, by some curious coincidence, happened to pass by the Ward Room.

"Supper in ten minutes, O'Riley," ordered Number One, giving Peter an enormous wink. "What is it tonight? Cockroach soup and corned dog?"

"Yes, sorr; how did you guess, sorr?" replied the black-haired Irishman, grinning all over his open face, "But there's veg with it tonight, sorr; fresh veg!" and he disappeared into the galley.

A few seconds later, in he came, bearing some limp lettuce leaves which looked like brown paper.

"There ye are, sorr! The red lights don't 'arf make it look nice, don't it, sorr?" asked O'Riley with an expressionless face, eyes glued to the revolting lettuce leaves. "Shall I bring in the soup, sorr?"

"No, hold on a minute."

"Very good, sorr. Would ye like…?"

His conversation remained unfinished, as the deafening hootings of the klaxons rent the air.

O'Riley dived into the Control Room. The First Lieutenant, pulling the tablecloth with him, hurtled past Peter. Peter heaved himself up and rushed to man the Fruit Machine. Past him, men moved swiftly fore and aft to their diving stations. The planesmen yanked at their wheels, the main vents flooded open above their heads as the rumble of the diesels died away.

The clanging of the brass telegraphs still rang in the air. The hands of the Outside E.R.A. snaked over the 'panel' like lightning, as he tugged at the levers. Thunk! Thunk! went the main vents, opening overhead and allowing the water to rush in.

With a lurch, the boat took up a steep bow-down angle, causing Peter to hold on to the Fruit Machine, while two overall-clad lookouts tumbled out from the canvas hood and made their way silently for'd. A faint clang in the conning tower echoed from above.

"First clip on!" hailed the Captain's incisive voice from the darkness — "eighty feet!"

The competent figure of Number One faced the depth gauges, one hand on his left hip, whilst, with the other, he flipped the knurled knob of the pump order instrument: 25 … 28 … 30 … 35 … 45 feet.

"Blow 'Q'," snapped the First Lieutenant. A hiss and a roar followed as the high-pressure air blew out ten tons of water, the tank venting its foul air directly into the compartment.

At sixty-five feet two distant jolts were felt by all on board.

"That's that!" said the Captain. "Junkers 88, wasn't it, Pilot?" he asked Hickey who had preceded him down the conning tower ladder.

"I thinks so, sir."

"We'll give him the routine fifteen minutes, Number One, and then I'll surface. It looks as if they will be ready for us off Benghazi, doesn't it?"

"Yes, sir," replied Number One.

"Rommel wants every gallon of petrol and every round of ammunition he can get at the moment," the Captain continued, "but I wonder which way the square heads will be driving this time?"

They were to know at dawn.

The battle that was to be one of the turning points of the Second World War was as yet unfought. General Alexander had not yet come to grips with Rommel and both sides were sparring for the final death grapple at Alamein.

Rommel's Afrika Korps, the crack corps of the German Army, nominally supported by Mussolini's hordes, was building up its strength to fight its way through to Alexandria. From thence their objectives were Suez and India, where the Japanese were knocking at the gates. One more shove and Rommel would be through.

But before he struck, he had to have more petrol, more guns and ammunition. Shipped in convoys which sailed from Naples and Palermo, the only way in which these essentials could be delivered was by sea. Heavily escorted, the shipping would steam at full speed down the narrow funnel to Tunis, a channel heavily mined on either side.

The convoys would then be reorganised, the smaller coasters and tankers being sent round Cape Bon and along the North African coast to Tripoli and Benghazi, coast-hugging all the way.

And that is where 'The Fighting Tenth' appeared on the scene — they struck along the whole route from Naples to Benghazi.

At dawn, a small, blue submarine slithered beneath the shallow waters off the low-lying coast of Tripolitania. Her intended landfall was a small port named Burat-el-Sun which was being used to full capacity by the Hun to unload his precious petrol supplies. Submarines, small tankers, and anything capable of floating were ferrying the precious liquid to the Afrika Korps.

Just before diving, the Captain had taken a star sight with his sextant. The low-lying coast was still invisible to the bridge personnel, the bridge being only some twelve feet above the waterline, and so their position was doubtful.

On diving, it was the navigator's duty to work out the calculation of the sight and, thereby, to determine the boat's position. It was a task that took some twenty minutes of careful working. Crouched over the minute chart table in the Control Room, Hickey was still labouring away after twenty-five minutes had elapsed.

"Got a position line, yet?" crackled the voice of the Captain.

"Not yet, sir."

"Then buck up! I want to go straight in. This is the one time we might see a U-boat."

The Captain was impatiently waiting in the Ward Room, while the First Lieutenant kept a periscope watch. Number One kept quiet, for he sensed the impending storm.

Another three minutes elapsed.

With a grunt, Joe sprang from his seat. He could stand it no longer.

"Get out of my way!" he blurted explosively into Hickey's ear. "Learn to do your job properly, so that others don't have to do it for you."

He barged against Hickey, pushing him from the chart table and sending the dividers clattering on to the corticene deck.

"Don't make such a blasted noise!" he snapped.

Hickey stooped down to pick up the dividers, his face flushing while the Captain's eye quickly ran up and down the rows of figures, stopping after half a minute's perusal, his eye stabbing at a blurred figure.

"Pencil?" he rapped out, not looking round.

"Here you are, sir."

"More haste, less speed, is my advice to you, Pilot. Slow but sure is a much better way of going about things. Look here!" — and he almost drove the pencil point through the paper as he indicated a careless subtraction.

Peter was forced to look away from Hickey's discomfiture. Both Peter and Number One seemed strangely preoccupied with the job in hand, Peter twiddling the knobs on his Fruit Machine, whilst Number One seemed to be concentrating on pumping.

Within a few minutes, the Captain had produced a position-line.

"Now get it on the chart, and for Heaven's sake get a move on."

Changing places, Hickey drew in the position-lines, the Captain scowling over his shoulder, flicking his fingers and thumbs impatiently.

"That's it, sir!" announced Hickey, a nervous smile of achievement creasing his pale face, as he stepped back to allow the Captain a sight of the chart.

"Humph! Five miles to the eastward," Joe grunted as he snapped shut the dividers. Then, carefully running the parallel ruler across the chart, he drew a pencil line which led to the shallow entrance of the little port of Burat-el-Sun.

"Port ten, steer two-two-five," the Captain ordered.

"Port ten, steer two-two-five, sir," repeated the First Lieutenant who was still on watch.

Already the helmsman, crouched by his wheel in the port for'd corner of the Control Room, had flicked the brass wheel over towards the ship's side, the spokes glinting in the glare of the bright electric light.

"Keep a good lookout for aircraft, Number One. Land should show up in about twenty minutes. I'm going to have my breakfast" — and the Captain strode three yards from the Control Room and into the Ward Room, Hickey following sheepishly behind him. Joe was a hard taskmaster but, once he delivered his reprimand, that was the end of it and life went on as before. This incident drove home to Peter the importance of knowing his job backwards and he intended never to cross Joe's path if he could possibly avoid it.

Half an hour elapsed before Number One called, "Captain in the Control Room!" — a cry which, later on, always secretly brought men's hearts into their mouths. Joe quietly rose from his seat, strode into the Control Room and took over the periscope which had been fixed on a set bearing by the First Lieutenant.

"Thank you, Number One. Bearing THAT," he rapped out, squinting through the eyepieces.

"Red five," reported the Outside E.R.A., as he read off the bearing from the brass sleeve which surrounded the periscope at the deckhead. Hickey scuttled to the chart.

"That's the entrance to Burat-el-Sun. Course for the entrance, please?"

"One-seven-oh, sir."

"Steer one-seven-oh."

Ten minutes later, they were on their patrol line, off the entrance to this vital little port, and three miles from the narrow approach channel.

"Be careful with that periscope, Number One. There are two aircraft to seaward of us," and, swinging round the periscope, the Captain steadied it on two black specks circling like buzzards, two miles away.

"See them?" he asked his First Lieutenant, handing the periscope over to him.

"Yes, sir," Number One answered, as he peered through the eyepieces.

"Down periscope," ordered the Captain, and from now on, for fear of detection, the periscope was only to be used for a few seconds at a time. The Captain then returned to the Ward Room, and, five minutes later, the watches changed.

"Blue watch, watch diving," ordered Number One.

The order was passed verbally throughout the little boat, men strolling from for'd to relieve their weary shipmates. This was always a difficult moment, because, in a boat of this small size, the sudden shift of weight from for'd to aft tended to tilt the bows upwards, which risked a disastrous 'break surface'.

"All right, Sinclair?" asked Number One after handing his watch over to Peter.

"Yes, thank you, Number One." With a thumping in his heart, Peter was taking his first diving watch alone, on war patrol, only some three miles distant from the enemy shore. It was a tremendous moment for him.

One false move, or one moment of carelessness, thought Peter to himself, *and I can send all of us, and this half a million pounds' worth of submarine, to Davy Jones's locker.*

"Up periscope," he ordered aloud, trying to appear unconcerned.

Swish! The steel tube streaked upwards.

Peter clamped himself on to the handles, swinging quickly round with the low-power lens to look for aircraft. Suddenly he stopped his sweep, his gaze riveted upon a small black dot which moved imperceptibly across his small circle of vision.

"Down periscope," Peter ordered, snapping the handles shut.

Pausing a moment, he strolled up to the depth gauges, conscious that all eyes in the Control Room were furtively watching their new Sub-Lieutenant. Hickey was still lounging on the chart table and Peter was very conscious of him.

"Up periscope," Peter ordered and then swung the lens farther round to the yellow shore. He was amazed that he could see German lorries, packed full of helmeted troops, driving eastwards along the brown coast road.

Is this really me, looking at the enemy at such close range? Peter asked himself incredulously. The lorries were driving wheel to wheel and sending great whorls of dust streaming across the desert.

"Down periscope." Peter was fascinated by the new excitement, hardly able to contain his astonishment before the next look.

"Up periscope."

To the right lay the harbour, if it could be so called. Guarded by two shallow sandbanks, the dirty brown water opened into an anchorage. He could just see a large pier which must have been where the petrol was discharged, because a small tanker lay alongside. In the harbour the topmasts of at least a dozen small ships were visible.

He swung the periscope across the coast and over the sea again. Slowly the lens swept the horizon, little wavelets drenching the periscope glass.

Peter stiffened. Into his circle of vision a black object, looking like a matchbox, grew larger at every second. A surging white crest of a bow wave gleamed intermittently, as the shape pushed its way through the still waters.

"Captain in the Control Room!" yelled Peter excitedly.

The Captain streaked into the Control Room and snatched the periscope from Peter's hands.

"Diving stations! Bearing THAT! Down periscope!" The periscope handles snapped shut. Swish! The flashing steel tube streaked down into the periscope well.

"Target — U-boat! Stand by all tubes!" the Captain snapped out his orders. "Starboard twenty, up periscope."

Swish! The periscope snaked upwards.

Swiftly, silently, men rushed to their diving stations to relieve those on watch, who, in their turn, disappeared to lonely stations in the more remote corners of the boat.

Number One, his watchful eyes lynx-like on the trim, flicked the knob of the pump order instrument.

"For Heaven's sake, watch your trim, Number One! It's very shallow," murmured the Captain, for he could feel the boat taking on a bow-up angle.

Peter had dashed to his box of tricks, the Fruit Machine, on which he was putting all the settings from the information that now streamed from the Captain's lips. By Peter's right hand were the 'tube ready' lamps and each mauve light flicked on in turn: Number two ready — Number three ready — Number four ready — Number one ready!

"All tubes ready, sir," reported Peter.

"Down periscope. Anything from the Asdics?" asked the Captain.

In his dark corner in the port after-end of the Control Room, Elliott, the Asdic operator, earphones clamped over his head, listened intently, while his right hand slowly moved a black ebony dial.

"H.E. increasing, sir: diesel, estimated speed, fifteen knots."

"Very good," acknowledged the Captain; "course for a one-two-oh track?"

"One-two-five, sir," replied Peter.

"Steady on one-two-five, up periscope."

The helmsman spun his wheel, checking her swing.

"Course one-two-five, sir."

Uncurling himself from the deck as the periscope flashed past him, the Captain snapped open the handles, a thin pencil of light stabbing the pupils of his eyes, as the glass broke surface.

"Bearing THAT!"

"Green-one-five."

Snap! The periscope handles banged shut. Down swept the gleaming tube.

"Don't dip me for Heaven's sake, Number One! Up periscope."

The Captain swung himself up with the periscope.

"Stand by!… Fire one!… Fire two!… Down periscope. Fire by Time Interval."

Swish! The periscope streaked downwards.

"Fire three … Fire four!" Peter passed over the telephone to the tube space.

Phumph! … phumph! … phumph! … phumph! … The jolt of the compressed air, as the torpedoes left the boat, jarred the whole atmosphere.

"Torpedoes running, sir," reported the Asdic operator.

"Starboard twenty," the Captain ordered quietly.

The helmsman's monotonous repetition of the order was the only sound to break the tense silence. No sound except the background hum and whine of the main motors. Strained faces watching dials and skilled hands spinning the brass hydroplane wheels, waiting — waiting for the shattering explosion which would mean a torpedo tearing into the vitals of an enemy U-boat.

CHAPTER 5

Gun Action!

Capitano di Corvetta Roberto Puzzi felt extraordinarily pleased with himself. He was a pompous little man, and had reason to feel deserving of Il Duce's commendation. Leaning on the bridge of his large submarine which was loaded to capacity with petrol for the victorious armies of Rommel and Graziani, he puffed at a rancid cigar. Three days previously, before the submarine left on her storing run, the Italian Admiral in Palermo had come to see him personally.

"I and Rommel," he had declared, "rely upon you, Puzzi. Viva Il Duce!" and they had exchanged their fascist salutes — rather smartly he thought.

Here he was, almost at his destination, a hellhole of a place called Burat-el-Sun, boasting the name of a port, the existence of which he had never even heard before the war. He was hot, sticky and dirty, and for two hours now he had been coast-crawling along this yellow strip of Tripolitania. He kept well inshore and in the shadows to avoid the arrogant British submarines which lurked so frequently in this area.

Ah! There was Burat-el-Sun! Five miles on his starboard bow, the masts of the shipping dancing in the mirage, for it was confoundedly hot, *sapristi!* In the wings of the bridge, the lookouts were singing their popular peasant songs. Although unshaven and sallow, they felt happy, for this cursed war, which nobody wanted, would soon be over. Did not Il Duce say so? Graziani and Rommel would soon be in Alexandria, and the *Capitano* flicked his thumb and forefinger together in a gesture of finality, and, smiling and singing to himself, he lightly tapped out the rhythm of the song with his sandalled foot.

There was the buoy, fine on the starboard bow! Crouching over the voicepipe, he gave the order, "Starboard fifteen, steer one-three-oh." The boat quickly answered to her helm and swung to her new course.

The voice of the port lookout stopped in the middle of his song. He stood transfixed, with his arm outstretched towards the port quarter, screaming at the top of his voice, his eyes bulging.

"*Guarda! Guarda! Torpedini, torpedini!*" he screamed and glanced round at the blanched face of Capitano di Corvetta Roberto Puzzi, who had spun round on the alarm, his cigar hanging limply from his lips.

"*Santa Maria!*" he shrieked, as his eyes fastened on the four parallel tracks of bubbling water, now only three hundred yards away and growing nearer every second.

"Hard-a-starboard," he whispered hoarsely down the voicepipe. Then he gripped the pipe with both hands, shaking it with frantic urgency and screaming down it at the top of his voice as the boat started to swing away to starboard.

"Midships! Steady!" the trembling voice of the *Capitano* mumbled down the brass voicepipe, as the stern of his boat steadied on a parallel course to the torpedoes which were now lunging upon them. Time stood still on the bridge. Not a sound, except for the faint coughing of the diesel exhausts in the hot, muggy air. The four lines of bubbles seemed to creep slowly, so slowly up their stern. And then suddenly, the first tracks streaked down their port side twenty feet clear, so close that the bubbles hissed as they broke surface. Mesmerised, the

Capitano could not tear his eyes away as the bubbles effervesced abreast the bridge.

"*Il Capitano, il Capitano!*" the agonised voice of the diminutive starboard lookout cried hoarsely. Tears streamed down his face and his grimy finger pointed over the side, where a line of bubbles slithered under the ballast tank. They held their breaths, crossing themselves rapidly and gabbling away in their native dialects. Looking up, they saw two further tracks hiss past them, but farther out to starboard.

Slowly the *Capitano* dragged his eyes away from the murderous tracks which now trailed away ahead of them, growing fainter with every second that elapsed.

"*Grazie, grazie!*" he sighed, averting his gaze. "Port twenty," he shouted, for the boat would soon be on the sandbanks. As if to emphasise the danger, four dull thuds shook the steel hull of the submarine, as four foaming spouts of water and spray leaped into the air, three hundred yards distant on their starboard side.

As the Italian U-boat rounded the black buoy at the narrow entrance to the shallow harbour, her ship's company and Capitano di Corvetta Roberto Puzzi were silent and thoughtful men.

The tension in *Rugged's* Control Room was shattered by four muffled thuds.

"Confound it! Those aren't hits. Up periscope," Joe barked.

Using the large for'd periscope, he quickly swept around the horizon for patrolling aircraft, but, seeing none, he continued his search until he fastened upon the U-boat's bearing. She was already hull down and steaming as fast as she knew how. Flicking the lens over to high-power, he could just see the gesticulating Italians on their bridge. At that very moment, the U-boat altered course to port towards the buoy.

"Down periscope," sighed Joe wearily. "Sorry about that, but she seems to have altered away just after firing. Those thuds were our 'fish' hitting the sandbanks, Number One. Tell the hands, 'Better luck next time — she's got to come out again!'" And, with that, Joe's face lit up with an endearing grin. His eyes met those of his men around him, eyes that met his with sympathetic understanding.

The First Lieutenant grinned at his Captain and spoke for the ship, "Bad luck, sir. Shall I go to patrol routine?"

"No, Number One. Let's get out of here, because they're bound to send something out to look for us. It's too shallow for us to go deep. Come round to north, and when we've got enough water under us, I'll go deep to reload."

"Aye, aye, sir. Port ten, steer north."

"Port ten, steer north, sir," the steady voice of the helmsman replied.

The Captain kept the periscope watch for the next five minutes, while they slowly circled away from the scene. He then handed the boat over to Peter, as the First Lieutenant was busy readjusting the trim which had inevitably been upset by the discharge of four tons of torpedoes. Orders were passed along the boat from man to man, like links in a chain. When the order had been carried out, back came the report to the Control Room that the order had been executed. Men relaxed and slouched against bulkhead doors, joking and yarning about the recent attack, and placing bets upon the next move.

In the tube space, Slater, the Torpedo Petty Officer, who was the senior rating responsible for the correct functioning of the precious torpedoes, moved nimbly, opening and shutting valves as he 'blew down' the tubes, thus draining them of the water that had rushed into them as the torpedoes sped on their journey to the sandbanks.

"Well! That's eight thousand pounds on the putty," grinned Petty Officer Slater, who was joking with Smith, the Seaman Torpedoman.

"Cor! What couldn't I do with that lot?" mused the black-haired cockney, wiping his glistening forehead with an oily wad of cotton waste.

In the Control Room, men bustled around the figure of the Captain, while his Navigator, Hickey, crouched low over the chart table, was busy laying fresh plans. As he picked off distances with the dividers, the Captain mused aloud.

"Go deep now, Number One. Take her down slowly to eighty feet."

"Aye, aye, sir. Eighty feet," ordered Number One.

The periscope was lowered, the pumps whined into life, as the boat slowly sank to her new depth. The Captain listened for the ominous scraping of sand on her bottom, but nothing save the routine whine of motors could be heard.

"Eighty feet, sir."

"Thank you, reload all tubes."

"Reload all tubes, sir."

This was a tricky operation, and all men who were not on duty went to the fore-ends to help. When reloading, the submarine was in a very vulnerable state, for a counter-attack could well cause a shambles in the fore-ends, the heavy 'fish' rolling about out of control.

Four steel-blue torpedoes, glistening in the bright lights, had to be hauled by tackles into the gaping mouths of the tubes whose rear doors were now open, because the bow caps were shut to hold out the engulfing sea. The First Lieutenant had to be extremely careful to prevent the boat taking on any bow-down angle, for it would be a calamity to have a torpedo crashing about in the fore-ends. Heaving and sweating, the men laid back on the tackles, as the gleaming 'fish' were hauled out from the racks. No voice was heard except that of the 'T.I.', as Slater was called, giving his precise orders; encouraging here, cursing there, until at last he nursed his 'children' into their tubes.

While this operation was being carried out, the Captain spoke his thoughts to his First Lieutenant who was busy trimming.

"What do you think about it, Number One?" he asked. "They've got to de-fuel the U-boat, and I don't think that she'll risk coming out again before dark, knowing that we are in this area."

"Yes, sir?" answered Number One encouragingly.

"Let's try a double bluff. The odds are that they think we will have left this area to avoid detection, as we have now jeopardised our position. Right?"

"Right, sir."

"Then let's take advantage of that, and go into the harbour at dark. We can't dive because it's too shallow. That means gun action, going in trimmed-down on the surface. We'll slink in amongst the shipping and play merry havoc with the gun, which will give the Sub some practice! They shouldn't know what's hitting 'em. In the confusion, we ought to be able to slip out again on the surface, diving as soon as we're clear of the entrance. Does that make sense to you, Number One?"

The First Lieutenant paused before replying.

"Yes, sir: providing we achieve surprise."

"Yes. We'll stay out until dusk to make sure of that. What time is moonrise, Pilot?" the Captain asked Hickey.

Hickey fumbled with the pages of the Nautical Almanac.

"About one-fifteen a.m., sir."

"Good! I'll do that, then. All set for your first gun action, Sub?" asked Joe, a twinkle in his eye as he addressed Peter.

"Yes, sir. All ready."

"Well, you'll have a bit of time to think about it. We'll approach the entrance at dusk."

From all corners of the submarine, men exchanged glances. *What about getting out of the harbour again? Once we're inside, we've got to get out. They've only got to 'wing' us or get a ship across the entrance, and we're caught like rats in a trap.* So the thoughts ran, but remained unsaid. Joe did not take unnecessary risks, and he knew what he was doing.

"All tubes reloaded," came the report from the tube space.

"Very good. Go to watch diving, Number One. Tell everyone to get some sleep as they're going to have a busy night. Go to supper early, and tell the cook to make it one of his 'specials'. And issue the rum at supper."

"Aye, aye, sir. Red watch, watch diving."

Slowly the men took over their watch, the remainder going for'd to get some rest and to discuss the hours that lay before them.

It was the waiting for action at a predetermined time that Peter disliked most. As he became more accustomed to the daily routine of intense excitement and split-hair decisions, he began more and more to dislike the long waits. The sudden emergency exhilarated him, tuned as he was to a fine pitch of alertness after his time in the English Channel, but now they had seven hours to wait, quietly patrolling fifteen miles to seaward, invisible to the inshore patrols. Except for the odd sea bird and distant patrolling aircraft, there was nothing to be seen.

In his mind Peter continuously found himself repeating every detail of the gun action drill. By six o'clock he had an aching void in his stomach, feeling again the agonies of the batsman, waiting in the pavilion for the next wicket to fall. He could almost see the green fields at Dartmouth, sprinkled with white figures as they played their leisurely games. Apart from an identical feeling in the pit of his stomach, however, that was the end of the comparison. The game that they were now playing was for the higher stakes of life or death. How would he conduct himself when the testing time came in exactly two and a half hours? And, as he felt his mouth go dry, he remembered his friends in the Chasers who had sold their lives so gallantly. Their example comforted him, as he looked round at his companions.

Unconcerned, the Captain was reading the latest detective thriller, thick horn-rimmed spectacles perched on the end of his nose. The spectacles were a secret he kept from their Lordships at the Admiralty, for it was only when reading that his eyesight needed help.

"This is exciting!" he mused quietly to the world in general, the ghost of a smile twitching at the corners of his lips, as he peered at the novel propped on the Ward Room table.

Lieutenant John Easton, Royal Navy, twenty-three years old and First Lieutenant of His Majesty's Submarine *Rugged*, lay on his bunk with feet against the Control Room bulkhead. His head lay on his arms which were folded beneath him. His eyes followed the antics of a cockroach which scuttled along one of the pipes six inches above his head. In his bunk, which lay fore and aft against the ship's side, John Easton found the privacy for which he craved. Though within two feet of his brother officers, once he reached his bunk, perched six inches above the level of the Ward Room table and across the outboard end of it, he entered into his own private world. His messmates respected his feelings, and, when Number One lay there, his eyes open and staring at the pipes above him, they left him alone with his thoughts.

Recently married, he had had but ten days with his bride before sailing for the most active submarine flotilla in the world. Less than a year ago, his brother Ian had been in command of an armed trawler off the Scottish coast, where he had been murdered in cold blood by the merciless machine-guns of a Junkers 88 whilst swimming for his life in the cold North Sea. Only three years previously, they had both spent a holiday with their parents in North Wales, enjoying every carefree moment on the golden sands. Now both his brother and father lay dead, his father dying from a heart attack in the middle of a London air raid whilst shielding an old flower seller from the blast of a near miss.

No, Number One did not say much, though on occasions he could be most amusing with his dry humour. Calm in all emergencies, he was a man in whom all, officers and ratings, had confidence.

"Seven-forty, sir." Hickey's pale face poked round the corner from the Control Room, where he was on watch.

"Thank you, Pilot. Go to diving stations," answered the Captain, slowly closing his book. Peter followed him into the Control Room, where he found Number One already at his station between the depth gauges, adjusting the trim while the hands came tumbling aft.

"Stand by to surface!" The red lights had already been shipped, throwing an eerie light upon the expectant faces.

"Lookouts in the tower!"

Three minutes later, the little boat slid to the surface, the phosphorescence sparkling like quicksilver from her dripping sides, as water drained from her conning tower and superstructure. It was almost dark when the diesels started to charge their batteries.

Weaving slowly towards the coast, *Rugged* took over an hour to sight the low strip of land, standing like a black ribbon against the indigo blue of the clear sky which lingered over the desert.

"Stop main engines. Group up, slow ahead together," came the order down the voicepipe.

Down below in the red gloom, the clatter of the diesels died away as the main electric motors took over. No chances now, for silent skill must achieve the surprise.

Peter, clad in gym shoes, shorts and blue polo-necked sweater, waited in the Control Room. Standing near him was his gun's crew of five, dressed also in dark clothes. The others wore knitted balaclavas, rolled turban-like upon their heads, and looked as motley a collection of cut-throats as you could ever meet.

Stacks of three-inch shells lay piled in the gangway, ready to be passed, by a chain of hands, up the conning tower and down through the chutes on either side of the bridge, to the waiting ammunition supply number at the gun.

The gunlayer, Able Seaman Stack, was a swarthy Cornishman who revelled in the barking of his gun. He was captain of the gun and was the mainspring of enthusiasm for the speed with which it was manned. Grinning now in the semi-darkness, he was itching to get up the conning tower ladder to man his waiting weapon.

"Vickers gun on the bridge!"

Up went the vicious little machine-gun with its long flame guard, to be manned by the signalman, Goddard, who was waiting for it on the bridge.

"Gun action!" the Captain barked.

As Peter's eyes became accustomed to the darkness, he leaned over the side of the bridge to watch his gun's crew manning their gun, now trained upon the harbour entrance. He heard nothing but the lapping of wavelets against the pressure hull and the undertones of the Captain's orders.

"There's the buoy, right ahead, Sub. I'm going in now."

"Aye, aye, sir," answered Peter in a steady voice.

"If we're lucky and find the enemy U-boat, open fire on her without further orders. If we're out of luck, have a go at the tanker at the petrol-unloading pier. Don't open fire on her until I give the order."

"Aye, aye, sir."

"Load," ordered the Captain.

"Load," repeated Peter over the fore-end of the bridge.

"Load," answered the eager voice of the gunlayer.

The submarine shuddered to the extra power, surging forward as she increased speed for the attack. The breeze whipped around Peter's ears as she gathered way, sending little drifts of spray over the fore-casing and prompting jocular, muffled oaths amongst the gun's crew.

Hickey and the signalman strained through their glasses to look for the target. The black buoy slid down the starboard side, and now Peter could see the open harbour. Against the sombre foreshore, the outlines of the small ships at anchor were silhouetted, their masts and crosstrees laced against the night sky in a weird, fantastic tracery. An occasional flicker of light in one dark corner caught Peter's eye. He strained his eyes in that direction — there it was again! It flickered and was as quickly extinguished. His heart leaped, for it was the petrol pier and a low shape lay alongside it.

"There she is, sir! Fine on the port bow."

"Very good — I've got her. Port twenty," ordered the Captain.

The submarine swung round fast, putting the target broad on her starboard bow, but between them and their target lay several small ships at anchor, with very little distance between them.

"I'm going in between those two, Sub," indicated the Captain with outstretched hand, as the black shapes of ships loomed closer.

"Signalman, take the port ships. Pepper their guns to stop their crews from manning them."

"Aye, aye, sir," a soft Irish voice replied calmly.

Now that they were almost on top of them, Peter could see a figure leaning over the rail of the nearest coaster, and shouting at them excitedly.

"Target — ship — starboard bow!" Peter yelled to the gun's crew. The gun barrel aimed point blank at the squat tanker's side.

"Open fire," came the Captain's quiet voice.

"Open fire!" yelled Peter.

Crash! The gun's detonation shattered the night.

The ejected shell case bounced, clanging on to the pressure hull, and splashed over the side. A yellow flash and a spurt of red flame tore into the steel plating of the little coaster.

Rat-a-tat-tat — rat-a-tat! barked the vicious little Vickers, spitting green tracer into the ship which lay on their port quarter. Bang! Another round whined into the stillness of the night.

Click! Slam! The breech block added its own cacophony as it opened and shut to the accompaniment of the gunlayer's shouts.

"Hard-a-starboard!" shouted the Captain down the voicepipe. The boat swerved close under the counter of the coaster, and now all bedlam was let loose! As they flashed by, Peter could see figures rushing to man the guns of their ships, while the clatter of their Vickers snapped and barked at the stumbling men who fell sprawling.

"Shift target — port bow — U-boat on petrol jetty!" Peter yelled above the din.

"Shift target, sir… TARGET — ON!" yelled the exulting gunlayer as another round slammed home in the breech.

"Open fire!" shouted Peter.

Bang! Crash! Bang! Crash! Yellow spurts of flame flashed along the petrol jetty, throwing black dust and debris into the air.

"Over!" yelled Peter. "Down one!"

"Down one!" screamed the gunlayer.

Bang! Crash!

"Hit!" yelled Peter. "You've hit her. Rapid fire!" The gun worked itself into a frenzy, slamming home round after round into the U-boat.

A blinding, searing sheet of flame tore into their consciousness as a fearful explosion rent the darkness. The target had disintegrated, but there was no time to watch the smoke clear away and see the terrible results.

As *Rugged* wove her way through the congested harbour, the chaos became pandemonium. Tracers flew in every direction, as ships fired one upon another and even the shore batteries joined in the fun and were spiritedly engaging each other.

Bullets whined in the darkness, smacking against the steel casing of the submarine. Above the din, Stack's voice yelled suddenly.

"Davis is hit bad, sir!"

Peter tore his eyes away from his glasses and glanced over the bridge at the gun's crew. Davis lay sprawled by the mounting, his body slumped near the edge of the casing, one arm trailing and flapping over the side but even by the light of the sporadic flashes, Peter could see that he was dead.

"Carry on firing, I'm coming down," Peter yelled.

"Davis is dead, sir. Permission to man the gun?" Peter shouted to his Captain.

"Carry on," Joe answered, crouched low over the voicepipe as he conned the boat through the crowded harbour.

Peter leaped over the bridge-side, scrambled down the iron rungs of the ladder and then ran forward to take Davis's place at the mounting.

On the shore, men could be seen running to man the launches which were secured to the jetties by slip-ropes, and then the throaty roar of an E-boat starting up her engines burst familiarly on Peter's ears.

"E-boat starting up," Peter shouted up to the Captain on the bridge, and he pointed towards the jetty to port.

"Let's get out of here!" muttered the Captain above the din as the gun banged away at any target that presented itself, yellow spurts of flame piercing the blackness. An overwhelming roar burst upon their ears as a small petrol tanker exploded and vivid tongues of flame shot hundreds of feet into the air.

Peter's stomach turned over at the horrifying sight and he looked away. Even at this stage of the war he could not enjoy the actual process of annihilation.

"Check! Check! Check! Cease firing — clear the gun!" the Captain shouted as he swung the boat seawards towards the entrance. "Clear the tower. Stand by to dive!"

Peter was by the gun and he heard the order above the tumult.

"Clear the gun!" he shouted, as he stooped over Davis's slumped body. He quickly turned the man over, but sickened at the sight. He could do nothing for him.

"Here, Stack, give me a hand."

Stack was crouching over Peter.

"Clear the gun, do you hear?" Joe's voice bellowed angrily. "Leave Davis and get below."

Peter looked at Stack who turned and made for the bridge.

"Aye, aye, sir," Peter yelled as he gently lowered the shattered body to the casing. "God rest your soul," he whispered as he sprang after Stack who was already disappearing over the lip of the bridge.

"Full ahead together!"

The boat surged forward, as Peter reached the bridge.

"Lookout astern, Pilot. Sub, keep a lookout ahead! Remainder, clear the bridge!"

The bridge was cleared in a few seconds, save for the Captain and his two officers. Already the entrance buoy was close on their port bow, looming larger with every second that passed.

"I can't dive until we're a mile outside, can I, Pilot?"

"No, sir: only thirty feet of water."

"Go below, Pilot, and start the echo sounder. Let me know as soon as I've got forty feet."

"Aye, aye, sir."

Peter was left alone with his Captain.

"Keep your eyes skinned astern, Sub, while I take her out.

Cleaving through the water, the little submarine strained forward to reach freedom before the pursuing hounds could pounce upon her in the shallows. "Six minutes should do it,

Sub," said the Captain, as the buoy slid past them. "Keep your fingers crossed!"

"E-boats astern, sir!" Peter interrupted, "I can just make out a bow wave."

"To blazes with them!"

Slowly the faint smudge astern gained upon them, becoming larger and splitting into two distinct V's of foaming bow waves. They were less than half a mile astern now and gaining at every second.

"Sounding?" the Captain shouted down the voicepipe.

"Thirty-two feet, sir," a voice replied.

Another agonising minute dragged by, while the overhauling shapes of the E-boats enlargened.

"Thirty-five feet, sir."

Long pencil lines of red tracer slowly spiralled towards them whistling overhead in the darkness, a shrill whine howling above the wind on the bridge. The E-boats, going like bats out of hell, had now opened out on either quarter, closing in for the kill, a mountain of white water building up astern of them as they closed in at forty knots.

Joe dared not risk waiting any longer, even though he had not received any further information on his depth of water.

"Hard-a-port! Dive! Dive! Dive!" he shouted down the voicepipe, while he pressed the diving alarm.

Peter jumped for the hatch and let himself down with a rush. The upper lid clanged behind him as the Captain shut it.

"Twenty-eight feet," he roared above the din.

Number One took her down in nineteen seconds, the boat still steaming at full speed. Tumbling out at the bottom, the Captain exchanged glances with Number One and nodded.

"Shut off for depth-charging!" the First Lieutenant rapped.

"Watch your trim," the Captain muttered, "or we'll be aground, Number One."

"Aye, aye, sir."

"Group down, slow ahead together."

Twenty-five feet — twenty-eight — thirty — thirty-three feet.

Poor Davis has found his grave, Peter thought to himself as a harsh scraping, like sandpaper along a stone floor, scratched along the metal sides. They were grounding on the seabed.

"Group up, full ahead together. Twenty-five feet, Number One."

In an agony of suspense, all eyes watched the pointers of the depth gauges stick at thirty-three feet. Overhead the rumble of propellers roared all about them, drowning everything in a tumult of sound. Strained faces waited, waited for the shattering explosions that would send them all to Kingdom Come.

Thirty-three — thirty-three — thirty-three feet. The pointers remained motionless.

Thirty-three — thirty-two — thirty feet — with a jerk she shuddered, trembled and started to shake herself free. At that instant, an overwhelming shock squeezed the minute submarine like an egg crushed in a man's hand. Men gasped as the surrounding air constricted them like a smothering blanket, and expanded again as quickly.

Lights flickered and went out. The pale emergency lighting clicked on. Men groped in the semi-darkness to hold themselves upright in the jumping boat which was now out of control, for she leaped at an alarming angle, almost breaking surface.

With his heart thumping, Peter watched the depth gauge.

Twenty — twenty — nineteen — nineteen feet.

"Flood Q. Full ahead together," the First Lieutenant snapped. All eyes were mesmerised by the depth gauges, for a break-surface at this moment, with the E-boats directly over them, meant disaster.

Nineteen — eighteen — eighteen — eighteen, and she hung, balancing between life and sudden death, with twelve inches as the margin.

Eighteen — eighteen — nineteen — nineteen — twenty — twenty-one…

Good old Number One! He'd got her!

A ripple of relief was audible throughout the boat, as the dreadful rumble of the E-boats faded away astern, followed by the muffled explosions of depth charges well away to starboard.

"Nice work, Number One," Joe said, looking his First Lieutenant straight in the eye. "Do you think that we gave the Sub enough to do?" he grinned.

With a roar of delight which released the tense atmosphere, the whole boat joined in the merriment and burst into deep, rumbling laughter. They were safe and could relax for a moment.

But an empty hammock swung lazily in the fore-ends.

CHAPTER 6

Too Close!

The area of Burat-el-Sun seemed an unlikely hunting ground for *Rugged* on the following day. Joe took her down the coast, keeping an eye on the motor traffic as it poured eastwards along the shore road but, apart from air patrols, they spent a quiet day, men snatching their rest while they had the chance.

Before turning in for the forenoon sleep, a small group of men mustered in the Control Room and when they had gathered round him in a semicircle, Joe addressed them by the for'd periscope.

He explained that Davis had given his life and how there had been no chance of recovering his body. Davis had found his last resting place in the way he would have liked: *Rugged* had committed him to the deep as she dived. The small band gathered round their Captain while he said a shortened Burial Service. Submariners said little, but the service ended with a murmured "Amen".

"Carry on," Joe said.

They went for'd slowly, and, as the Coxswain passed Joe, he held out his hand. "Thank you, sir," he said.

The day passed and the night, dark and cheerless, soon stole upon them. *Rugged* surfaced and charged her batteries.

"Permission for the Officer of the Watch on the bridge?" asked Peter, glancing at the clock which showed five minutes to eleven.

"Yes," Hickey's voice grunted from the voicepipe.

After taking over the Watch from Hickey, Peter settled down to his second night's watch 'on the billet', as the patrol area was called. At the back of the bridge, the Captain slept fitfully on a camp stool while the figures of the two lookouts leaned over their respective sides of the bridge, glasses to their tired eyes, as they methodically swept through their sectors of the horizon.

It was very dark, but shortly after midnight a golden orb climbed out of the sea, throwing a pale shaft of dancing light on the black water. The moon, aloof and cold, slipped slowly and majestically high into the night sky, throwing the submarine into relief.

It's like being caught in the nude! thought Peter as the moonlight shimmered off the boat's sides, making her visible for miles. Though trimmed right down so that her casing was barely visible, her conning tower stood out like a house. Slowly weaving across the moon's track, the submarine zigzagged her way, the diesels roaring and coughing into the night.

As Peter's glasses swept the horizon, a grey smudge checked him so that he looked again. Yes! There it was. A small dark object, then another and another.

"Captain, sir!" he shouted, keeping his eyes on the target.

"Yes?" mumbled a hoarse voice, as the Captain stumbled to his feet.

"Three small objects right ahead," reported Peter.

The Captain picked them up almost immediately.

"E-boats, I think," he murmured. "Can you see any more, Sub?"

Straining his eyes, Peter waited a full minute before replying.

"Yes, sir … five … six. Looks like a small convoy."

"Yes, that's what it is. Sound the night alarm."

Peter jumped for the night-alarm knob and pushed it. Below, in the red gloom, the alarm rattlers awoke the boat, sending men still drowsy from the sleep of exhaustion pell-mell to their diving stations.

"Stand by all tubes, stand by gun action!" the Captain sang out down the voicepipe.

In the moonlight ahead, Peter could just pick out a dozen small tankers, plodding their way in the same direction westwards. *Rugged* was slowly overhauling them from astern.

"They often keep no lookout astern, and we are down-moon of them, so I'll stalk them, Sub. Let's see whether we can get within range so that we can use the gun. I think that those two escorts are F-lighters, armed with eighty-eights. We want to look out for them. It's not worth wasting our 'fish' on small coasters as they would probably run under anyway."

"Gun's crew ready, sir," a voice reported up the voicepipe.

"Gun action! Load with flashless H.E.," the Captain ordered.

Once more the agile gun's crew emerged from the conning tower hatch and nipped nimbly over the bridge to bring their gun to the 'ready'.

"Target — first ship on the port bow," yelled Peter.

"On target, sir," roared the gunlayer.

It was another game of cat and mouse, however, for *Rugged*, her diesels at maximum speed, was only just able to overhaul the small silhouettes which slowly, so slowly, grew in size. She was now less than a mile from them, yet they showed no sign of alarm.

"Haven't those F-lighters got closer?" asked Joe suspiciously.

"Don't think so, sir," replied Peter, who had been glaring at them for so long that he hadn't noticed any enlargement of their outlines.

"They must see us soon," murmured the Captain to himself, and then spoke out loud. "Do you reckon that you can hit at this range, Sub? It's about twelve hundred yards."

Peter could now see the tiny ships pitching and yawing on their erratic courses, the pale moonlight stippling their rusty sides. But the F-lighters showed no sign, keeping rigidly on their station.

"Could we get a little closer, sir?" he asked.

"All right, but I don't like the smell of it," replied the Captain as he ordered down the voicepipe. "Stop the generators!"

The roar of the diesels died away and the following silence seemed uncanny. There was nothing to be heard except the lapping of the wavelets along the rounded pressure hull.

One thousand yards. Nine hundred yards. The inaction was suspicious. Surely they must have been sighted?

"Open fire, Sub."

"Open fire!" yelled Peter, leaning over the lip of the bridge.

"Trainer on!" the voice of the new trainer growled.

Able Seaman Bowles had taken Davis's place at the gun. Peter watched the gunlayer. With his eyes glued to the sights, he squeezed the trigger as the crosswires came on.

Peter was watching for the fall of shot, waiting for it to burst on the silver shape fine on the port bow, but the Captain was concentrating on the F-lighters, barely nine hundred yards away, their washes streaming in sparkling bubbles astern of them.

At the very moment that the gun's first round crashed into the night, the nearest F-lighter spun round on its tail, pushing a surging bow wave ahead of it. As it came beam on, its familiar and sinister shape became apparent, whilst it leapt forward with green tracer spurting from its guns.

"E-boats!"

The warning rang out through the night.

"Clear the gun! Dive! Dive! Dive!"

The urgent summons of the klaxons could be heard even above the din. The gun's crew, for the second time in twenty-four hours, leaped up the bridge-side and hurled themselves down into the gaping cavity of the conning tower hatch. The Captain stood alone, waiting for the last man up from the gun. Already the water was lapping up the side of the bridge as the boat gathered way, but not until the gunlayer had dropped into the void below him, did the Captain swing himself down, pulling the upper lid shut after him.

"This is too close," he muttered to himself, before shouting to the Control Room "— one clip on! Port twenty, one hundred and twenty feet. Shut off for depth-charging!"

The last glimpse that Joe had before shutting the hatch remained etched on his memory for the remainder of his life. Bright moonlight washed the sea with its pale beauty, the phosphorescence of the disturbed seawater sparkling on the calm surface. This peaceful background seemed to accentuate the savage shapes of the leaping E-boats which thrashed towards him. As Joe dipped below the rim of the bridge, the leading boat was barely two hundred yards away. Her gleaming bows lunged hungrily through the cascade of spume and spray. Green and white tracer smacked about the side of the conning tower, but already only the periscope standards remained visible in the flurry of sparkling foam, as *Rugged* gained speed in her desperate dive.

The leading E-boat, engines roaring in the stillness of the night, saw the swirl of the standards as they dipped ahead of her. The young German Ober-Leutnant held his breath as he waited for the crash of his propellers against the submarine. His hands twitched nervously on the depth-charge firing lever, as he waited to give the *coup de grace* to this English swine. Another three seconds now! As he leaned over the side of his small armoured bridge, he saw the swirling water where the standards had disappeared.

"Fire!" he yelled as his hand jerked on the firing lever. "*Gott strafe England!*"

Two wicked depth charges rolled over the foaming stern. Almost instantaneously, two shattering explosions rent the night, hurling spouts of cascading water high into the moonlight. The E-boat heeled over to port to make way for the other three boats now tearing into the attack.

Down below in *Rugged*, the First Lieutenant heard the "Dive, dive, dive!" order from the voicepipe, even before the klaxons shattered the silence below. He nodded quickly to the Outside E.R.A. who jumped for the panel and pulled the main vent operating levers. The vents clunked open, as the first man tumbled into the Control Room from the canvas trunking, stumbling as he swiftly moved for'd to his diving station. The hum of the main motors rose to a shriller whine as the submarine gathered speed to take up a steep bow-down angle, while the planesmen spun their handwheels over to 'hard-a-dive'.

"Shut off for depth-charging," Easton ordered quietly, his eyes fixed on the depth gauges, hands swiftly flicking the pump order instrument. The bulkhead doors swung ponderously, shutting off each compartment from the next. It was difficult to stand upright now, for the boat had taken on a steeper angle — thirty-five — thirty-eight — forty-two feet and men were still tumbling out of the canvas trunking when the crash came.

A savage wrench jolted the whole boat. The curved steel sides jumped towards them and then as suddenly bounced out again. The boat plunged into darkness as the lights shattered from the shock. Mercifully, a few emergency lights clicked on automatically, and threw a thin light on the confused scene in the Control Room.

Fifty — fifty-five — sixty-five — seventy-eight feet. The luminous pointers spun round the dials of the depth gauges alarmingly fast, for the boat was now out of control as she shot into the black depths of the ocean. Men lay struggling in heaps at the forward end of the Control Room.

"Blow Q!" shouted Number One. The air rushed into the boat as the tank was vented inboard, but still she plunged on downwards, now at a twenty-five-degree bow-down angle.

"After-planes jammed, sir," the voice of the grey-haired coxswain on the after-planes calmly reported. "At hard-a-dive!"

"Thank you, Coxswain. Pass by phone to the after-ends. After-planes in hand," snapped the First Lieutenant.

"Aye, aye, sir."

Hanging on to a pipe with one hand, the telegraphsman spun the telephone handle and passed the order.

A hundred and sixty — a hundred and eighty — two hundred feet. The rate of dive had increased rapidly and now only fifty feet remained before the boat's safe diving depth of two hundred and fifty feet would be reached. On trials she had been tested to this depth, but below that, the designers could not predict at what depth she would disintegrate like a squashed fruit.

Down — down — down… She seemed to slide away from under their very feet, the pointers on the gauges now racing by the luminous numbers on the dials.

Two hundred and forty — two hundred and fifty — two hundred and sixty — two hundred and seventy … jumping in 'tens' now!

Providing there was enough high-pressure air left in the bottles, and that the high-pressure lines were intact, there always remained one last resort when plunging to destruction.

"Why doesn't he blow the main ballast tanks? Please God, let him blow those main ballast tanks," Peter whispered to himself, remembering his training course which seemed so far away in murky, dreary, bleak but oh-so-friendly Blyth.

The Captain gripped the rungs of the steel ladder.

"Blow number one main ballast!" he ordered crisply.

Eagerly the Outside E.R.A. spun the air valve open, to send the high-pressure air screaming along the airlines to the main ballast tanks in the eyes of the boat.

"Stop blowing!"

All eyes hung on the quivering needles of the gauges — it was now or never, for the pointers showed three hundred and ten — three hundred and fifteen — three hundred and eighteen — three hundred and twenty feet. The pointers hung motionless, while at any moment sudden calamity must surely burst upon them. Peter held his breath. A pin dropped at this moment would have sounded like a steam hammer.

Suddenly he felt the bows begin to lift under his feet, as she started to take up her new level. Abruptly the bows sheered up and away from the hungry expectant depths and then canted upwards at an alarming bow-up angle. She started to shoot upwards, as the water was expelled from the for'd main ballast tank.

Three hundred and fifteen — three hundred and ten — three hundred feet … she swooped upwards.

"Crack number two main ballast," ordered the Captain.

The air screamed to the after main ballast tank in the stern.

"Stop blowing!" Joe snapped.

The boat levelled off to a five-degree bow-down angle but, in spite of the planes being at hard-a-dive, she was still surging upwards out of control. Two hundred and ten — two hundred — one hundred and eighty — one hundred and sixty feet…

"Don't speed up, Number One, they're waiting for us up top," the Captain murmured to the First Lieutenant. "I'll try and catch a main ballast trim. Try to hold her on the planes — we'll have to risk the bubbles."

One hundred feet. Eighty feet.

"Open main vents," the calm tones of the Captain ordered.

The main vents thunked open, allowing the air in the main ballast tanks to escape to the surface in enormous bubbles, and thereby giving away their position to the waiting enemy.

"Shut main vents. Port ten. Half ahead together."

The whine of the motors slowly rose in pitch, as the boat gathered speed and turned to port, opening her distance as far away as possible from her pursuers. With the air in her main ballast tanks partly liberated, more water flooded in to check her crazy upward swoop. The pointer dithered at fifty feet and she slowly sank back to eighty, ninety, one hundred feet, Number One just holding her on the planes.

"Slow ahead together. Steady … steer one-eight-oh," ordered the Captain. By taking the boat through the wake of the convoy, he hoped to confuse the attackers.

"H.E. increasing, red six-oh, sir," reported Elliott on his Asdic set.

Already the noise of fast-running propellers thrashed above them, and the noise drummed into a roar as the hunter rumbled overhead. Not a sound in the boat as every man waited for the sickening crash of depth charges.

"Passed over, sir," quietly reported Elliott, "H.E. fading on…"

Crash! … Crash! Crash!

The charges, which exploded some yards away on the starboard bow, shook the boat slightly, but were too far away to cause anxiety. The pursuers were dropping all that they had on to the tell-tale streams of bubbles, now seething and frothing in the moonlit sea, but hundreds of yards astern of the submarine. Joe had acted wisely by scurrying away from the scene of the tell-tale bubbles which he had been forced to vent.

"Well done, everybody!" Joe grinned. "I think we'll slide out of this while the going's good."

The next day was comparatively quiet. Following the abortive moonlight attack, *Rugged* had surfaced an hour after the last depth-charge attack to recharge her batteries. After surfacing they had been put down three times by low-flying search aircraft, before they finally dived at dawn.

Joe was not in jocular mood at breakfast. Tired after the fruitless efforts of the night, he grimaced as his teeth sank into the mushy baked beans.

"O'Riley!" he shouted.

"Sorr?" O'Riley's face registered innocent inquiry, as it popped round the bulkhead door.

"Take these frightful beans away and bring me some more coffee."

"Yes, sorr."

O'Riley scuttled into the Ward Room and left it more quickly than he had come.

"It isn't as if we'd hit anything for all our trouble and the 'heat' we got — and they almost had me for a 'sucker'!" continued Joe with his one-sided conversation.

"Yes, sir," smiled Number One, cannily feeling his way.

"Don't say 'Yes, sir', blast you!" Joe roared. "You just sit there, grinning like a Cheshire cat."

"No, sir," replied Number One, poker-faced.

Joe exploded into a gust of laughter. The storm was over.

"Good old Number One, he won't be drawn! He's too used to the edge of my tongue, Sub!" said Joe, addressing Peter, while Hickey kept the periscope watch in the Control Room.

"Well, Number One? What do you suggest now?"

"Let's get out of the area, as they are obviously alerted in these parts, sir. Let's go up to our old hunting grounds at Hammamet. We had better luck there last time."

"Yes, and catch 'em as they come round the corner. The snag is that there's not much water for us there. I don't like that but beggars can't be choosers! Sub, take over from the Pilot and tell him to let me have a course and E.T.A. for Hammamet. It's about two hundred miles away. Care for a game of 'liars', Number One?"

"Yes, I'd love one when the Sub gets back."

Peter went into the Control Room.

The Captain lowered his voice. "How's Sinclair doing with you?"

"Very well, sir. Reliable."

"Good. That's what I hoped you'd say. Let's get on with the game. Aces up and Kings towards." Then he carefully adjusted the grimy dice in front of him.

When Peter re-joined them, the Control Room crew could hear nothing but bursts of laughter from the Ward Room, mixed with the rattling of tumbling dice on the mahogany table.

The storm was over, but Joe had hated letting them down and all aboard knew it.

The moon slowly sank behind the high mountains, leaving a cold glow as a backdrop to the silhouetted peaks. The darkness closed in rapidly, enfolding *Rugged* in a mantle of invisibility. It was three-fifteen a.m. and Hickey had just taken over from Number One on the bridge. He shivered as the first of the dawn's clammy coldness enveloped him. Trimmed right down, the submarine's small conning tower was almost invisible, as she slid silently through the darkness. The lookouts shook themselves and drew their Ursula jackets closer around them. Hickey swept the landward horizon with his binoculars for the twentieth time. In his last sweep, a faint blur, darker than the rest of the horizon, checked him. He swung across it again, but the other way this time and — yes, there WAS something there!

"Captain, sir!" shouted Hickey to the back of the bridge.

"Ye-e-s?" mumbled Joe, stumbling sleepily to Hickey's side.

Lining up his glasses with Hickey's, he soon found the object.

"Small ship, about two thousand tons. Sound the night alarm!" the Captain ordered Hickey.

Down below, the night-alarm rattlers clattered, once more bringing sleep-hungry men scrambling to their feet.

"No blooming peace for the blooming wicked," the Coxswain muttered to himself, as he rushed to his position at the after-planes in the Control Room. The Captain's voice could just be heard as the muffled orders came down the voicepipe.

"Group up, full ahead together. Stand by all tubes!" The boat shuddered as she sped forward to work up to her utmost speed, the white bow wave creaming ahead of her and the phosphorescence gleaming and tumbling down the wet sides of her hull.

Manoeuvring into a position ahead of the target, the Captain stopped and waited on the steamer's port bow. Slowly the target grew larger. The men on the bridge waited breathlessly, while they continued to sweep their own sectors with their binoculars, just in case of errors.

The ship bore down upon them, growing larger at every second. Her blunt bow shoved a massive wall of white water as she wallowed her ponderous way down the coast, oblivious of her lurking danger.

"Confound it. I'm too close," muttered Joe to himself. "Still, it's too late now. I'll have to stay where I am."

Slowly the target bore down upon them, her bearing drawing quickly ahead of *Rugged's* bows. Now she seemed right on top of them, looming down upon them, ready to rip them open.

But Joe never wavered. His knuckles gleamed white on the side of the bridge as he waited, his long body crouched low over the starboard torpedo sight, his eye glued along the bar.

"Fire one!" his voice snapped.

A slight tremor…

"Fire two!"

Another tremor, as the second torpedo loosed into the night.

The thin trail of white bubbles spurted like a pencil line ahead of them, and then there was an explosion that seemed to rend the heavens apart. A vivid, electric-blue flash split the night and a sheet of orange flame swept upwards, blinding the bridge personnel. A roar, which nearly split their eardrums, rolled over them, reverberating again and again far into the night, while strange sighings and hissings gradually replaced the diabolic pandemonium. Then a loud splash, close on their starboard bow, shot a shower of seawater slopping over the bridge.

"Down, all of you! Cover up! She's an ammunition ship!" roared Joe.

The four men on the bridge needed no reminding! They dropped to the deck instinctively and shielded their heads with crossed arms as the splashes, sizzling and hissing, seethed in the water around them. A great clang rent the air, and *Rugged* shivered from stem to stern, as a large hunk of metal fell from the skies to land on her after-ends.

Down below, the Leading Torpedoman, Flint, was watching his switches and ammeters in the Motor Room. Suddenly the boat quivered and the air split above his head and he fell to the steel deckplates, stunned by the concussion. When he came to his senses seawater was streaming on to his sweating face.

"Water! Water!" he screamed through to the Engine Room. "Water's pouring into the Motor Room! Tell the bridge!" and he tore frantically at his switches, where blue flashes spurted, choking from the acrid smell of burning and from the billows of brown fumes which circled about the Motor Room.

On the bridge, the Captain had felt the boat shudder from the blow on the after-ends, so he was not surprised when he received the report from the Motor Room.

"Blow number two main ballast tank!" he shouted down the voicepipe.

The air roared into the after tank and cocked the submarine's stern high into the air, free from the water; while in the Motor Room Flint, dazed by the fumes which swirled about him, gradually noticed that only a trickle of water was now seeping in from the jagged rent in the steel plating above the port switchboard. Through this he saw stars twinkling, and he laughed. He was quickly sobered, however, by the realisation that the boat was now unable to dive.

"Here, Joey, take over while I report to the Old Man," Flint said as he dashed out of the Motor Room, sliding neatly past the Engine Room's silent crew. He received permission to go on to the bridge, where he reported to his Captain.

Ahead of them, apart from the bubbling of confused water, there was nothing to show that a ship had been afloat here a few seconds before. In this appalling explosion, she had disappeared in a sheet of flame to leave the submarine's personnel shocked by their success.

"Well, that's torn it, literally!" joked the Captain, having heard Flint's report. "We can't dive until we get it patched up, if that's possible, and dawn is in two hours' time. We'd better get cracking. Send the First Lieutenant on to the bridge."

Number One came scuttling up into the moonlight.

"Number One, you realise the position? We can't dive. Dawn is only two hours away and Malta two hundred miles. If we are to get back at periscope depth, we've got to plug that hole within the next one hundred minutes. Would both you and the Chief have a go? You may, of course, refuse if you wish, for I should have to dive if we were savaged, leaving you to fend for yourselves."

"Of course. We'll fix it, sir. I'll get the Chief."

Within two minutes, Number One and Chief E.R.A. Reginald Potts, clad in gym shoes, bathing trunks and sweaters, and each with a heaving line around his chest, slithered down to the slippery roundness of the after-ends.

The gash was nine inches long and two inches wide: quite sufficient to sink the boat. She would be unable to dive below periscope depth, even if the plug held as deep as that, because the increasing pressure would force the water through the gash and into the boat in an irresistible deluge.

Working steadily and surely, the Chief would not be hurried. His skilful fingers chopped at the wooden chocks with a seaman's knife. Full well he realised that at dawn all their lives depended upon his present skill for there would be no second chance. As he was knocking the last chock home into the mass of cotton waste which acted as a wad in the rent, the dull purr of a prowling aircraft grew louder and louder somewhere astern of them. The Chief stopped, head cocked on one side, automatically trying to determine from whence the sound came.

Peering aft, the Captain kept his thumb on the diving alarm knob. The angry hum throbbed into a rough moan, bursting into a roar as the aircraft swept directly over them. In a moment of time that no one would ever forget, they saw the dim lights in the pilot's cockpit of the Cant 52 on its anti-submarine patrol.

They held their breaths. They watched and waited for her to lurch into a steep bank and circle, to hurtle in upon them with all guns blazing. Waiting … waiting, the Chief licked his lips — and then suddenly it was gone.

"Thank God," the Chief whispered, and to give vent to his feelings, he smacked the wedge home, as hard as he could.

Fifteen minutes later, just as dawn was breaking, the Chief and Number One, blue with cold, were helped down below. With a grateful grunt, they accepted hot mugs of cocoa which were thrust into their hands. Number One went to his depth gauges in the Control Room and the Chief to his warm Engine Room. The klaxon brayed, the upper lid in the conning tower clanged shut.

"Take her down to twenty-eight feet, Number One — slowly," sang out the Captain from the tower.

"Aye, aye, sir."

Peter looked at his watch. Fifteen minutes to go before daylight. It had been a close shave! If this plug did not hold… Peter thrust the thought from his mind although the next thirty seconds would show.

"Eighteen feet, sir," Number One reported quietly.

For once the Captain was not in the Control Room. He had gone aft to the Motor Room, where, amid the filth and stench from the burning switchboard, the Chief and Flint crouched to watch the plug.

"Twenty-three feet, sir," came the report from the Control Room.

The plug started to drip as the cotton waste became saturated. The drip flooded to a trickle which splashed on to the back of the switchboard. Would it swell to a gushing torrent? The steady drip continued, and the plug held, as the Chief sighed audibly.

"Twenty-eight feet, sir," came the report.

"Very good. Tell the First Lieutenant, 'Twenty-eight feet and keep her there'."

"Aye, aye, sir."

"Rig up drip-tins and drain that water away from the switchboard and lead it into the bilges, Flint."

"Aye, aye, sir."

" — and, Flint."

"Yes, sir?"

"Well done."

"Thank you, sir."

Joe returned to the Control Room through the Engine Room.

"Well done, Chief," he said as he passed. "Thanks."

"Thank you, sir. All in a day's work, as they say."

"Come into the Ward Room on your way for'd and have a drop of medical comforts."

"Yes, sir, thank you" — and with a grin on his wrinkled face, which was now losing the blue shadows around the jowls, the Chief wiped his greasy hands on the seat of his swimming trunks.

And so, for the next two days, *Rugged* proceeded at periscope depth, steaming on the surface at night. On the morning after the second night, the friendly bluffs of Malta showed ahead.

To Peter, entering harbour after his first patrol, a black Jolly Roger flapping proudly from the attack periscope, it was a moment of fierce happiness. The barefooted children yelled and clapped their hands on the breakwater as *Rugged* swept past the boom and into the blue waters of Lazaretto. The Creek was washed by the early morning sun, the willowy reflections of the yellow buildings eddying lazily upon the ripples made by the rust-splotched submarine. Slowly she entered harbour.

They were home.

CHAPTER 7

Iron Ring

Ten days later, only one submarine lay at her mooring in Lazaretto Creek. The whole flotilla had been sent out to form two iron rings — one round Naples and the other off Cape St. Vito, at the north-western tip of Sicily. Operation 'Torch', the code name for the Allied landings in North Africa, was planned to begin at any moment. Every submarine sailed under sealed orders and, apart from the position allocated to them, they knew not on what day the operation was due to start.

In the room of the Captain of the Tenth Submarine Flotilla, the Commanding Officers assembled in conference. Their orders were brief.

"Sink at sight," remarked their humorous-faced leader who was beloved and respected by all in the flotilla. Short and stocky of build, he had been an intrepid submarine captain in his own right, and now, day and night, he conducted the strategy of his 'Fighting Tenth'. Because the flotilla was the only unit of the Royal Navy left in the Mediterranean, he was inflexibly determined to hit the enemy hard and often on his own doorstep.

Peter had never forgotten the day when the whole flotilla had been assembled in the stone courtyard, to be addressed by its Captain. It had been customary for the sailors to give cigarettes to their German and Italian prisoners, and to look after them, if survivors were ever retrieved from the sinkings. The Captain now believed that such actions were leading to a certain softening in morale towards the enemy and Peter would never forget listening to his short speech. In acid and blistering terms the Captain had withered his audience and reminded them of the way the enemy had behaved, first as conquerors and then as whining captives. Everyone, officers and ratings alike, had left that courtyard with a burning desire to renew the fight with ruthlessness and determination.

"Sink at sight," he now said to the conference in his room. "When in your patrol positions, you are to be five miles apart. Do not fire at U-boats, when on your billets, for obvious reasons. Don't allow one enemy ship to get past you. There are no restrictions on passage. God bless and good luck."

With a smile, he shook each Captain by the hand, as they left his room to take their boats to sea.

A few days before sailing, however, a local sickness known as sandfly fever, which was contracted by sleeping in the sandstone caves, took its toll of *Rugged*'s ship's company. The few men unaffected by the fever regretfully watched the remainder of the flotilla depart.

"It's a shame, isn't it, Sub? We're going to miss this party," John Easton said to Peter as they stood by the water's edge ruefully waving to the departing submarines as they slipped from their moorings.

"Yes, Number One, but…"

A hoarse cough behind him had made Peter turn round.

"But what, Sub?" Easton asked irritably.

He turned to finish his conversation, but he was left talking to thin air.

Peter was busy pumping the hand of a burly rating who was grinning from ear to ear. The sailor was obviously one of the new spare crew which had arrived from England yesterday. The man was stocky, with enormous shoulders, and blue eyes twinkling beneath a crop of fair hair.

"Crippin, sir! I didn't think to meet you so soon!"

Peter grinned foolishly. "Nor did I, Hawkins! But it's good to see you. This is Able Seaman Hawkins, sir, gunnery rating," Peter continued, introducing the man to his First Lieutenant.

"And who is Hawkins, Sub-Lieutenant Sinclair?" Easton replied with a flicker of a smile, as he proffered his hand.

"We're old shipmates, sir," Peter went on. "We were both in my Chaser, and we both repaid a debt."

"Oh, yes — gunnery rating, did you say, Hawkins?" Number One hesitated.

"Yes, sir, and…"

"Yes?"

"Well, sir, it's not for me to ask, but, er…" Hawkins stuttered.

"Well, what do you want?"

Hawkins looked hopelessly out of his depth.

Peter spoke.

"I have a feeling he wants to join *Rugged*, sir."

"Oh, does he? Well, he'd better put in a request in the proper manner."

"Yes, sir. I will, sir. Thank you, sir."

"Carry on, Able Seaman Hawkins."

"Aye, aye, sir."

The burly figure turned away, but not before his eyes rolled sheepishly in an imploring glance at Peter.

"You and he seem to be buddies, Sub," Easton grinned.

"Yes, we are, Number One. He saved my life."

"Oh, I see. Is he a good hand?"

"First rate."

"Since Davis was killed, we're down one in complement — and a gunnery rating at that."

"Yes, Number One. Hawkins is a gunnery rating."

"I'll see if the Captain approves."

"Thank you, Number One."

But Easton was already striding up the stone steps which led to Joe's cabin.

So it was that a few days later, *Rugged's* complement was complete once more. Able Seaman W. Hawkins had replaced Able Seaman Davis, and all had recovered sufficiently for *Rugged* to sail. She slipped from her moorings, her destination the iron ring off Cape St. Vito, at the north-western tip of Sicily.

By proceeding at full speed on the surface at night, she would be just in time to fill her position in the ring, before the operation was set in motion. Her billet was between *Rapid* and *Restless*, the latter being commanded by Lieutenant Harold Arkwright, Peter's old friend and Term Cadet Captain at Dartmouth. As soon as Peter had landed in Malta, Arkwright had renewed his friendship with him.

So, for the second time, Peter found himself standing on the windblown fore-casing, as little *Rugged* quietly slid between the black necklaces of buoys which formed the defensive boom at the harbour entrance. Already the boyishness had vanished from his youthful face. A faraway look clouded his eyes, and his cheekbones had begun to show their prominence beneath the windblown skin, which was no longer tanned by Channel weather, but was quickly assuming the faint greyness of most submariners.

Instinctively, he carried out his routine duties for securing the fore-casing, and, going below after a lingering look at the fading battlements of Valetta against the evening sky, he changed into his patrol rig of white shorts, khaki shirt and sandals.

After the trim dive had been successfully completed, *Rugged* remained on the surface, as night enveloped them like a comforting blanket. When clear of the little island of Gozo, *Rugged* set a course for Cape St. Vito. This meant steaming all night to the minefield off Sicily, where she dived at dawn to proceed all day through the 'blazed trail' in the minefield affectionately known as Piccadilly.

Glancing through the periscope, Peter was amazed to see how close this Sicilian shore seemed to his inexperienced eye. The white houses showed boldly, shining in the dazzling sunlight like small cardboard boxes as they nestled in the green fields of the low-lying foreshore.

"Don't use the stick so long, Sub," snapped Joe when he strode into the Control Room. "I don't want to be sighted in Piccadilly. We would jeopardise the whole channel and everyone else into the bargain. Watch me. Use it like this. 'Down periscope'," he ordered.

In a series of quick looks, Joe took some swift bearings of shore objects, before handing the periscope back to Peter; then, using these bearings, the Captain quickly put the fix of the ship's position on the chart.

"Look here, Sub. This is our position," he said as he indicated a small circle which was right on their course line.

"Take a fix every ten minutes, and inform me at once if we veer off our course. We can't afford to do that in this minefield" — and he gave Peter an odd glance.

"Aye, aye, sir."

The long day wore on. The circles on the chart crept slowly along the course line, while the silent submarine slunk through the treacherous water, the mines growing like mushrooms from their swinging wires on either side of her. The enemy were known to have hydrophones spaced at intervals along the minefield, so all conversation was carried out in low voices, the men changing watches in slippered or gym-shoed feet. Silently, remorselessly, the submarine nosed her way through the barrier.

In the afternoon, all hands tried to snatch sleep. Even Bill Hawkins knew that a hectic night awaited them, because they had to slip in between the enemy E-boat patrols, lying stopped and listening for them off Marittimo Island.

Peter lay on his bunk and stared at the disporting cockroaches on the pipes above him. Out of the corner of his eye he could see Easton, the First Lieutenant, turn on his side, obviously making a fruitless effort at sleep. Below Peter, and across the other side of the table, the Captain lay reading, stretched out on his settee, but now he seemed to take longer in finishing a page.

Yes, thought Peter, *the strain of listening for the scraping mine wires is not only worrying me* — and, sighing, he turned on his side. His eyelids closed and he began to feel the drowsy half-world of sleep enfolding him when, from somewhere miles away in the fore-ends, there came to his dozing subconsciousness a faint burring, like a file on hard metal.

Suddenly, a sharp twang brought him jerkingly awake. He turned on his back, to see the Captain lay down his book quickly while the First Lieutenant rolled over with his eyes wide open. No word passed. The Captain's eyes met those of his First Lieutenant and they held each other's gaze. There was a slight pause in the ominous sound.

Then came the sinister scraping that all submariners feared and as the mine's mooring wire clattered along the hull, the jarring clangour thrummed to fill the boat with a spine-chilling resonance.

Inexorably, the submarine was dragging down the lethal mine upon herself. Inevitably, it must swiftly blow them to eternity.

The Captain held Number One's gaze and deliberately crossed his fingers. Peter swallowed and closed his eyes, to shut out the dreadful picture painted by his imagination. The scraping twanged into a scream as it passed directly over them. If it fouled in the conning tower...? Each man shut his eyes. Prayed. Held his breath. The infernal twanging shrieked hideously through the boat and, as suddenly, was gone.

The Captain picked up his book. He turned over a page, deliberately placed the novel face down upon the table and quietly rose from his settee. He walked into the Control Room. Number One looked across at Peter. They smiled and Peter swallowed. He saw Number One turn over upon his side to grope for elusive sleep.

But nobody slept much for the rest of that day, which slowly dragged on to its merciful close. Before surfacing that night, Joe called his officers around him and wasted no time. Drumming his fingers upon the chart, which was spread out on the Ward Room table, he grinned at them all.

"Well, Number One, this may all seem rather pompous, but I particularly want no misunderstanding during the next night or two. We are going through the E-boat patrol lines off Marittimo Island tonight. We should be there in two hours' time."

He glanced at his wristwatch, a slight frown puckering his bushy eyebrows, as he continued, "That means nine o'clock and the moon will have just risen. To reach our position off Cape St. Vito on time, I shall have to proceed on the surface on main engines, at full speed and trimmed right down. I don't like it but there 'tis, as they say in Devonshire. The E-boats will be lying stopped and listening for us, so they may easily hear us before we sight them. However, we'll have to risk it, and I expect a particularly good lookout, as it seems like being a flat calm tonight. Any questions, any of you?" he asked, looking at his three officers.

Peter felt the steady eyes boring through him, weighing his worth. Then the gaze shifted to Hickey, and so to Number One. Each man slowly shook his head.

"Right!" continued the Captain. "Tomorrow night we should be well through the E-boats but we will continue on main engines at full speed, and should reach our billet at dawn. Intelligence reports that we may meet enemy U-boats, so watch out. You are to fire on sight, even if I am unable to see the target. All our own boats will be in position off Cape St. Vito so there is no possibility of wrong identification. Any questions? No? Then stand by to surface, Number One" — and, grinning again, Joe dispersed the meeting.

"Aye, aye, sir," replied Number One.

He squeezed his way past the Captain on the settee and, raising his voice, gave the order, "Shift to night lighting. Diving stations!"

Quickly and silently, men scurried to and fro to their diving stations. The Ursula suits rustled as the lookouts, Officer of the Watch and signalmen donned them awkwardly in the passage outside the Ward Room. Swiftly the canvas trunking was lowered from the conning tower hatch, whilst the last red lamp was fitted to replace the white lighting. The eerie red glow shining on greasy faces now enveloped them all. The lower conning tower hatch clunked open and, slipping their binocular straps over their necks, the signalmen, lookouts and Officer of the Watch disappeared into the darkness of the conning tower. The Captain, dark blue, polo-necked sweater pulled over his khaki shirt, binoculars dangling from his neck, sat patiently waiting on the Ward Room settee.

The boat was deep during this dangerous period of twilight, for the periscope was useless as soon as the light started to fade.

"No H.E., sir. All-round sweep completed," said the Asdic operator, Leading Seaman David Elliott.

"Ready to surface, sir," reported the First Lieutenant to his Captain who then strolled into the Control Room.

"Periscope depth," he ordered quietly.

Slowly, the depth-gauge pointers swung to twenty-eight feet as Number One, murmuring to the planesmen, brought her up to periscope depth, while he operated the pump order instrument with his left hand.

"Twenty-eight feet, sir."

"Up periscope," the Captain ordered.

The steel tube hissed as it slithered swiftly upwards. The Captain swung round rapidly to ensure that the coast was clear, though he could see little in the darkness.

"Surface," he snapped.

"Blow one … blow two," Number One ordered and the boat wallowed to the surface, rolling gently in the swell. Several long minutes passed, while the Captain, who was now on the bridge, swept the horizon.

"Start the generators! Half ahead together," came his muffled voice down the voicepipe, and, a few minutes later when she had enough buoyancy, "Stop the blowers!"

The little submarine surged ahead, trimmed right down so that she was hardly visible, while the roar of the diesels filled the boat. To starboard, the black land mass of the western tip of Sicily loomed blackly against the night sky, the razor-like ridge of mountains dropping sheer into the sea. Huge and sombre, they looked like a menacing backdrop to a stage set for tragedy.

Alert, and strung taut like banjo strings, the bridge personnel restlessly peered through their binoculars, and swept their respective sectors, so that the whole horizon was covered. They sensed the mountains brooding over them, watching like giant guardians of the Sicilian shore, waiting to repulse all marauders of their *Mare Nostrum*.

Not a breath of wind shivered the glassy surface of the sea which reflected with pinpoints of dancing light the glittering stars in the indigo sky. The undulating water stretched astern in curving lines, as the submarine zigzagged through the mirror-like sea leaving willowy lines etching their tell-tale presence to the lurking enemy.

The first glimpse of the rocky chain of islets came into view ahead. They stretched out from the western tip of the mainland, emerging from the ocean depths like turrets on fairyland castles. Woe betide any submarine that careered out of control into these depths, for here the ocean was two miles deep, and the pressure at such depths would squeeze the steel pressure-hull like a man's foot crushing a beetle.

The roar of the diesels coughed and rumbled into the night, heralding *Rugged*'s approach as she scythed her way swiftly towards the point where she would round the last islet in the chain, the notorious and dreaded island of Marittimo.

When Peter came on watch at eleven o'clock, Marittimo was already abeam now some two miles distant and was already passing out of sight, because a thin haze of fog was blanketing the land.

Hickey quickly turned over his watch to Peter.

"Mind they don't bite, Sub," he said jokingly, as he dropped down into the conning tower.

"They won't," replied Peter, not knowing clearly what Hickey meant. He had no time for riddles, for his whole concentration was focused upon searching the horizon for E-boats. This was now doubly difficult, for the haze had reduced visibility on the starboard quarter to less than half a mile.

At the after-end of the bridge, the Captain dozed fitfully. The moon had risen behind the mountains to throw its pale beam behind the haze, so that a ghostly whiteness shivered over the whole north-eastern horizon.

Peter looked over the side to port and his heart leaped into his mouth at the sight of thin white lines of phosphorescence weaving and streaking towards him, gleaming eerily in the glasses.

"Phew! Thought they were torpedo tracks!" he sighed with relief. "Must be those electric eels I've heard about," and he realised what Hickey had meant. They were now right in the middle of the E-boat lines, and Peter's heart thumped anxiously until he settled down to the routine of watch-keeping.

There was a grunt by his elbow. The Captain stood by him and leaned over the bridge-rail.

"How goes it, Sub?"

"All right, sir. Those electric eels shook me, though!" Peter replied.

"Yes, they look uncommonly like torpedo tracks, don't they? We'll soon be able to round up to clear Marittimo. I shall be glad when this is over," he murmured, more to himself than to Peter. "I'm sure that these E-boats lie stopped, just listening on their hydrophones. We must be sounding like an express train tonight, mustn't we, Sub?"

"Yes, sir. The engines make an infernal din," replied Peter, and continued, "I don't like this starboard quarter, sir — visibility is very low over there."

"Yes, I know, Sub, but we must press on," the Captain replied, gazing out to port.

Peter picked up his glasses and shifted his body round to starboard to start yet another sweep from aft. The wind from their own speed gently soughed past his head, the quiet swishing and gurgling of the water lapping along the swirling casing. It was so peaceful, so still. He shifted his weight to the other foot to readjust his binoculars and as he did so, he was aware of more phosphorescent trails far out to starboard.

These eels, he thought, *confound them!* — and then he froze where he stood. These two trails seemed broader than the others. They were dead straight and approaching on a steady bearing. Then he saw a third, equidistant from the rest.

His heart leapt, his hand outstretched to starboard.

"Torpedoes, green nine-oh, sir!" he cried.

Instinctively, he yelled down the voicepipe, "Hard-a-port!"

The Captain sprang to Peter's side.

"Fish!" he muttered. "Dive! Dive! Dive!" — and his hand shot out to press the diving klaxon.

Peter's eyes were mesmerised by the steady line of bubbles, now only a few hundred feet away. It seemed an eternity before *Rugged* started swinging to port. Slowly the jumping wire started to traverse the horizon line … slowly … so slowly…

"Oh God!" Peter whispered. "Will she never move?"

Then suddenly she started to swing swiftly to port, turning her stern towards the tracks, in order to comb them. Faster! Faster! But now the hideously bubbling tracks seemed to be on top of them. The lookouts jumped down the hatch, faces deathly pale and the sea hissed around the conning tower as she plummeted downwards.

Mesmerised, Peter stood transfixed. Closer … and closer! At any moment a sheet of flame would blast them to eternity. The first track ploughed remorselessly onwards and passed slowly up the port side. The second one would have them then! But it, too, slid slowly up the starboard side, whispering with a sibilant gurgle.

"Steady!" yelled Joe down the voicepipe to the helmsman and then he saw Peter standing there, eyes fastened on the tracks.

"What the devil are you doing here, Sub? Get below!" he yelled.

Peter sprang to life. As he dropped down the hatch, he saw the third track, and then water splashed down upon him, as he heard the upper lid shut with a bang!

"First clip on!" the Captain shouted. "One hundred and twenty feet. Full ahead together, steer two-three-oh. Shut off for depth-charging!"

In the Control Room, the sound of Number One's orders rose above the clatter of operating valves. Men were still rushing to their stations, changing places silently and quickly. The whine of the main motors rose shrilly above the ordered confusion, as the telegraphs clanged their urgent summons to the Motor Room.

Still no pulverising explosion! The torpedoes must have run past them by now.

"Blow Q!" Number One's voice jerked across the pregnant tension.

The roar of the escaping air, which vented inboard, reverberated throughout the boat, filling it with an acrid, stale stench.

"Sixty feet, sir."

Down, down, she plunged steeply, gaining momentum at every second. Eighty — ninety feet.

"Shut main ballast Kingstons," ordered Number One quietly. "Pump on 'O'."

One hundred — hundred and ten — hundred and twenty — hundred and twenty-five feet. The pointers started to slow their rate of descent, while the boat began to level out again.

"H.E. closing, red one-four-oh, sir," sang out the black-haired Elliott from his Asdic corner.

"Group down, stop port," ordered the Captain calmly, now standing astride near the canvas trunking. "Open main vents."

Thunk! The vents opened above their heads. When the boat had shut off from depth-charging, all the bulkhead doors had banged shut, so that each compartment was now a small world on its own.

"Port ten."

"Port ten, sir," repeated the helmsman slowly, swinging over his wheel.

The drumming of the E-boat's fast-running engines quickly increased up their port side.

"Hold your hats on!" grinned Joe.

Waiting was the worst part of this business — but still no depth charges. Nothing but the clattering and tinkling of the E-boat's progress as it flashed overhead, quickly decreasing when it had passed over them.

And then it came! A sharp crack! crack! as two charges split the sea asunder, but well clear on their port side.

"Rotten shots!" murmured the Captain. "We'll go right round and give them the slip."

Hickey leaned over the chart, and indicated *Rugged*'s position to the Captain. "Another hour at 'slow one', sir, and then I reckon we can turn up to the northward around the island."

"Thank you, Pilot, we'll do that. I'm glad that this isn't the Trapani First Eleven — those boys are good! But no doubt they will be after us soon."

They were on the doorstep of the crack Italian destroyer flotilla, based upon Trapani to deal with the British submarines. Highly skilled and extremely efficient, the First Eleven were much respected by our submariners.

Still showering depth charges in all directions, and sore at losing their quarry, the hunting E-boats gradually dropped astern. Fainter and fainter came the jarring shocks from the exploding charges.

An hour later, *Rugged* surfaced two miles north-west of the island of Marittimo. This jagged rock, rearing menacingly from the placid depths, stood in sharp contrast against a moon-kissed sky. The moon hung like a tiny lantern above them, but the low haze still drifted in long, trailing wisps of greyness along the foreshore, hiding the bases of the mountains.

To Peter, now on watch again on the bridge, it did not seem four hours since he had stood transfixed by the terrifying sight of the hungry torpedo tracks.

An hour and a half before dawn, the clammy wet and the cold of approaching fog chilled his tired body. Joe stood by him for a while, staring into the opaqueness, with visibility now down to about half a mile. Sweeping his glasses along the landward horizon, Peter stiffened.

Surely the murkiness seemed thicker just there? Yes! He wiped his eyes. He searched again.

"U-boat, sir, red two-oh! We're about sixty degrees on her starboard bow," he yelled excitedly.

Joe's body hurled itself at the voicepipe.

"Night alarm! Stand by all tubes!"

Once again, tired men hauled themselves to their stations. Tubes were brought to the ready and, within half a minute, the report "all tubes ready!" was passed up the voicepipe.

"Blowed if I can see her, Sub! Are you absolutely sure? Point with your hand."

Peter, peering intently through his glasses, could just see the outline of a submarine drawing slowly across the torpedo sights.

"There, sir!" — his arm indicating the bearing.

The Captain strained his eyes along Peter's outstretched arm.

"Yes, I think I can see her. *You'll* have to fire, Sub. Starboard ten."

The Captain quickly set the torpedo sight with his estimations of the target's course and speed.

Straining his eyes hard, Peter could only just see the ghostly shape. It was more of a shadow than a definite outline and as *Rugged* swung slowly past the target again, Peter steadied the ship and waited for the sights to come on the target.

"Lay off ten degrees, Sub. Fire when your sights come on!"

"I can only just see her, sir. Stand by!"

"Stand by!" the Captain repeated down the voicepipe.

Peter was trembling with excitement while Joe, calm but swearing under his breath, waited impatiently by him, every moment an agony of suspense.

"Fire one!" yelled Peter, as the shadowy shape slid slowly across the sights.

Joe waited two seconds. "Fire two," he shouted. A further pause.

"Fire three! … Fire four!"

The jolt of torpedoes spilling out into the night shivered the boat.

"Down lookouts!"

An interminable wait for the explosion.

If I miss, Peter thought, *I shall never be believed*.

The ghostly apparition slowly vanished into the murkiness.

"Port twenty," the Captain snapped, his eyes meeting Peter's across the bridge.

Peter felt himself flushing with shame, and looked the other way just as a distant orange flash, followed by an intense golden glow which suffused the greyness of the dawn, burst upon their consciousness. After a slight pause, an ear-splitting rumble shook the eastern horizon.

"Well done, Sub!" shouted the Captain, beaming all over his face. "Dive, dive, dive!"

Rugged slowly disappeared into the greyness, leaving only a threshing swirl to mark her lethal whereabouts.

Six hours later, *Rugged* was at periscope depth and in position off Cape St. Vito. To the eastward, the familiar precipice rose vertically from the black depths like the blade of a knife. At five-mile intervals, a semicircle of submarines lay in wait for the Italian battle fleet. Two miles from the Cape, *Reliant* lay dived. Next to her, Arkwright in *Restless*, *Rugged's* easterly next-door neighbour. Then *Rugged*, *Rapid* and, at the western extremity, *Renegade*.

The Captain was at the periscope, checking their position. He had left Elliott, the Asdic operator, crouching over his set in the far corner of the Control Room.

"Make the challenge on a bearing from red six-oh to red one-two-oh."

"Aye, aye, sir."

With his left hand, Elliott, an open-faced man from Norfolk, slowly turned the black knob, step by step. With his right, he transmitted a letter in Morse code. He then listened intently. He repeated these actions until he reached red one-oh-five, when his back stiffened. All eyes fastened upon him, for it was always fascinating to feel that there were friends in contact with them, within a few miles. Somehow, the depths seemed more hospitable.

"Red one-oh-five, submarine making 'Q' for Queenie, sir," Elliott reported.

Joe, hands thrust into the pockets of his khaki shorts and leaning with his back against the Fruit Machine, shifted his legs and nodded.

"That's *Rapid*. Make the same on the starboard side, between green eight-oh and one-one-oh."

"Aye, aye, sir," replied Elliott, a faint smile of pride on his raw-boned face.

Twiddling the black knob quickly, he went around to the other side, and started transmitting step by step, pausing only to listen for reply, while the Captain, with a faintly bored expression, shifted his weight to the other foot and waited for the answer to his challenge.

Slowly Elliott swept through the whole sector.

"They must be asleep in *Restless*. Try again, Leading Seaman Elliott. This time, increase your arc to green four-oh and green one-four-oh."

Deliberately, precisely, Elliott swept and transmitted.

"No reply, sir."

Joe uncrossed his gangling legs and heaved himself upright. He scratched the side of his head and came over to Elliott's Asdic cabinet.

"Try again," he said quietly, leaning over the man.

Once more there was no reply.

"Humph! — odd," growled Joe. "Let's go a bit nearer their billet and see if that will wake them up. Starboard ten."

Twenty minutes later, now on the edge of her billet, *Rugged* resumed her course.

"Try again."

Elliott repeated his drill, his body stiffening as he reached green eight-oh.

"Green eight-oh, sir. Submarine transmitting letter 'Y' for 'Yorker'."

"Thank you, check the transmission."

Elliott bent low over the dimly lit instrument, his right hand adjusting his headphones.

"Checked, sir. Submarine transmitting 'Y' for 'Yorker'."

"Odd! That's *Reliance*'s letter."

Joe's face was thoughtful, a slight pucker tracing a deep line between his jutting eyebrows.

Elliott crouched, still waiting.

"Submarine transmitting challenge, sir."

"Make the reply," ordered Joe wearily.

On the ebonite key, Elliott slowly and deliberately tapped the letter 'F'. He listened intently as three 'R's came back to him from the depths.

"Reply acknowledged, sir," he reported, half turning on his wooden seat to meet the questioning eyes of his Captain.

"Strange, very strange," muttered Joe as he crossed over to the chart table. He was worried. A horrible suspicion, a wrenching doubt tore his mind. Swiftly the news swept through the boat.

Restless was missing from her station.

CHAPTER 8

Tragedy

The major campaign of the North African landings has now passed into history.

The enormous Allied convoys assembled off the North African coast on the same day that *Rugged* took up her position off Cape St. Vito. At the western half of the North African continent, the ambitious plan to link up with the British Eighth Army on the other side now rolled into action.

To the five British submarines lurking off Cape St. Vito, Operation 'Torch' was a disappointment, only *Reliance* and *Rugged* being presented with targets.

In the early hours of the morning following the African landings, an Italian cruiser and six destroyers swept round the Cape. Inshore of *Rugged*, *Reliance* scored one hit on the stern of the cruiser, which promptly tried to turn back to safer waters. *Rugged* took up the action where *Reliance*, saturated by the depth-charging from the counter-attacking destroyers, had left off. It was a most nerve-racking attack in glassy calm conditions for *Rugged*, in trying to sink the cruiser and to finish the job *Reliance* had started, sank an escorting destroyer which crossed the torpedo tracks at the wrong moment.

Two days later, tired but jubilant, *Rugged* was recalled from patrol, with only one torpedo remaining and was the first to enter Lazaretto harbour, under the protective walls of Malta.

As she turned in a wide sweep to come alongside the catamarans, the lonely figure of the Captain of the flotilla could be seen waiting to welcome them back from patrol. Joe

Croxton was surprised when he did not receive the familiar wave for he had sunk a U-boat and a destroyer, as the flapping Jolly Roger plainly indicated.

Joe looked down from the conning tower upon the white-clad bulk of his Captain standing astride upon the pontoon. The venerated figure smiled quizzically up at him.

"Well done, Joe," he said.

There was something in the way in which he said it, however, that set Joe's heart racing and, looking carefully at him again, Joe detected an unaccustomed air of sadness, a resignation in the stoop of the broad shoulders.

Wearily, Joe swung himself over the edge of the conning tower and dropped down to the casing with a clatter, to walk off the bouncing plank which served as a 'brow'.

"Well, Joe, come and have a drink," greeted Captain 'S', and turning, they both walked slowly ashore over the thin line of bobbing pontoons.

Twenty minutes later, as Peter was collecting his gear to go ashore, a messenger, cap tucked under his arm, coughed discreetly and spoke to him.

"Captain's compliments, sir, and would you report to Captain 'S' as soon as possible?"

Overhearing the message, Number One looked up towards Peter.

"You lucky old devil, Sub! That'll be about the U-boat," he grinned.

"Much more likely to be a rocket — I'm more used to them," Peter replied, brushing his hair and buckling the clips on his shorts. Giving them a hitch, he hurried out of the Ward Room, clambered his way through the litter and confusion of men hungry to get ashore, and clattered up the fore-hatch ladder.

"Good to get ashore again!" he muttered to himself, as his feet touched the Maltese sandstone, his eyes blinking and dazzled by the unaccustomed brightness. However hard he tried to control it, his heart had started to thump faster, so that he could hear his pulse pounding in his eardrums. He hated interviews with Senior Officers, feeling as if he were reporting outside the headmaster's study again. But this was a pleasant visit, he told himself; for, after all, there were not many Sub-Lieutenants who had sunk a U-boat, and he did feel rather proud of it in his secret moments.

The large white door with its rusty hinges barred his way. "Captain 'S', Tenth Submarine Flotilla", the white-lettered nameplate proudly announced. To one side was the open window of Captain 'S''s cabin and the low drone of conversation drifted through the aperture.

"Here goes," sighed Peter, taking off his cap and squashing it under his left arm. He knocked softly.

"Come in!"

After the dazzling whiteness outside, Peter was surprised by the darkness of the bare sandstone room. For the rest of his days, Peter never forgot this scene.

A bottle and glasses stood on a table in the middle of the room. A green mat failed dismally to lend comfort to the cold, flagstoned floor. A white chest of drawers, hairbrush and comb neatly in the middle of its shining surface, furnished the far wall, while two wicker chairs were drawn up by the open window. A doorless opening led through to the small bedroom. The only lighting, as throughout the whole base, seemed to be an Admiralty-pattern candle, stuck by its own grease on to the upturned lid of an empty tobacco tin which stood squarely between the brush and comb on the chest of drawers.

Captain 'S' smiled at Peter, motioning him to join them. Joe stood next to him and each held an empty glass in his hand.

"Gin, Sub?"

"Thank you, sir."

Slowly Captain 'S' poured them a drink. Peter could have cut the silence with a knife. He took a gulp and was thankful to feel the unaccustomed warmth flow through him.

"I want you to tell me exactly what happened, Sub, when you thought that you saw the U-boat."

"Yes, sir."

Peter sickened. *Thought I saw? But I did see it. What is he getting at?*

Peter jerkily warmed to his story, recounting exactly what he remembered, while Joe nodded and grunted in assent when Peter paused for confirmation. As Peter talked, Captain 'S' gazed out of the window, a distant look in his wise eyes. He said nothing, and, when Peter had finished with "… that's all, sir", there was a long pause.

Joe met Peter's eyes and seemed to be sending him a message of sympathy and understanding, which was unusual for such a man. Captain 'S' turned slowly from the window and motioned Peter to a chair. He sat down. From the breast pocket of his tropical white shirt, the elder man took a few sheaves of paper and handed them to Peter.

"Read that, Sub," he said quietly. "I am not blaming you in the least…"

Looking upwards at the kindly face above him, Peter could see the wealth of compassion in the shrewd eyes and his hand was trembling as he took the paper and read:

Extract from the Italian Monitoring Service, relayed from Rome and broadcast at 1600 hours on the Italian Radio Band:

News flash! Brave Italians! Today our victorious airmen, with naval assistance, captured the crew of a British submarine, some miles north-west of our base at Trapani.

This enemy submarine was bombed the night before by our gallant airmen and was crippled so that she could not dive. Returning on the surface at dawn to her base at Malta, a mysterious explosion occurred at her stern. This, miraculously, caused no casualties, but the enemy submarine filled with water and sank immediately. The explosion was seen by our alert observers ashore and a Cant 52 reconnaissance aircraft was sent to investigate. The intrepid pilot, Leonarda Guzzi, of Palermo, reported survivors swimming in the water. Fifteen minutes later, our E-boats picked up the whole crew, including their Captain, one Lieutenant Harold Arkwright, Royal Navy, holder of the enemy's Distinguished Service Order, who comes from Bridport, England. The crew are safe and are now prisoners at our camp in Marsala. The men seemed dazed and mystified by their experience.

Once again, our victorious airmen and sailors have struck another blow for their Duce and Motherland. Long live Il Duce, saviour of Italy, Benito Mussolini!… Message ends.

Peter could no longer read. Hot tears blinded him as he got up and stared through the window and minutes passed before he recovered his self-control. The tears had splashed like globules to the windowsill. His taut nerves felt like snapping under the strain. Surreptitiously, he groped for his handkerchief, feigned a cough and blew his nose violently. When he turned to face his superiors, there was little trace of his agony, except for the bright glitter in the eyes.

"I don't know what to say, sir." From far away he heard his voice croaking, a queer, strangled sound.

'S' came over and put his hand gently on Peter's shoulder. Coughing and clearing his throat, he shook him by the hand.

"I'm to blame, Sub, not you. They are all alive to fight another day. That's the miracle, that's what matters, isn't it, Joe?"

From far away, Joe's voice grunted in agreement, and went on, "Would you show him the other one too, sir?"

Captain 'S' gave Peter another signal. It was short and timed eighteen hundred hours:

Countrymen! The Captain and crew of the British submarine, which was captured earlier today, are from the submarine Restless, *as announced in our last bulletin. Churchill should learn a lesson from this episode. The Royal Navy is being swept from Mare Nostrum!*

The prisoners are now enjoying our hospitality in the dungeons of Castellare Poliano, near Marsala. Long live Il Duce!

Peter handed the message back to Captain 'S', whose kindly mouth twitched into the beginnings of a smile, and in whose eyes there was once again a mischievous sparkle. He turned to Joe.

"Joe, I have an idea."

"Sir?"

"It's good of the Wops to vaunt their success. They have told us exactly where Harold Arkwright and his boys are. What say you to going and getting them back?"

Joe took a pace backwards and whistled.

"Strike while the iron is hot, you mean, sir?"

"That's it. Have another drink?"

The bottle gurgled before he continued: "Before telling you my plans, I think that you and your Sub, Sinclair, have, by miraculous good fortune, saved the lives of all aboard *Restless*.

Harry had been bombed the night before" — 'S' sipped his drink and slowly turned the glass, holding it to the light and squinting at it with one eye — "Harry had been bombed and couldn't dive and may have been unable to steam at more than a few knots. He was forced to attempt the impossible. He had to pass Trapani in daylight and get back past Marittimo on the surface. He hadn't a chance! The first aircraft would have whistled up the whole Wop Air Force, and the Trapani First Eleven as well!"

He paused as they raised their glasses.

"They would have made mincemeat of Harry and his boys. Harry would have fought back with his Vickers against hopeless odds. Any survivors would have been butchered in the water," continued 'S'. Then, with a twinkle glinting in his eyes he went on:

"And then you and your Sub, Joe, kindly sent *Restless* to the bottom without scratching one of them, thus saving Harry the indignity of scuttling. The Wops obligingly picked them out of the drink! Yes, it's a miracle!" 'S' sighed and laughed.

"Now, Sub, before taking you into my confidence, I imagine that you would like to put things straight. Am I right?"

Peter felt his face muscles relaxing slowly. When he answered, his voice sounded normal again.

"Of course, sir, if it's possible."

"I'm asking you to lead a pretty tricky jaunt ashore to rescue Lieutenant Arkwright. Before putting you on your oath to secrecy, do you volunteer? It may mean that you won't come back."

Peter nodded.

"I'll go, sir."

An imperceptible glance passed between 'S' and Joe, who leaned broodingly across the table, unrolling a chart.

Swiftly and brilliantly, for 'S' was not the Captain of this crack flotilla for nothing, he unfolded his plan. After intensive night training in Lazaretto harbour, and with the aid of an Army Commando unit, two folboat canoes would reconnoitre off the cliff at Castellare Poliano. Peter's party would try and force their way into the castle to bring back Arkwright.

"Harry Arkwright is all ready for you," he continued. "I've already got in touch with him on the bush telegraph, and he will be waiting for you on the nights of next Tuesday, Wednesday and Thursday. He's billeted with his officers, apart from his troops, in the second tower to the westward of the main gate of this castle" — and 'S' unrolled another chart which was a plan of Castellare Poliano. How he got it, Peter never found out, but the skill with which 'S' amassed information was legendary.

Captain 'S' continued, "Harry relies upon you to get inside and contact him in any way you like. I know no more, except that Huns are their gaolers."

"I know Lieutenant Arkwright well, sir; we were almost brought up together and were at the same school," Peter said.

"All the better, Sub," nodded 'S'. "Joe! Remember that you've only got six days. That means that you must leave harbour the day after tomorrow, having stored and reloaded with torpedoes. You must get your folboats aboard, train your Commandos who are ready and waiting for you. Your ship's company will be tired, but you may tell them briefly what's up because I know that they will respond. Sub-Lieutenant Benson, just in from the U.K., will relieve Sinclair temporarily as Third Hand of the boat. It will do him good to have a crack at rescuing Arkwright. This is secret. I am admitting that we are risking *Rugged*. But I think that we owe it to *Restless* and that we all feel better, don't we, gentlemen?" 'S' continued, reaching for his cap, "I am going to tell the ships' companies what's happened to *Restless* as soon as they get back from the Iron Ring, so that there can be no recriminations."

Joe followed 'S' out of the doorway.

"Thank you, sir, for giving us the chance to get him back," he said.

"That's all right. Good luck to both of you" — and 'S' started to walk off.

But Peter, against all Service regulations and etiquette, shyly held out his hand.

Captain 'S' grasped it, shaking it in a vice-like grip. He did not speak, but held Peter's eyes momentarily. For an instant, Service barriers were down, and wisdom looked to youth, and youth responded.

"I'll do my best, sir," Peter whispered.

"I know, I know. Carry on, both of you!" Captain 'S' replied testily, and nodding, he turned away, looking across the water at the yellow battlements of the ancient fortress.

Joe and Peter had gone.

Am I right? 'S' asked himself. *Am I right? I may be sending him to his certain death. May God bless him!* — and his distressed eyes followed the English youth who was disappearing down the flagged balcony.

At dusk two nights later, one of the flotilla, so recently returned from blockading the enemy's bases, slipped from her moorings and proceeded silently out of the harbour and into the night.

Down below, the submarine looked like the left-luggage department of some great London terminus. A full outfit of torpedoes was in the racks, but in addition, two lean, light folboats filled the fore-ends. These flimsily built canoes were made of canvas, stretched across wooden frames. A collapsible canvas Army boat, known as a dory, lay propped against the stanchions. Bren guns, their magazines and boxes of ammunition, hand grenades and red-painted boxes of 'sticky bombs' cluttered every square inch of deck space. Amongst this shambles lived the burly figures of the Commandos in their green camouflaged battledress. There was, however, one sailor in the beach party, Able Seaman Hawkins. Peter had asked Easton for him, and Number One had reluctantly consented to let Hawkins go.

"I must have one seaman amongst all these Pongos, hang it, Number One!" Peter had said, using his trump card.

That settled it, and Hawkins joined in with the training. He was good with the folboats, and his general handiness was soon appreciated by the remainder of the Commando party.

"If we must have a matelot, you'll do," one of them had graciously said, and it was not long before Hawkins was rigged in Commando battledress.

During the passage to the area, Peter spent his time checking and rechecking his plans with the Commando Army Captain, already renowned for many successful and daring exploits. Such a one had been a dawn raid on a German-held lighthouse off the Channel Isles, where he had disturbed the enemy at breakfast by kicking open the door and lobbing hand grenades on to their frankfurters.

Of necessity, the plan had to be simple, daring and swift. Only by boldness could it succeed. The first landing would be a reconnaissance to determine the lie of the land. Their presence must never be suspected, or the rescue attempt on the following night would be compromised.

The hours dragged by. Peter looked at his watch. Only seven-thirty. In two hours they would be landing.

He looked across at his comrade-in-arms. Jan Widdecombe, the Commando Army Captain, was dressed in the field-grey uniform of a German trooper, an iron cross pinned on the left breast of his tunic. He had borrowed Peter's razor to shave his fair head, which made him look every inch a Teuton. His eyes wrinkled at the corners as his weather-beaten face, old for its twenty-eight years, creased into a friendly grin of appreciation. He was strapping a large Luger pistol into his belt and filling his pockets with spare magazines. Four Mills bombs on sticks slung from a bandolier, and the thin Commando knife, shining blue-black in the bright lights of the Ward Room, clove neatly to his left hip. He placed the German helmet squarely on his head, the two ventilation holes on either side giving him a grotesque appearance. Peter laughed and rolled feebly across the table.

"You don't look so British yourself, Sub!" retorted Jan, scowling at Peter.

Then Peter remembered that, in his Italian garb, he must have looked just as incongruous. The black gabardine of his trousers and jacket gave him the sinister air, down to the last detail, of an officer in the crack Guarda Fascista. By mixing their uniforms, it was hoped that confusion might be added to distract the German sentries.

In the fore-ends the three Commandos were having their legs pulled unmercifully by seamen who were volunteering unfamiliar phrases in the broadest cockney-German so that the soldiers might be able to make themselves at home ashore.

"*Ein grosse bier, bitte, mein liebeling Fräulein!*" grinned Smith, the Seaman Torpedoman. "That ought to get you somewhere!"

"Nark it!" returned Graves, the largest of the three Commandos. "I can't breathe with this perishin' titfer on!"

The Canadian, Jarvis, who was the smallest of the party, looked like a walking armoury.

"Got my silencer, anyway," he grinned, holding up the brass cheese wire, toggle-fitted at each end. "They croak quiet!" he concluded wickedly.

He caused a sensation while he demonstrated the efficiency of his primitive weapon by a horribly realistic demonstration of a potential victim's fate. Even the sailors were shocked to silence when he rolled his eyeballs upwards and drew the wire slowly across his throat.

The third Commando was a burly, red-headed young man who hailed from Fife.

"Och! Ye bloodthirsty Canuc!" he growled to his confederate. "Can ye no' leave it alone for a wee while?"

Surprised, Jarvis stopped his act. "Sorry, Jock!" he said quietly, in the silence that followed.

"Then let's check up on these folboats and see that they're all right," said Bill Hawkins and they turned to see that the canoes and paddles were rigged and ready to shift outboard when the moment came. The larger collapsible dory would not be assembled until they surfaced, for, after heaving it through the fore-hatch, it would be put together on the casing and then taken in by one of them and used to bring off any rescued men.

"Shift to night lighting!" The sudden order, with its foreboding message of the impending operation, made Peter's stomach sink. The eerie red glow slowly flooded the boat and instinctively, men's voices hushed.

The landing party was privileged. A bowl of hot soup and a large tot of rum made their blood course warmly.

"Ah, that's better!" Jan said, smacking his lips and rubbing his stomach with a circular motion. "After looking through a periscope all day, it's a pleasure to have something to do. I hate creeping about below the surface. I'm looking forward to getting ashore!"

He echoed the sentiments of all the beach party for the day had been spent peering furtively through the periscope and making sketches of the cliff below the towering castle. They had chosen a reddish gash which seemed to be a steep slide in the two-hundred-foot cliff.

Dressed in a dark blue polo-necked sweater, Number One came into the Control Room. As he had to open the fore-hatch and take the boats through it on to the casing, he could not risk light-coloured clothes which might be seen from ashore.

"Ready to surface, sir," he reported to the Captain.

"Thank you, Number One. Stand by to surface."

Jan and Peter stood by the trunking, the latter feeling sad not to be taking part in the routine of his submarine. His thoughts were interrupted by Joe.

"Remember this, both of you: I will surface and wait for you for half an hour at one-thirty a.m., half an hour before moonrise, if the Pilot's got his times right! It should be very dark. We will flash our infra-red lamp towards the shore. Have you both got your infra-red receivers with you?"

"Yes, sir," said Peter, patting his breast pocket.

Joe nodded and continued, "Look through that glass and you will see us flashing. When I surface, I can't dive with my fore-hatch open and as we are at our most vulnerable then, make your return snappy. If I am detected, I shall be forced to leave the area, but I will pick you up five miles farther down the coast, by the large rock upon which we agreed yesterday. I will be there for two nights running, but daren't risk any longer. If you want me to surface in emergency, throw two hand grenades into the water. Is everything clear and are we all agreed?"

"Yes, sir, thank you," Jan answered.

"All right, let's get on with it and..." Joe coughed and an embarrassing pause followed. He mumbled something about "... good luck!" and held out his hand which Jan took firmly.

Rugged broke surface a quarter of an hour later. Trimmed right down, with very little of her casing awash, she crept on her electric motors to within half a mile of the shore, the massive cliffs looming menacingly above her. It was a perfect night for the operation — dark as pitch, the blackness clinging about them and almost tangible.

"Not a sound from anyone now," the Captain reminded them all on the bridge. "Open the fore-hatch."

A few moments elapsed and then the bridge saw the dull red glow appear from a hole in the fore-casing, through which swiftly slid the dark figure of Number One. He drew the boat through the void, his gym-shoed feet moving silently on the steel plating. When the third boat was through, the aperture faded as the hatch slowly shut, clipped from the inside by unseen hands.

Joe breathed again.

"Over you go," he whispered to Peter.

Peter, followed by Jan and his men, slid silently over the bridge, pattering along the slippery casing in their noiseless, rubber-soled boots.

Already Number One and the Second Coxswain had juggled the first folboat into the water and, as it bumped against the pressure hull, Peter and Hawkins nimbly slid down into it, sitting down quickly to prevent a capsize. As Peter fended off from the side, he heard Number One whisper, "Good luck, Sub."

Peter gave a few strong strokes with his paddle, and lay off to await the others who joined him three minutes later. He waved his hand which was acknowledged by Jan in the other canoe, and by Graves in the Army dory. With a flick of their paddles, Peter and Hawkins turned their folboat towards the cliffs and disappeared into the darkness, the other two following at fifty-yard intervals.

At once Peter felt a great loneliness. When he looked over his shoulder, he saw a slight swirl at *Rugged*'s stem as she slowly went astern on her motors, sliding back into the night.

Swish — swish, swish — swish!

The licking of their paddles was the only sound he could hear on this placid sea, save for the ominous growl of the breakers pounding upon the beach a few hundred yards ahead of them. Already he could see a white pencil line of surf, where the waves slapped down on the rocky shelf.

Ah! There was the small black rock to the left. He turned slightly to port to leave a larger rock on his starboard hand, farther away. Passing between these two, he should be able to run straight into the small sandy cove which they had spied at the bottom of the fissure. He held water to allow the others to catch them up. Only the surge and the sigh of the swell, as it heaved and swirled around the jagged rocks, disturbed the stillness of the peaceful night. Peter had only to rip the canvas of his boat on some hidden rock to render her waterlogged and useless.

He looked back over his shoulder. There was the faint outline of Jan's boat, his paddle motionless. So far, so good! Peter swept his arm forward in a signal, and they started paddling cautiously. On alternate strokes, he dipped his blade into the water to see whether he could touch bottom. He paddled onwards. The small breakers were now swirling on top of him and suddenly he was in the flurry of foam.

Clutching the paddle in his left hand, he heaved himself out of the tiny cockpit, and dropped into the pounding surf. He was surprised to feel his boots touch bottom immediately, and to realise that the water was only knee-deep. Keeping the boat's stern towards the swell while Hawkins jumped out, Peter hove the canoe on to the beach, clear of the breakers.

They stood motionless, feeling stark naked in their loneliness, and sensing that an unseen enemy was waiting for them on the towering cliffs. Instinctively they dropped flat, listening and straining their eyes. For a full minute they lay prone.

Then Peter sat up and produced his shaded blue flashlamp. The thin blue pencil of light flickered seawards.

"O-K," he flashed.

Jan thrashed his way in, two minutes later, Bill helping him from the canoe. Two folboats now lay side by side on the sand. The dory grated on the beach, and three ponderous figures splashed nimbly ashore. Jan took command.

"Graves, get the boats out of sight. Have them ready for instant launching if you hear anything. Guard them well for they're our only return ticket!"

"Yes, sir, and good luck, sir."

Jan's teeth gleamed in the darkness as his mouth parted in a wide grin. Peter chuckled as he thought that never had he seen such a sinister bunch of Germans!

Peter followed Jan in single file, Jarvis, Jock and Bill bringing up the rear. A few steps brought them to the foot of the fissure. Jan looked upwards.

"Easier than I thought," he whispered. "I'll nip up and sling you down the rope."

Instantly he was gone, crouched against the clay landslide. Agile as a cat, he disappeared. Three minutes later the end of the rope snaked down from the darkness to drop at their feet. Peter gave Jan a moment to belay it, then, hand over hand, he shinned to the top, followed in quick succession by the other three.

Far below, the blackness of the sea merged with the invisible horizon, and already the sound of the surf soughed more distantly.

"Perfect night for this job!" whispered Jan, leaving the rope belayed around a large boulder. "And we mustn't forget that," he reminded Peter, patting the lifeline.

They turned their backs on the sea. Against the skyline, barely four hundred yards away, the bleak walls of the old fortress were faintly visible against the night sky. Its castellated battlements, broken by its immense rounded towers, had defied many invaders. Already Peter could see the two main towers which formed the gateway and, to the left of them, the main corner towers.

"Harry's in that one," he whispered, pointing.

It was odd to be so near and yet so far.

"Let's go round to the back, where you'll go over the wall," whispered Jan. "Jarvis, you stay here at the top of this cliff. Jock, I'll leave you to cover us by those bushes at the main gate. Hawkins, come with us. Let's go, Peter!"

Jan loped into the night, Peter and Bill close at his heels. So quietly and lithely did Jan move that Peter almost lost him by the north-western corner. The Commando's movements were uncanny. Suddenly he would stop, crouched and motionless, his nostrils sniffing the air like some pointing setter. Instinctively, he seemed to feel where danger lurked and to sense an atmosphere with a skill that only comes to men who hold their lives in their hands. For so long now, he had lived on a taut string, like an acrobat on the high wire. One false move, and all is over, but Jan's experiences during the last two years had given him a sixth sense that he was now using to the full.

Small, scrubby bushes dotted the area around the massive walls, and these cheered the three conspirators, for they gave them ample cover. Unless they ran blindly into an outlying patrol, their chances of remaining undetected seemed good.

As they slowly reconnoitred the castle walls, they tried to memorise the whole scene detail by detail, for use on the morrow. Creeping slowly to the foot of the wall, Peter looked upward and saw the castellated top some twenty feet above him.

"A grapnel here," Peter whispered to Jan who was lying on the ground beside him. "A grapnel here, and I could nip inside."

"Better take Hawkins with you tomorrow," said Jan. "You can both climb inside. He could guard the grapnel on the battlements, just in case of accidents."

Peter nodded, as Jan beckoned him and Bill to follow. Bill was already mastering the technique of moving in the dark, and he was remarkably light on his feet. Like three flitting shadows, they slunk through the scrub, some twenty yards from the walls, until they had travelled right round the northern and eastern flanks of the castle. Cautiously now, Jan dropped flat, crawling on his stomach as he reached the south-eastern tower. The open gatehouse, a massively timbered arrangement, sagging at the hinges and obviously long overdue for repair, was only thirty yards distant.

A sentry box stood by the right-hand tower and the sentry, a mug of soup in his hand, meandered to and fro across the entrance. The dim, blue light from the arch above him showed the steam wisping from the soup in rising vapours. Coils of barbed wire blocked the entrance on either side, while the gate itself was a white swinging pole which was operated by the sentry.

Slithering backwards on their stomachs, Jan, Peter and Bill disappeared into the night. As they made a detour round the gatehouse, they could see into the courtyard within the castle where wire-protected Nissen huts filled the open square. Here another sentry paced backwards and forwards under an arc lamp, his rifle slung from his shoulder.

Jan nudged Peter and they gave the entrance a clear berth before returning to the wall by the south-western tower where Bill's heart leaped as he bumped into something soft which gave to his touch.

"Don't, ye flat-footed matelot — you're tickling," Jock giggled feebly.

Bill had forgotten Jock, waiting there by the gate!

Peter looked upward, and noticed the dim, yellow lights glowing dismally from the slits of windows in the south-western tower, although all the other towers were in darkness. Peter whispered to Jan:

"I reckon this is Harry's room."

"All right. Go ahead."

When they were boys, Peter and Harold Arkwright had often spent their holidays together. Harry's father would take them wild-fowling on the tidal mudflats off Bideford, and there they had learned the calls of such sea birds as the wigeon and redshank, the curlew and snipe. At home they learned to imitate the weird cry of the curlew, and they would whistle it across the mudflats to each other.

As Peter's cheeks retracted to whistle the plaintive note, Jan's fingers fumbled for his Luger pistol…

Tweeet — tweeet, tweee — tweee — tweee, twee — tweeee—

It was superbly done. Peter's head slowly turned from the gateway to seawards, as he threw the sad cry through the still night. In Morse code, the slow, plaintive note clearly spelled out the word 'morrow'.

Their hearts beating, they waited long moments for enemy reaction. There was none.

They watched the lights at the top of the tower, expectantly, hopefully. There was no sign. Still the dim lights shone. Looking at the luminous dial on his watch, which glowed in the darkness, Jan gave Peter another five minutes.

"Again," he whispered.

The curlew's weird cry floated plaintively again through the stillness.

"*Donner und blitzen!*" swore the thickset sentry under the gatehouse.

Peter and Jan half rolled over on their sides, as they reached for their pistols while Bill covered his head with his hands, one eye balefully open.

Peering carefully towards the gate, they heard the sentry still cursing. He stooped down and, still with the steaming soup bowl in his hand, hurled something in their direction. Peter and Jan ducked, and heard the stone land a few feet from them. The sentry's cursing grew louder as he wiped the slopped soup from his sleeve.

"Rotten shot!" grinned Jan. "He doesn't like birds!"

Suddenly Peter jabbed Jan with his elbow. He pointed above them. The dim light in the top aperture was slowly flicking on and off: 'dot, dash, dot' — it slowly blinked out its message — 'R!'.

"He's received it, Jan, he's received it!" whispered Peter excitedly as they smiled at each other.

Jan looked at his watch. One o'clock.

"Let's get out of here and wait on the beach. Come on!"

Creeping on their stomachs to pick up Jock, all four started loping back to the cliff edge.

Jan suddenly froze in his tracks, then flung himself down behind the nearest scrub, and frantically waved his arm at Peter, whilst the other two silently melted into the gloom beside Jan. Holding their breaths, they felt, rather than saw, a dark figure loom up in front of them. Whistling the 'Horst Wessel', the German lumbered straight at them. There was no avoiding the patrol now, for he blundered unconsciously onwards.

Jan reacted instinctively and as the German's heavy boots crunched around his head, he sprang upwards at the soldier's throat.

Peter heard the sharp intake of breath as the German, frightened out of his senses, gasped with fear and then crumpled as his steel helmet clattered to the ground. Shocked more by fright than anything else, the Hun lost consciousness.

"Curse it!" said Jan, as he crouched over him, Commando knife in hand, "I can't murder him in cold blood. Come on! Let's lug him back on board. He may be of use to us."

For a fraction of time they waited, but the sentry at the gate still gulped his soup.

"Come on!" Jan hissed again.

They heaved the limp body across Bill's huge shoulders. Peter took the German's rifle, while Jan went ahead with his revolver cocked, to search for Jarvis and the rope on the clifftop.

The slumped body jerked, the arms and hands swinging limply as Bill loped seawards. When they reached the cliff edge, Bill twisted his huge frame and the body slipped to the ground.

Jan was untying the rope when a fearful, nerve-racking squeal pierced the night. The jolt had shaken the Hun into consciousness, and the shock had reduced him to hysterical screaming.

Jan leaped through the air, landed astride the man's chest and drew his gun.

"Shut up!" he hissed as he jabbed the gun into the man's chest but the German was by now almost insane with fear and the sight of the gun only made him scream the more hysterically.

"Get on down, all of you!" ordered Jan. "I'll bring up the rear."

Peter swung off into space down the rope and Jock followed. As Peter's head disappeared below the clifftop, he glimpsed the beam of a large searchlight sweeping the approaches to the castle. Lights flashed on at the gatehouse from whence sharp, guttural shouts and the clatter of nailed boots disturbed the night. Peter slithered downwards until his feet dropped on to the rocks below and then Jock landed with a lurch alongside him.

"Get the boats ready," Peter hissed.

On the clifftop, Jan shoved his cupped hand across the German's mouth, but it only made him squeal and choke the more. In a moment of frantic exasperation, Jan pushed his left fist into the man's gullet but the German's teeth sank into Jan's hand, causing searing pain.

Jan grunted. With his right hand he groped for his revolver and slipped it from its holster. He grabbed it by the barrel and smacked the butt across the soldier's temple. The body jerked and Jan quickly withdrew his torn hand from the man's mouth, as the slack jaws relaxed. The Hun's eyes rolled upwards and glazed into unconsciousness again.

"Grab him, Hawkins. Get cracking!" snapped Jan urgently.

Bill disappeared over the edge holding the unconscious body over one enormous shoulder, while he shinned down the rope with amazing dexterity. As his head dipped below the clifftop, he could hear the enemy almost on top of them.

Jan jerked a grenade from his belt. While he fumbled for another, he pulled out the pin of the first grenade with his teeth, and, with an overhand lob, he hurled it far out into the sea. The noise of running soldiers was now behind him and almost over his shoulder as he heaved the second grenade into the sea below.

Tearing the pin out of the third grenade, he counted two, turned round with his back to the sea, and lobbed the hand grenade as far as he could at the lumbering enemy. Then, as he slipped the rope off the rock and started to slither over the edge, a brilliant orange flash seared the darkness and outlined the castle walls in sharp relief. The shouting stopped.

Jan dipped his head below the edge, as bullets whined into the darkness over him and green tracer criss-crossed the clifftop. When his bruised body slumped at the foot of the cliff, eager hands picked him up and dumped him into the waiting dory in which sat Bill with his unconscious prisoner. Wading up to their chests, Peter and Jock launched it out into the breakers, out and beyond the white line of surf with Graves paddling furiously.

Like two marathon swimmers, Peter and Jock returned to the beach and, half swimming, half running, forced the folboats like arrows into the sea. Then they straddled them and slipped inboard driving them with long, desperate strokes.

"Go on!" shouted Peter stupidly, his voice almost inaudible in the bedlam now loosed above his head. Jock surged ahead, overhauling the dory to lead the way back to the invisible submarine while the plopping of bullets hitting the water, ricocheting and whining into the night, spurred the little convoy to frantic efforts.

Peter turned his head over his shoulder. On the clifftop, now already beginning to fade, he saw lights blinking like puzzled glow-worms, twinkling in the confusion. Green tracer crisscrossed in large arcs, well out to the right and crawling across the sky. He slowly overtook the dory, and saw that Jan had added his own efforts to the flailing paddles. Peter drew ahead and shouted to Jock to follow as the exhausted little convoy disappeared out to sea.

Peter peered into the darkness until his eyes ached and then stopped paddling and drew the red glass from his pocket. He put it before his eyes and slowly searched the horizon. No sign, not a glimmer of a red flashing light.

He felt desperately lonely and a wave of panic swept over him. Had *Rugged* heard the two grenade explosions? Perhaps she was too far out and out of range? Why, in the name of goodness, couldn't they wake up, so snug and warm in their bunks? Already, twinkling lights were tumbling like a necklace down the cliff about half a mile to the northward. The enemy were close on their heels, their tracer sweeping and flying into the night in short bursts, kicking up the sea where it hit.

He found his hand shaking as he searched again through the red glass. Where was she? Was that smudge something, or merely imagination playing him false? No. Yes, oh yes! There she was! A dim red flash, then another and another. Very, very, close.

"There they are!" yelled Peter, a sob of relief catching his voice, while he stretched out his arm to port, to point the way. He grasped his paddle and gave a few quick strokes and almost collided into the gleaming sides of the submarine whose black conning tower loomed above them. A heaving line rattled across the bows of his canvas boat. He grabbed it and passed it across to Jock who had bumped into him. Half a minute later, the dory was alongside.

A blue pencil of light was sweeping the surface of the sea, half a mile to the northward of the submarine. Somehow, they never knew how, they were dragged inboard, sprawling helplessly over the fore-casing, completely exhausted. Willing hands picked them up and handed them swiftly over the conning tower and down to the warmth below. Lines were passed around and under the folboats, and they were yanked out of the water, slipped through the fore-hatch, and secured safely.

The searchlight slowly swung up to them, casting an oval circle of weird light as it went while the men on the bridge held their breath. It crept right up to within a hundred yards of their port side, stopped, and slowly swept back again. Then they dropped the limp body of the German down the fore-hatch, the boat being ready to dive immediately it was secured. Already the submarine was sliding away from the shore, stern first, the white line of foam licking along her sides.

The fore-hatch was shut. The klaxon roared and the upper lid clanged shut.

"First clip on! Sixty feet." Joe's familiar voice, so firm and confident, sounded like music in Peter's ears, as he picked himself up from the Control Room deck.

He laughed. Jan was in front and crawling on all fours into the Ward Room, his green Commando's overalls leaving a snail-like trail after him.

"You seem to be in a hurry!" Joe murmured.

CHAPTER 9

The Spider ...

Kapitan Ulrich von Kramer, Officer Commanding the S.S. garrison guarding the Castellare Poliano Prisoner of War Camp, had lunched well. He sat at the head of the rectangular polished table, his four junior officers on either side of him.

Although von Kramer was just six feet high, he did not give the impression of being tall and this was due perhaps to his bulk, for he had a massive barrel of a chest. Yet he was as hard as seasoned oak, with no spare flesh on his whipcord body. What little hair he had was flecking grey at the temples and short bristles of stubble jutted from his bullet-shaped head, which protruded pinkly, like an oblong egg, from the deep collar of his field-grey jacket.

It was difficult to describe the mobile face that had made him such a master of his profession for he was ranked by Himmler as being among one of the six foremost espionage agents in the German S.S.

A commonplace face was the first requirement of a spy, and von Kramer's appearance would have been very difficult to memorise. His features seemed to change with his environment, so that one could not identify anything definite. Just as the shadows of the clouds sweep across the valleys on blustery days, his face would melt and then fix in a completely different expression in as many seconds.

Apart from this natural ability, he also possessed the instinctive art of disguise and it was this quality that had gained him so many successes and triumphs for the Fatherland. He had been in England during 1941 and the repulse of the attack on Dieppe had been mainly because of von Kramer's information when, disguised as an innkeeper in one of the south coast resorts, his perfect command of the English language had stood him in good stead.

He was a dangerous and efficient man.

As Commandant of this new concentration camp, his post was temporary. Himmler had thought that von Kramer was showing signs of strain and needed three months' rest, so the new camp at Castellare Poliano seemed the right appointment for a man of Kramer's bullying nature. Himmler was not over-fussy about the survival of enemy submarine crews, and Kramer could not count squeamishness as one of his failings. As he had no nerves or scruples, he was, in fact, just the man for the job.

But last night's fiasco had touched his vanity. His brown eyes, close-set and sunk in their sockets, glinted dangerously. Bullying was his speciality and he now had ample opportunity to give full rein to his whim.

"*Gott und dämmerung!*" he roared, snatching the white napkin from his collar with one hand, while the other fist crashed on the table, setting the cutlery and glass a-jingling. Nervously the younger officers coughed and waited for the wrath to subside, but this seemed to be a storm above all storms, for the President of the Mess, their bullying Kapitan, had even forgotten to rise for the toast to "The Führer", whose photograph hung on the wall of their vault of a dining hall. For hours during the long forenoon, the officers had kept well clear of him on some pretext or other, but now they had to face the music.

"You lily-livered idiots. You should never have left your mothers' knees. Here we are, only a week in this accursed Italian island castle, and you let down the German S.S. like this!"

Von Kramer had resented his appointment to Castellare Poliano, feeling that he had been given a back-number of an appointment. Himmler was a fool! He did not recognise talent when he saw it, but he, von Kramer, would show these Sicilian ice-cream merchants which was the master race — he'd show them, yes, and that short-sighted Himmler, too, for all his big talk!

Slowly his wicked eyes glittered at the pale faces before him! What a lot! Even his officers were second-rate.

"Seidlitz!"

"*Jawohl, mein Kapitan?*"

"Why did you fail to call me when you heard the scream? You were on duty, weren't you?"

"*Ja, mein Herr, but I…*"

Von Kramer interrupted him ruthlessly. "Stop talking! You're too incompetent and soft for the S.S. I shall see that you are transferred to something more appropriate."

Seidlitz did not look up, but comforted himself with the thought that Kramer would not dare to report the inefficiency to headquarters. The incident reflected upon the Commanding Officer as much as anyone else, so Seidlitz kept silent, knowing that it was useless to offer any defence.

"But why am I wasting my time with imbeciles like you? I have a plan," von Kramer hissed between his teeth. "You will do me the honour of listening extremely carefully, and this time, for the Führer's sake, and for your own necks too, see that you don't bungle it. Fritz! Shut the door."

When the youngest officer had reseated himself, von Kramer warmed to his theme. His face started to glisten with tiny beads of perspiration, while his little eyes almost disappeared into the creases of his eye sockets.

His enormous fists hung by his sides, and it was the action of his long fingers that betrayed an identifiable peculiarity. The fists opened and shut, the short fingers crackling in their joints as they clenched and unclenched rhythmically. The knuckles showed white, and the snapping of the tendons sent shivers down the spines of his onlookers.

"I couldn't dispose of these English pig-dogs today. These inefficient spaghetti-mongers of Italians do not understand us Germans and were too tired to have the barracks at Taormina ready before Tuesday. We'll move all the prisoners the day after tomorrow, lock, stock and torpedo-tubes."

He burst into uncontrollable laughter at his own heavy joke, so that his shaking body set the glassware on the table jingling again while the officers' faces cracked into obsequious smiles of appreciation.

"Tonight these English swine may try another rescue attempt for their much-respected friend" — and he nodded his head towards the site of the south-western tower. "It would be a pity," he continued, "if we had to shoot him for attempted escape, wouldn't it?" he leered.

"But, Herr Kapitan, that would…"

The insolence of the interrupter was checked instantly.

"Silence, you infant! Listen to what I have to say," snapped von Kramer truculently, his anger abated, his hands motionless. Then he pushed his chair back from the table, so that it slid swaying for a moment before it clattered back upon the paved floor.

"Lieutenant Arkwright of the accursed Royal Navy is a large man. But not," he continued, coughing modestly, "quite so well built as I. But, nevertheless, the similarity is close enough."

The officers gave each other amused glances as Kramer continued. "Let him remain in his cell" — again the bullet head nodded upwards — "let him remain there, but let us allow him to watch the play enacted before his eyes. Let him witness with his own eyes the scene of his own friends crushed between my fingers."

He pressed his short, stubby fingers together, so that his knuckles crackled.

"Like beetles beneath my boots."

Again came a burst of maniacal laughter, which caused surreptitious glances among the officers.

"You see, gentlemen, I will take Arkwright's place. He shall be chained to the wall in the small annexe which leads from his cell. He will thereby have a first-class seat. He shall watch the flies crawling into my web," Kramer continued. "We shall welcome these English pigs, quietly and without any fuss but Arkwright will be unable to warn them. We'll see to that. We'll — er — liquidate him afterwards for attempted escape. His men will be told that he tried to bolt."

As the officers leaned forward to hear the final details of the parts they had to play, the sun had already passed over the southern tower, casting a longer shadow across the grim courtyard with its guarded huts. The faces of the prisoners could be seen pressing against the windowpanes as they craved for the warmth of the sun.

From the top of his western tower, Harry Arkwright slowly paced his damp cell. He heard faintly the triumphant laughter gusting across the courtyard from the Officers' Mess, and was very worried. What had gone wrong last night? Surely Peter wouldn't try again? How could they be warned, for he was sure that the Germans were going to use him for bait for some fiendish scheme? He felt like the morsel of cheese on the spikes of a rat-trap, the jaws sprung and ready to snap.

Slowly, inch by inch, the first rays of the afternoon sun crept through the slit that was his window, leaving a sliver of sunlight patterned on the slimy floor. He could not drag his eyes away.

"My ray of hope," he smiled ruefully to himself.

CHAPTER 10

... and the Fly

At long last their plans were ready. It was five o'clock. in the afternoon, and already the air in the little submarine was becoming stale.

Jan and Peter both nodded in silent assent, as the Captain closed the conference on a serious note.

"You must realise, of course, that, whatever happens to you, I cannot jeopardise my submarine and ship's company. Captain 'S' was insistent upon this condition, and I must abide by his decision. I know that you chaps will understand. If you don't show up by one thirty a.m., I will withdraw and rendezvous off the Spella rocks, five miles to the south-eastward. I will remain there until dawn, unless I am forced into the 'deep field'. I will be there again on the following night if possible. We seem to have stirred up a hornets' nest already!"

Thus were their final plans made. They would land in the same cove, for the Huns seemed to think they had landed farther to the northward.

Jan had struck the German too hard. The unfortunate prisoner had died, the corpse still lying stiff in the after-ends, a blanket over it. They would bury it at sea on surfacing.

Poor devil! thought Peter. *He never really knew what hit him.*

They were to take Very lights and pistols. One green star from the submarine would mean that *Rugged* would open fire with flashless cordite on a point inland, a mile to the northward to divert the Germans for a while. The Commando, Graves, was to lie up there in order to lend a hand by firing, with small arms, in all possible directions, and then dash back to the landing beach to prepare the boats for immediate launching.

One red Very light from the shore party would tell *Rugged* that the Commandos had failed and were making for the rendezvous. They would find some way of getting there — by swimming if need be — for the current was in the right direction. But, in their hearts, they all knew that the red light meant shooting against a wall, or, at the best, captivity for the duration of the war.

Jan, Jarvis and Jock, skilled men with their small arms, would assemble opposite the main gate. They would allow Peter and Bill Hawkins enough time to scout round to the north-westward, and to scale the north-west corner wall, where Harry was a prisoner, with a grappling iron. When they heard Peter give his cry of the curlew twice, they would open fire with everything they had to simulate a frontal attack upon the main gate.

This would give Peter and Harry Arkwright time to retreat back along the walls to the grapnel which Bill would be guarding and by which Peter had entered the castle. While Jan and his party attracted the Germans to the area which *Rugged* was bombarding to the north-westward, Peter, Bill and Harry would work round the exterior of the eastern and southern walls, and back to the cliffs. They would then turn east until they found the fissure in the cliff, and paddle off in the first folboat.

When Jan had given them enough time, and with *Rugged* still bombarding, Jan's party would break off the action and cut back to the cliff, where they would bring up the rear in the two remaining boats which had already been prepared and launched by Graves.

Bold and simple, thought Peter as he checked his Very pistol and lights. *Bold and simple, but it all depends upon perfect timing and a great measure of good luck.*

Dusk had started to fall like a mantle on the azure Mediterranean, as the Captain peered through the for'd periscope.

"Another perfect, flat, calm night. Overcast and, God willing, too much cloud for the moon at three-thirty," he said to Jan.

"We'd better synchronise our watches," Jan replied tersely.

Peter could see that Jan's nerves were strung taut, and that he was itching to get into action. The shore party stood in a quiet group, Bill with the grapnel coiled round him. They were all dressed in the sombre green of the British Commandos as they did not relish being shot as spies if they all failed.

Half an hour later, *Rugged* surfaced and the previous night's routine was repeated. Trimmed right down, she crept slowly in on her main motors.

Peter, now numbed by excitement, manned his folboat and paddled a few yards clear, Bill in the bows, and waited until all the others were bobbing around them. Then he waved his hand and started paddling, his eyes straining straight before him. *Rugged* slid silently astern, slowly merging into the horizon. They were alone.

Ahead, the familiar cliffs and beaches looked menacingly close. An ominous silence brooded as Peter shivered, goose pimples prickling his battledress. The shadow of the black cliffs reached out as if to smother them and once again the surge of the heavy seas licked round the base of the snarling rocks.

Suddenly there was a bump, followed by a harsh grating along the keel, and as Bill jumped out Peter was already ashore.

The others followed as soon as his tiny blue light flickered, 'O-K'.

Graves immediately started to hide the boats. No one spoke. This was no time for heroics. Up the cliff scrambled Jan. They reached the top, hearts thumping hard, and expecting a short volley to end the attempt.

But there was nothing, absolutely nothing. Peter pinched himself. Yes, he was still in this world. He saw the mark on the boulder which had held the rope on the previous night. They had been right, then: the Hun thought that they had landed farther up the coast.

Agile as a cat, Jan slipped into the scrub, Peter and Bill following close on his heels. When they had gone two hundred yards, Jan stopped in his tracks. He gripped Peter's hand.

"God bless," he whispered.

"Thank you, Jan. Come on, Bill!"

Peter and Bill broke off and slipped away to the left, some three hundred yards from the castle walls. Peter looked back. It was entirely up to him now — like the moment he was alone when he made his first trial escape from the diving tank at the submarine school. He braced himself and took a deep breath.

Cautiously and silently they crept from bush to bush, and soon reached the north corner. There was the massive tower, rising hugely before them. Up in the western tower, a hundred yards to their right, the dull light glowed in the top slit of the window.

Peter crept forward to the last patch of scrub, some twenty feet from the wall, and lay still for a few moments to recover his breath. Bill was close behind him. Peter looked at his watch. Just right. Another three minutes and *Rugged* would be opening fire on the beach farther up the coast. That would be his moment. No going back now. He was committed. Success or failure — which would it be? Peter pushed the thought far from his mind and concentrated on the task which lay before him.

His blood chilled as an owl flapped overhead, its doleful hooting disturbing the silent night. No other sound. Only a treacherous silence. What were the Huns scheming?

He stiffened. A bright flash was followed by a dull boom from seawards. *Rugged* had opened the first round. Half rising on one shoulder, he saw the last of the burst. Then another and another. They were doing well, clouds of black dust flying about on the cliff-edge, well to the northward of their cove. The orange glow lit up the black line of the clifftop, throwing the area into pale relief against the horizon of the sea.

Gruff shouts and a pounding of feet sounded from inside the castle. Lights went on in the lower cells at the southern end.

"Now!" Peter whispered to Bill.

Crouching low, they sprang for the foot of the wall, and then lay prone against the damp stone, not daring to breathe. Still nothing, except the confused shouting of disturbed men.

Then, a hundred yards to the right, a squad of figures doubled out from the gates and went crashing through the undergrowth. Flattening themselves in the shadows, Peter and Bill lay still and waited for the Germans to pass. The stumbling grew fainter as the enemy disappeared towards the cliffs. Bill uncoiled the rope from his shoulders, quickly and surely making it into a coil in his left hand.

He took the heavy, four-pronged grapnel, set his feet firmly astride, and hove upwards and over. Whistling and snaking upwards, it whirled in a neat parabola over the top of the castellated wall. He allowed the rope to remain slack and threw himself into the deeper shadows. As the iron clattered on the stonework, the noise seemed deafening, but fortunately it was drowned by one of *Rugged*'s salvoes.

Gingerly Peter pulled at the rope, but it came away slowly in his hand.

"Must we do it again?" he whispered to himself.

And then the rope no longer came home. He pulled evenly. It held, it was fast. He gave a strong tug. Still no movement.

"Here goes, Bill!" He heaved himself up the rope, hand over hand in the shadows.

Just like the gym at school! flashed through his mind. His fingers clasped the top, masonry crumbling under his palms. He took a firm hold, hauled himself over the ledge and dropped on to a parapet. He found himself on a platform about eight feet wide and matted with lichen. Mercifully it was dark and gloomy at this end of the castle so he crept cautiously to the edge of the parapet, and gently raised his head until his eyes took in the scene.

Below him, four corrugated iron huts, surrounded by a barbed-wire fence, some ten yards clear, formed a rectangle in the centre of the castle courtyard. Through the small windows of the huts he could see the excited faces of British sailors evidently hugely enjoying the discomfiture of the enemy, who had a dozen guards nervously fingering their guns surrounding the huts. They faced inwards and held their submachine guns at the ready, resting on their right hips. The strains of 'Rule, Britannia!' which roared out from the huts added to the general confusion.

But already the hubbub was dying down and there was no movement or sound from Jan, lying hidden in the scrub. Time was slipping away fast and Peter would have to move quickly, for all too soon the party of Germans would be returning from the clifftop. He crawled to the top of the wall and as he looked down a shadow slid to the rope.

"O.K.," Peter hissed, and in a few seconds, Bill stood beside him.

"Stay here and cover me, Bill — I'm going in!"

"Good luck, sir," Bill whispered, drawing his revolver.

Blessing the sailors in the huts, who were so successfully distracting the guards, Peter wriggled for fifteen yards on his stomach, until he reached some steep steps. These led down to the balcony which ran outside the door of the top room in the western tower.

This balcony was edged by a six-foot parapet which formed a safety wall from the drop to the courtyard below. The steps curled to the left at a sharp angle, flanking the round tower. Peter estimated that the door to Harry's cell must be at the bottom of these steps, and was probably guarded by a sentry. Where the steps curved, a small slit, about nine inches wide and two feet high, served as an inner window to the cell in the tower. He could see the dull glow from the internal lighting.

He quickly withdrew his head as the back view of a bulky, steel-helmeted sentry loomed into view from behind the curvature of the stone wall. The sentry was replacing his submachine gun and slinging it across the back of his broad shoulders. He seemed fidgety, but kept his eyes on the hut below and on the bustle at the main gate. He moved slowly forward and leaned over the inner parapet, his chest resting on the coping, with his back to the tower.

Already the clamour in the castle was subsiding. Peter had to act quickly if he was to act at all, for already the scouting parties must surely be returning. It was tantalising not to be able to see through Harry's inner window because of the sentry who guarded the door. Peter made up his mind that he must first dispose of the sentry.

Swiftly he crawled back into the gloom at the end of the north-western parapet. In the deep shadow made by the northern tower, he stood upright, his head just reaching over the outside wall. He took a deep breath, and then the weird and plaintive call of the curlew floated twice through the disturbed night.

Jan, Jarvis and Jock, Tommy-guns in front of them, lay flat on their stomachs, concealed by the dense scrub at the main gate. They could not see each other, as they were some twenty yards apart, but ahead of them they could make out the glow of the lights by the castle entrance. Already the commotion of the excited German patrols was dying away.

Jan peered at his watch. Another four minutes to go. What had happened to Peter? What on earth were the Huns playing at? They must have been ready for something, but their reaction was so un-Germanic. Had Peter walked right into a trap, and was he now lying stiff with a bullet between his temples?

The strange and plaintive cry of a curlew floated weirdly through the night, followed quickly by another.

"Thank Heaven," grinned Jan. "Action at last!"

He picked up his gun and fired a prolonged burst at the gate. To his left, Jarvis took up his cue and blazed away, pumping tracer low into the entrance. Soon they were all three emptying their magazines erratically and yelling at the tops of their voices while spraying the general direction of the gateway with short bursts of fire, and so giving a realistic appearance of a determined frontal attack.

Between bursts, Jan could just hear the blowing of whistles as the remaining guards were called out from their quarters and it was not long before the rattle of rifles and machine-gun fire sputtered from the parapet on each side of the gateway, firing at the elusive Englishmen hidden in the scrub.

Suddenly, a blue-white shaft of light pierced the night from the top of the gatehouse and swept the foreground in front of the castle. Jan felt almost naked as the beam of the searchlight swung over his head, stopped and focused on a clump of bushes near Jarvis. Taking deliberate aim, he put the Bren to his shoulder. His left eye closed as he squinted along the sights, the luminous foresight standing neatly between the 'V' of the backsight. He squeezed and held on to the trigger. A long burst of tracer spouted in from the darkness, a high squeal rent the night, and the light plunged into nothingness as the mirror shivered into a thousand fragments.

The battle was joined.

As fast as he was able, Peter regained his position above the stairs, some ten feet from the burly, great-coated sentry, who, by now, was thoroughly alarmed. The German fingered the trigger of his submachine gun and, after ducking his head from each burst of fire, peered dimly over the parapet, fascinated by the scene at the gate. Peter glanced at his watch, hardly believing that twenty-eight minutes had elapsed since he had entered the fortress. Lying in the shadow, he drew his Commando knife from its sheath; then he pulled out his revolver, cocked it and laid it carefully on the flagstones.

Just in case I miss! he thought.

A clatter of musketry roused him to action and he drew the tip of his tongue across his dry lips as he carefully brought himself to his full height by the shadow in the wall. His soft-soled boots made no sound as he balanced with his feet astride, his weight on his right foot and his left arm outstretched towards the broad back which formed his target. Holding the point of the shining blade in his right hand, he slowly bent his arm back behind his right ear. Then, unconsciously shutting his left eye, with all his might he concentrated on a point between the massive shoulder blades which were hunched over the parapet. With all his strength, quicker than his eye could follow, he hurled the flashing blade at the unsuspecting sentry.

There was no need for Peter to drop flat, as he slowly and deliberately picked up his cocked .45 Colt. Covering the massive bulk with his revolver, and sickened by his action, Peter watched his victim slide gurgling to the ground. As it fell, the body half turned, the surprised eyes glaring towards him, mouth opening as if in protest, one hand sliding from the parapet while the other tightened on the submachine gun.

A wave of nausea swept over Peter, who had never killed a man in cold blood before. He slipped silently down the steps, two at a time, until he was on the level of the slit window. Spread-eagled against the clammy wall, he strained his ears. Silence from inside. Only the pale yellow light glimmered. If he peered through the window, a bullet might blow out his brains, but how was he to see whether Harry was guarded? Then he realised his luck. As the cell was lighted inside, the inmates would not be able to see any onlookers peering through the window because the view from inside, looking towards the northern walls of the castle, would be a rectangle of blackness.

Slowly Peter turned his head and raised himself so that his eye was above the level of the sill. A huge figure had its back to him. It peered out of the opposite window and was watching developments on the clifftop. Large, massive arms were grasping for support on the windowsill. Harry! Oh, Harry! How good it was to see him.

Even muffled as he was in that huge, enveloping cloak, his back was unmistakable!

Peter cupped his hands and whispered in a sibilant hiss.

"Boat ahoy, Harry? Boat ahoy?"

To this traditional naval challenge, Harry, being Captain of a ship, should perforce reply with the name of his ship — *Restless*. No other reply would suffice.

The huge figure slowly stiffened. In the gloom, Peter recognised Harry's immense frame, but it was odd of him not to reply instinctively with the correct response.

"Strange… I wonder…?"

Some primeval instinct pierced Peter with fear. He quickly jerked his head away from the slit as a shattering report split his ears and a bullet thudded and spattered against the stones. Peter dropped flat.

So it wasn't Harry! Some fat Prussian was playing possum to lure him into a deadly trap. Peter's blood was up and he saw red.

"Thank Heaven!" he whispered, groping for a grenade at his belt. In a flash, he pulled out the pin, counted three, and, without exposing his head above the sill, he lobbed the grenade through the window-slit.

He jumped for the door on the parapet in a flying leap as a muffled explosion came from inside the cell. Acrid smoke blew back from under the door.

Fifty yards away, the guards had their backs to him, and were firing over the walls and into the night. Careless as to concealment now, Peter thrust the barrel of his Colt into the lock of the door and fired, shattering the lock. He put his shoulder to the massive timbers and heaved with all his might.

The door moved slowly at first, then gave suddenly with clouds of dense smoke belching outwards. As Peter plunged into the darkness, the bitter taste of the fumes tore at his throat and choked him. The huddled body, which had prevented the door from opening, tripped him and sent him flying headlong on to his face. It was as well that he did so, for the floundering figure of a steel-helmeted guard loomed across him, firing at the doorway. Rolling on to his side, Peter emptied his revolver into the Hun, who slumped to the floor.

Peter crawled across to the far wall, feeling for his torch and at last his fumbling hands found the light. Holding it in his left hand, he reloaded the pistol and then, holding the torch well away from him, he saw the little beam light the way to an alcove which led off from the main cell.

Peter remained on his knees and held the light above him. Another murderous guard might be lurking! But no sound came, save an odd, muffled groan from within the alcove. Swiftly Peter crawled inside. The blue beam slid over the blank wall opposite. Slowly it explored the alcove and stopped by a small buttress, inside which a large figure loomed, writhing and kicking its legs. The beam fastened on the face, which was gagged.

"Harry!" Peter shouted, leaping to his side.

He tore at the bandages and stripped them from Harry's face.

"Bless you, Peter!" Harry gasped, his face cracking into a smile. "My hands — chained," he went on, as he shook his manacled wrists. Two shots reverberated through the cell, and the shattered chains fell to the ground.

"Follow me! Crawl!" Peter commanded.

Feeling their way over the bodies, they floundered to the doorway and Peter was feeling for the latch, when a guttural voice drawled in perfect English from the darkness.

"Not so fast, my friend! Drop your gun and stay where you are."

Peter spun round, the beam of his torch falling upon a dark figure that knelt in the far corner, and then his revolver clattered to the ground by the doorway.

Kapitan von Kramer, crouched on one knee, covered them with a weaving Luger. He had been knocked unconscious by the grenade and was lucky to be alive, but blood oozed from a scratch on his cheek.

"Against the wall!" Kramer snapped, his finger tightening on the trigger.

Peter considered rushing him, but, with Harry in poor shape, there would be no chance so they both backed to the wall. Kramer drew himself to his feet and sidled to the door.

"Come on, round to the other wall so I can see you."

Kramer's gun emphasised the order. Peter and Harry moved quickly, so that they were now facing the door which Kramer kicked open with his boot. The door creaked on its hinges and the bright glow from outside lit the cell. Kramer stood in the doorway with his back to the courtyard, his eyes blazing with hatred.

"Now, you English swine!" he blurted, "I am going to liquidate you. People don't trifle with Kapitan Ulrich von Kramer!"

Peter's heart jumped into his mouth. So this was to be the end, was it? Death in a squalid prison, with no one the wiser. His eyes watched Kramer, fascinated by the man's working face. The German was livid with rage.

"But before I do," he hissed softly, "let me just get one or two things straight. Firstly, you English haven't got a chance — not a chance."

He had worked himself into a frenzy, and his left hand hung by his side, flexing spasmodically so that the tendons crackled. It was a hideous sound and Peter shivered.

"That's what you think, mate!"

A glorious cockney voice rang through the cell. There was a flash and a loud report. Kramer held his wrist as the Luger clattered to the ground on to the battlement outside.

He turned round to meet the gaze of a blue-eyed Commando, wearing a sailor's cap. Kramer's eyes dropped to the blue barrel of a revolver from whose spout wisps of smoke still spiralled. The barrel jumped.

"Come on, cock, get weaving! Over against the wall, there. Move!" Bill's voice snapped.

Kramer jumped.

"Tie him up in Harry's chains," cried Peter.

While Bill guarded the door, Peter and Harry shoved Kramer into the annexe and bound and then gagged him with a ripped jacket. Bill's voice cut in from the doorway.

"Come on, sir, there's a party of Huns coming down the parapet. Let's get out of here!"

He was already loosening a grenade in his belt, as Peter and Harry cleared the doorway. Over their shoulders they saw a group of Germans, charging down upon them, rifles at the ready.

Whilst Peter and Harry rushed for the grapnel, Bill tore the pin out of a grenade and hurled it at the rushing Germans. Then he hurtled after Peter and Harry who were already scrambling over the parapet.

Behind him there was a vivid, orange flash.

While the dust and smoke cleared away to reveal the slaughter on the parapet, Bill nipped over the battlements and shinned down the rope. He let himself slide down the fifteen feet, burning his hands into raw weals and then collapsed on top of Harry.

"Beg pardon, sir!"

They picked themselves up and rushed for the scrub. Peter looked over his shoulder as bobbing heads appeared on the parapet and shots whined after them, ricocheting into the night.

"Come on!" Peter shouted, half dragging Arkwright who was still dazed from the explosion and the rapid turn of events. Head down, Peter streaked across the twenty feet of open ground and hurled himself rolling and twisting into the merciful blackness of the night.

"Harry?" said Peter.

"Coming!" a voice shouted nearby.

Harry crawled close to him. There was another crash!

"It's me, sir," Bill panted hoarsely.

"Follow me round to the other side. We'll work across and round to the gate. Come on, for all you're worth."

Now disregarding concealment, Peter stood up and raced through the scrub, stumbling and staggering as he went. He could hear Harry and Bill panting and gasping behind him but he kept on, on — ever onwards, opening the distance between themselves and the dreaded castle walls, streaking for safety and freedom, so near — and yet so very far away.

The southern tower was now abreast of them. Peter reduced his pace to allow the others to catch up. To his right, the twin towers of the gatehouse stood gauntly, still bathed in floodlights.

They dropped flat and, pausing not for breath or rest, crawled as best they could across the open space in front of the gatehouse, until they could see directly inside the courtyard. For an instant, Peter paused, for, from his vantage point, he could see the shattered masonry alongside the western tower which had been damaged by grenades. From here, Jan must have seen Peter's retreat along the parapet and even now would be drawing the Germans after him and retreating northwards along the clifftop towards the bombardment point, in order to give Peter and Harry time and room in which to reach the boats.

The three fugitives were past the gate now. They rushed for the cliff which was only three hundred yards away, but the desultory firing had grown into a swiftly moving battle. *Rugged* had stopped bombarding, but now the short stabs of Jan's fire were only intermittent. His bursts seemed but a few hundred yards away, for Jan was hard pressed by an encircling fire, some of which seemed horribly close to the descent on the clifftop.

Then Peter saw two figures striding backwards, Brens spitting from their hips in wide arcs of fire, and realized that the Commandos had reached the fissure two hundred yards ahead of them.

Peter, Harry and Bill hurled themselves down again, as a crashing in the scrub only a few yards distant bore down upon them. Peter could have reached out and tackled the nearest figure in the group which was advancing in short rushes towards Jan, who had now disappeared over the cliff edge. Peter's last glimpse of this magnificent Commando was of a shadowy figure hurling grenades towards the pursuing Germans, who advanced only cautiously now, none of them relishing suicide.

Peter groaned, "Too late, Harry, we're cut off. Come on! Let's try the beach farther down, and try to catch up with them."

As they doubled back on their tracks before bearing right to the cliff edge, each knew in his heart that their efforts would be in vain. Already the folboats would be well out to sea.

Panting and gasping, they hurled themselves despairingly upon the soft turf at the edge of the cliff while the wind rustled gently through Peter's hair as he peered towards the little cove. Following the lines of tracer which wandered slowly eastwards, he thought he could just see the faint phosphorescence of thrashing paddles as Jan and his party drove their exhausted way out to sea. Then, still sobbing for breath, Peter and Harry discussed the hopeless situation.

"If I fire one Very light to tell Joe to pick us up tomorrow at the rendezvous, it will give away our position," Peter said.

"We daren't do that," Harry replied. "Can't we signal them?"

"Of course we can!" Peter answered. "At least we can try. Come on, let's get out of sight below the clifftop just here, and have a shot!"

From below an overhanging cluster of rocks, fifteen feet below the clifftop, three lonely Britons in a very hostile world watched their chances, so nearly successful, fade into dismal failure. The blue beam of the torch flickered out its pathetic message hopelessly in the general direction of the waiting submarine. If Peter had removed the blue shade, he would have given away their hiding place. For some minutes, his trembling hand, now shaking with a long overdue reaction of nervous strain, flicked out the message, 'R V — R V — R V…'

With moist eyes, unseen by Harry and Bill in the darkness, Peter replaced the torch in his pocket. Never in his life had he known so deeply the meaning of despair.

"Look, sir!" Bill whispered, pointing with outstretched arm to seaward, and shaking Peter excitedly.

Peter flung round. Well out to sea, he glimpsed a trailing arc of curving white sparks. As they reached their zenith, a small red star exploded unheard, to fall like thistledown, gently, slowly, falling … falling … and was gone.

Rugged had received their message. She would keep her appointment at the rendezvous.

CHAPTER 11

On the Scent

"I don't like this, Number One," the Captain grunted to his First Lieutenant who was standing by him in the darkness on the bridge.

"No, sir, nor do I," replied Number One, sweeping the horizon through his binoculars as another round from the guns sent them reeling.

Sub-Lieutenant Benson, Sinclair's temporary relief, was down at the gun directing the fire and they had been firing now for over half an hour. Half an hour too long, in the Captain's opinion. Everything was ominously quiet to seaward, particularly as Trapani, the home base of the destroyer First Eleven, was less than ten miles distant.

The Captain could not prevent himself from continually looking over his shoulder, expecting to see the white gleam of attacking bow waves. There is nothing a submariner dislikes more than advertising his position, for his whole life is spent in concealment.

"No, I don't like it; I don't like it at all," Joe repeated to himself.

Ashore, the chatter and fireworks of the gun battle suddenly intensified. Slowly the centre of the commotion was moving to the right along the cliff. Faster, faster, the green tracer from Jan's men moved nearer to the landing place, then, as suddenly, was followed by the crack of exploding grenades drifting across the water.

"Cease firing. Check, check, check! Secure the gun. Stand by to recover landing parties!" shouted the Captain. "Don't worry about the fore-hatch, Number One. Keep it shut. I'll leave the folboats. As soon as we've fished the landing party out of the water, I'm getting out of here. I smell a rat!"

"Aye, aye, sir. Shall I go below, sir?" asked Number One, reading his Captain's thoughts.

The Captain nodded. To him, the strain of waiting was the worst part of it all and already the tracer was following the invisible boats out to sea, and drawing the fire nearer and nearer to the submarine.

The slow swish of the swell hissed along the pressure hull, silkily caressing the low casing and another distant chatter of gunfire barely broke in upon the silence of Joe's thoughts. His knuckles showed white in the darkness, as he gripped the bridge-rail. At any moment, he expected E-boats or destroyers to pounce down upon them, or heavy artillery to start pinpointing the vulnerable submarine.

"Keep your eyes skinned for the folboats," he said to the men who, waiting on the casing with heaving lines coiled in their hands and arms hanging by their sides, peered into the night until their eyes ached.

Joe saw them first. Two hundred yards on the port beam, paddling like fury out to sea. "Full ahead starboard, hard-a-port."

Two minutes later, heaving lines hissed through the air to rattle down upon the canvas of the dory and only one folboat.

As Jan's folboat wallowed and slithered in the swell, his choking voice hoarsely gasped from the darkness.

"This is the lot — lost Peter, Arkwright and Bill."

The exhausted men wallowed in the sea, too far gone to drag themselves up the slippery pressure hull.

"Secure these lines round you, we'll heave you up."

Desperately slowly they were hauled on to the casing, where they lay floundering like beached trout, gasping for air. Jan was the first on the bridge, his face an agony of reproach.

"If only I could have held on another few minutes. I'm sure they weren't far away."

"Stay here, Jan," answered the Captain kindly. "I must get the others below. Clear the casing!" his sharp voice crackled over the bridge-rail.

Already the wavelets were playing over the casing, as the submarine swiftly gathered way and turned her stern to the land and three soldiers, dripping and exhausted, were firmly and gently hauled over the bridge by kindly hands and taken through the conning tower hatch to the warmth below.

"I'm sure they're there, sir," Jan said when he had recovered his breath, pointing over the stern. "I saw Peter and Arkwright clearing out of the castle."

"Signalman!" shouted the Captain to the after-end of the bridge.

"Sir?"

"Keep a good lookout along the cliff edge."

"Aye, aye, sir."

Already the menacing cliffs were merging into an unbroken line of blackness as Goddard, the signalman, carefully searched them through his binoculars, sweeping from side to side.

"We so darned nearly pulled it off," Jan said bitterly, coming to a choking halt. Exhaustion was now overcoming him and emotion welled to the surface.

"Dim flashing blue light, sir!" interrupted Goddard, shouting from the after-end of the bridge, his glasses fixed on a distant point farther down the coast. Slowly he spelled out the message, "R V — R V — R V, sir,… RV confirmed, sir."

For a moment the Captain hesitated, his face creased into an odd smile.

"Fire the red Very light, Signalman."

"Aye, aye, sir. One red Very light, sir," Goddard answered triumphantly.

He dashed to the side of the bridge, pulled out the bell-mouthed pistol and looked at the cartridge, feeling its serrated edge. He inserted the cartridge in the barrel, which shut with a click. He stretched out his arm, turned his face away and pulled the trigger. The trail of sparks showered the bridge and, looking upwards, Joe saw the red star plop out from the shower of sparklets. Slowly it floated down, gradually falling astern of them.

"Starboard twenty, steer three-five-oh," Joe spoke down the voicepipe.

The submarine quickly swung to starboard.

"I'm going to put the Hun off the scent, Jan. Do you agree to opening up with another barrage a few miles farther north? That should draw them away from Peter and give him a chance of reaching the rendezvous."

"Yes. Anything we can do — just anything," mumbled Jan hopelessly.

They remained on main motors and, ten minutes later, the submarine again opened fire on the distant headland.

Once more the screaming shells burst upon the cliffs, three miles north of the previous position.

"And now let's get out of it. Cease firing, check, check, check! Secure the gun. Clear the casing!"

The submarine turned hard-a-port and disappeared into the night to charge her batteries which were now dangerously low.

Two hours later she dived at dawn and the Captain, alone on the bridge as the water swirled around the conning tower, peered through his glasses for the last time that night.

"Confound it! Just as I feared," he muttered, jumping through the hatch. Etched into his mind was the image of three sleek shapes, still mere blurs on the lightening horizon but, unmistakably, the familiar silhouettes of hunting destroyers.

"The First Eleven," he whispered to himself, as he snapped on the first clip of the upper conning tower hatch.

CHAPTER 12

Flotsam

If the three fugitives, Peter, Harry and Bill, had expected a few hours' rest, they would have been greatly mistaken. Crouched under the overhanging ledge of rock, they watched the wild firing from the clifftop gradually fade away to sporadic bursts, and then, as suddenly, cease. Distant whistles blew. On the light breeze, which had sprung up with the first light of dawn and which chilled their very marrows now that they were motionless, the guttural orders of the returning patrols floated downwind to them.

"What's our next move?" Peter asked Harold Arkwright.

Gone were the official references peculiar to Service rank and etiquette. Instead, the years had rolled away and they might have been two boys again, stalking on their native moor. But this time the stakes were higher — imprisonment, or death by shooting against a wall.

"We ought to lie up by day, and sneak down at sunset to the rendezvous off the Spella rocks," replied Harold, "but that is exactly what the Hun would expect us to do, isn't it?"

Once more, Harold Arkwright was a submariner, moving stealthily, step by step, and always trying to be one jump ahead of the enemy — by bluff and double-bluff.

"Yes," Peter answered, "only he doesn't know whether the rendezvous, if there is one, would be north or south of our landing place."

"Couldn't very well be north, because of the islands and the proximity of Trapani," argued Harold.

"Yes, you're right, there. So they must assume that, if we are still alive, it must be down this way — right?"

"Right! They must also guess that another attempt will be made to take us off by sea, and that the attempt will be made by the same submarine, as soon as possible," continued Harold.

Bill listened to the discussion and scratched his head.

"Surely the destroyers of the Trapani First Eleven will be out today, looking for *Rugged*?" Peter went on.

"You may bet your shirt on that," Harry said, and continued, "The First Eleven will probably make it so hot for Joe that he will be unable to keep the rendezvous. The enemy are sure to have their offshore patrols looking for Joe and us tonight."

Round and round went their thoughts as the net seemed to be drawing closer about them. As they discarded plan after plan, talking in low voices, Bill suddenly stiffened.

"What's that, sir?" he asked.

A distant baying of hounds drifted down on the wind and was gone.

"Bloodhounds!" Peter gasped. "I never knew that they kept them in Italy."

"Well, you've learned something then — probably trained police dogs: Alsatians or German dogs of some sort," snapped Harold. "Let's get cracking!"

"Wait!" said Peter. "If we run, they'll follow our scent and they're bound to trail us. Remember Dartmoor?"

"Yes, I do," Harold replied.

"Remember the day we were out fishing in the mist and were mistaken for escaped convicts from Princetown?"

"Water! The only thing to beat them is water," said Peter. "There's plenty of that around here!" — and he swept his arm to seawards.

They all looked at each other.

"I'm game," Harry said. "How about you two?"

"It's our only chance. Come on, Harry!"

Bill nodded, "Proper skylark, sir!"

They all laughed. After they had stretched their aching joints, they cautiously clambered up the edge of the cliffs. Once clear of their hiding place, there was no mistaking the baying of hounds which seemed much nearer — less than half a mile away.

Anxiously searching for a break in the sheer cliffs, Peter spied a possible descent, little more than a hundred yards away.

"Come on! It's now or never!" he whispered.

He hauled himself over the top, and, bent double, ran desperately for the gap, Harry and Bill following close on his heels. Already the eastern horizon was flaking into the cold strips of the first light of dawn.

Peter held his breath as he dropped over the edge of the cliff. If the descent was impassable, they were done! But, slithering and falling with their backs to the rough volcanic rock, they tumbled down the fifty-foot cliff, digging their heels into the rough surface to check their descent.

With a jolt that knocked the breath from their bodies, they fell, half stunned, on to the pebbles on the beach below. Peter swayed as he stood up, not knowing where he was. A dark figure loomed up against him.

"Are you all right?" asked Harold anxiously, dragging Peter's numbed mind back to consciousness. "For Heaven's sake, Peter! Peter! Peter, snap out of it and come on!"

It was Bill's turn to lead the way while Harold pulled Peter's stumbling frame after him. Years of training and severe discipline once again forced Peter's protesting body to obey.

He shook his head like a befuddled spaniel and, reeling and staggering, quickly recovered his senses.

Doubling back along the beach, in ten minutes they were within two hundred yards of the little cove on which they had landed — so long ago, it seemed. The familiar shapes of the black rocks jutting out to sea jerked sense into Peter's mind; while behind them, the cries of the remorseless hounds filled their ears with most horrible sound. Already the brutes were baying with triumphant yelps, as they snuffled round their recent hiding place below the clifftop.

"That's the cove where we landed, Harry! Be careful — they may have posted sentries."

"We'll have to risk it! Come on!"

Peter was now in full control of himself and they followed Bill swiftly and silently to the foot of the cliff, and peered round it.

"No one 'ere, sir! Come on!" Bill whispered.

"Look, Harry, look!"

On its side lay a large baulk of timber, a piece of flotsam washed up by the tide and which doubtless was from a ship torpedoed by one of The Fighting Tenth; they hauled it to the water's edge and turned it end-on to the waves.

"Take off your jacket and leave everything except your forty-five and ammunition," ordered Arkwright, who was already tearing off his jacket and kicking it to the water's edge. While the others followed his example, the sound of their relentless pursuers grew no louder, for they must have been checked by the steep cliff descent.

"They don't like our way down," grinned Harold, a smile appearing on his face for the first time that day. "Here goes!"

Grasping the front end of the baulk of timber, he waded into the water while Peter and Bill steadied the other end. They pushed their way out to sea, until they no longer felt the bottom beneath them. The dawn had brought its morning breeze, and little wavelets now flustered the sea.

Kicking with their legs, they drove the timber out before them. Surely, steadily, the cliffs receded until they were now some three hundred yards from them. Peter glanced back over his shoulder. Above the sobs of his lungs clamouring for air, he heard the snarling and baying of their pursuers on the beach, incited by hoarse shouts of encouragement from the German guards who were stumbling along the pebbled shore.

Out, out, and still farther out, keeping the end of the timber pointing directly seawards, they pushed and kicked, paddling with their free arms. Five hundred yards now — over a quarter of a mile!

Peter could continue no longer. "Stop, Harold, please stop!"

Harold held up his hand and, turning round to look at Peter and Bill he whispered, "They may not spot us, but if they do, I'll turn the log beam-on to the beach. Get on the far side and it will protect us."

The sinister baying of the hounds in the cove followed by the mumble of German curses which came to them across the water suggested that their sodden clothes had been discovered.

The grey dawn had now drifted into another day. A small black object, some six hundred yards distant from the shore, jutted up and was gone again. The German patrol leader blinked, peered seawards and then rubbed his eyes. There it was again, rising and falling in the slight sea that was now running.

"*Achtung!*" he expostulated, pointing out to sea.

"*Nein, Herr Leutnant!*" a shaggy-haired sergeant replied, wagging his head, and then raised voices denoted that a heated argument was in progress, but the Leutnant was not satisfied.

"Make sure, Karl — it won't be wasting ammunition. Open fire, just in case," ordered the young officer.

Harold heard the snapping of bolts as the rifles were loaded, so the three hunted men slowly paddled the log round until it was floating parallel to the beach.

"Look out, men!" Harold hissed.

Crack! Wheee-ee!

The bullet whined when it passed overhead, kicking up a spurt of spray as it hit the water twenty feet beyond them. Bill's head slowly subsided beneath the surface, and Peter filled his lungs, keeping himself under by pushing against the underside of the timber.

As he was doing so, a loud crack split the water above him. Then another, and another. Peter's ears sang with a sharp pain. His hand felt the jarring as bullet after bullet thudded into the baulk of wood. His lungs were bursting. He would have to come up for air soon. He couldn't hold on any longer — thud! thud! … thud! Slowly he exhaled, letting the air globules slowly bubble from his open mouth. Still keeping his wits, he rolled slowly on to his back and allowed his head to surface so that his mouth and nose just appeared above the water. He gulped, sucking in a lungful of life-giving air. His ears drummed as he turned over again, once more out of sight below the timber, and then, suddenly, he realised that the jarring and the ear-splitting crashes had ceased.

His head slowly returned to the surface to see Bill's grinning face, six feet away, one eye closed in an enormous wink. Then Harold surfaced, jerked his head and started to paddle with his disengaged arm, while Peter helped to bring the log slowly back, end-on to the beach. Out of the corner of his eye, he saw the last of the patrol disappearing round the sharp outline of the cliff down which they had scrambled.

Harold murmured, "In half an hour's time it will be daylight, Peter. Let's paddle eastwards, until we get well down the coast. Luckily, we've got the inshore current with us which ought to take us well down. Then we'll ease inshore and lie up. What say you?"

"All right, Captain, but it's blinking cold!"

Slowly the unnoticed baulk of timber floated down the coast of Sicily. Within an hour, it was near the Spella rocks, and bobbing up and down in the sea's white horses. Half an hour later, it disappeared to seawards of the black rock which was now lashed by the spray.

Peter could hardly hear Harold's voice. Shaking his head from side to side, he tried to remain awake, although almost overcome by the cold.

"Wake up, sir, wake up!" Peter heard Bill's urgent summons close to his ears. He dragged his eyelids open, to see Bill's grey face close by him.

"Hold on, Peter! Hold on! We're nearly there. Let's go in now, as we're round the point," Harold's urgent voice implored from the forward end of the timber. "Are you all right, Peter?"

Once again, Peter felt his numb hand slipping from the slimy log. Imperceptibly, the timber turned towards the land. Bill now worked his way round to Peter, half supporting him on the log, while at the same time kicking with his legs.

"Well done, sir! Keep it up — nearly there, nearly there, sir," Bill pleaded, a note of despairing urgency on his chattering lips. He looked to his left and saw the rocks slowly moving by them; and then faster — were they really moving faster? Surely not! Yes, they were! An inshore current was sweeping them towards the beach, swirling and spinning past the white-foamed rocks which, with their jagged pinnacles, formed a terrifying sight.

"Hold on, Peter! Hold on for all you're worth!" Harold shouted above the foaming tumult and as Peter dimly heard the distant voice his blue hands closed desperately on the timber.

A smother of whiteness engulfed them. Down, down, spinning and spiralling, down, down and down they went. A roaring blackness swept chokingly around Peter. In a frenzy of instinctive self-preservation, a sudden flash of consciousness pierced his deadened brain.

He lashed out with his legs, kicking and thrashing. Groping, struggling, tearing his way upwards, the light of day burst once more into his listless eyes, to be smothered instantly by a white flurry of foam.

Down, down, down… He dimly realised that this had been his last glimpse of life, when he felt his knees buckling under him. His feet were no longer descending. A sharp pain shot through his left foot. He had touched bottom. A roaring, smothering greenness hurled him forwards, throwing him headlong. Instinctively, he stretched his hands before him, softening the blow as he was crushed beneath the wall of water. Then a horrible whiteness enveloped him, a thunderous din drummed in his ears, and he knew no more.

CHAPTER 13

The First Eleven

The silence in the lurking submarine seemed uncanny after the pandemonium of the night. The crash of the gun's recoil overhead and the clatter of the shell cases as they bounced off the pressure hull, still rang in the ears of everyone in the boat.

To the shaken men, this strange contrast was unnerving. They had nothing to do but to wait for the inevitable retaliation that must surely soon crash around them.

Ordinary Seaman Smith lay on the oily corticene floor in the fore-ends, his arms folded beneath his greasy head. Around him sprawled the exhausted figures of Jock, Graves and Jarvis, too tired to make even whispered conversation. They had unbuttoned their tunics, and their revolvers and weapons lay in an untidy heap beneath the torpedo racks. Over them all hung the musty and pervading smell of Torpoil, the vapour drifting in a blue haze about the compartment.

"What wouldn't I give for a fag, just now?" croaked Graves as the whites of his eyes rolled in his blackened forehead, his face streaky from the night's escapades.

"Och! When will we be allowed to smoke, Smithy?" asked Jock plaintively, as he leaned upon one elbow to loosen his belt in a fruitless effort at comfort.

"You 'eard what the Old Man said, didn't yer?" Smith replied, a grin on his grey face. "This hunt may go on for a blinkin' long time. We ain't up against no beginners, chum! We'll be needing all the air we can get before this lark's over. I reckon old Bill Hawkins is well out of this. I hope he's all right."

Smith scratched his head, and added with a touch of pride, "This Trapani lot, the First Eleven, as the Captain told yer, is all right. They're good. They're blinkin' good. Why, I remember once, two patrols ago, when we were … 'ullo! 'ere we go!"

The slight 'burr' of the telephone on the bulkhead interrupted his soliloquising, much to the relief of the seasoned Commandos who did not relish or appreciate the finer points of this game of cat and mouse.

"… Yes, sir? Dead quiet, sir? Aye, aye, sir," repeated Smith in a low voice down the telephone.

Deliberately, he carefully replaced the receiver on the bulkhead, and then turned to the T.I., Petty Officer Slater, who sprawled between the doors of the tube space. He was the Petty Officer in charge of this compartment, and of his precious torpedoes.

"Don't talk so loud, any of you," he snapped curtly, "or else…" And he jerked his head upwards expressively. "As Smithy said, these boys are good. They can find you in the dark. I don't know how they do it" — and he shook his head resignedly.

These five men were now boxed up in their steel compartment, isolated from the rest of the boat. Joe had ordered "Shut off from depth-charging" when shutting the upper lid above him, and the bulkhead doors had been slammed shut, with all clips on. Each compartment was now an isolated world on its own.

"If possible, no talking to save oxygen. No eating, to save oxygen. Get your sleep and don't move about. That saves oxygen too," Joe had said, and each compartment obeyed his instructions. Their survival depended upon it.

In the Control Room, as in the rest of the boat, all unnecessary lights were extinguished to save the precious batteries and to keep down the temperature, which was already too high. A dim glow from the luminous dials and gauges and from the solitary bulb over the helmsman and the Fruit Machine bathed the Control Room in a peculiar light. The pointers on the depth gauges were steady at eighty feet. With the solid figures of the Coxswain on the after-planes and the Second Coxswain on the fore-planes, both spasmodically turning their shining brass wheels, a feeling almost of security pervaded the enclosed space.

The Outside E.R.A., Joe Saunders, an imperturbable Cornishman, sat on his toolbox by the panel. He was making a leather belt across his knees and was waiting. Sub-Lieutenant Benson, Peter's young relief, was engrossed at the chart table and was plotting the boat's course, but he, too, like everyone else, was waiting anxiously for the terror to come.

Number One, with one hand on a rung of the lower conning tower ladder, was waiting also. Joe leaned nonchalantly against the Fruit Machine, one hand in his pocket. He, too, was waiting… His eye turned to the clock above the dimly lit chart table. Eight-fifteen.

"They're in no hurry, Number One. Seem to be taking their time over this."

"Yes, sir, the mark of the professional!"

Joe smiled. "Any luck on the Asdic?" he asked Elliott.

The operator's black mop of hair bent low over the luminous dial as he twiddled the ebonite knob.

"There may be something on red eight-oh, sir. Sounds like slow-turning turbine propellers. Destroyer's propellers."

"Thank you. Carry on with all-round sweep."

So they weren't far away! It was only eight o'clock, with the whole day before them.

"I won't start evasive tactics yet, Number One, as we've got to close the Spella rocks to make our rendezvous with Sinclair and Arkwright — if we can", and, in an undertone, he added, "The First Eleven are slipping. They aren't in contact, yet, anyway!"

But, as if to refute him, very, very faintly from all quarters around the circular sphere in the Control Room, a faint 'tick-ticking' had crept in upon their consciousness. It was like the sound that is made between finger and thumb when they are flicked gently together.

Elliott looked up at the Captain, a faint smile twitching at the corners of his thin mouth. "Destroyer in contact, bearing green six-oh, sir."

"I spoke too soon!" replied Joe. "Starboard ten."

"Starboard ten, sir," the burly helmsman repeated, as his tattooed arms slowly turned the brass wheel.

The submarine was now keeping end-on to the hunting destroyer which was in contact on her starboard bow.

Slowly, very slowly, the sound of the 'tick-ticking' of the destroyer's Asdic impulses decreased, as *Rugged* turned end-on.

"Can you pick up the third blighter, Elliott?"

"Not yet, sir."

"We'll soon know where she is, anyway," Joe retorted.

"Course one-two-oh, sir," reported the helmsman, as the submarine steadied on her new course.

This game of cat and mouse was becoming more and more unbearable as the months wore on. Now, no one in *Rugged* bragged about 'the heat' in jocular terms as they had once done

— long ago it seemed. Elliott's voice cut into the brooding silence like a knife.

"Destroyer's H.E. increasing, red one-two-oh, sir."

"Confound them, they're in contact all right! I wonder how they do it?" Joe murmured to himself, as one professional grudgingly acknowledges another's skill. "Here we go!"

"Bearing steady on one-two-oh, sir. H.E. loud and increasing."

Now all ears in the boat could hear the increasing 'thrum-thrum' of beating propellers above them.

"Starboard fifteen," snapped Joe.

"Starboard fifteen, sir," repeated the helmsman eagerly, but, even at this moment, his training ensured that his movements were unhurried. Haste meant water noise, and noise spelled disaster. Elliott did not alter the pitch of his voice.

"Destroyer decreasing transmission interval, sir."

"That means five hundred yards, then, doesn't it?"

"Yes, sir."

"Hold on, everyone," Joe murmured.

Men's bodies stiffened for the shock that was remorselessly showering down upon them, perhaps to burst their steel coffin wide open. The knuckles of Number One's hand showed white on the ladder rungs. The Outside E.R.A. looked up from his belt. Then he slowly put down the unfinished leather and stood up quietly. He remained poised by his panel, wheel-spanner in hand, waiting…

All about them was the swish! swish! swish! of rapidly beating propellers. Then the clatter, whirl and whistling of water noises, as the hunter rumbled overhead.

Click-click…! Click-click…!

The precise noise was heard distinctly in the midst of the din.

Depth-charge detonators springing home, thought Number One. *They are always close when you can hear that.*

As depth charges tumble from the destroyers' racks or are hurled from the throwers, they smack down on the surface of the water and this sound can also be heard by the hunted submarine. When these sounds are audible, the enemy may be said to be close.

The rumble and clatter of the destroyer overhead had started to work across the submarine's starboard quarter when a devastating shock exploded all round them. Pandemonium shattered the eerie stillness in the Control Room, as charge after charge exploded alongside the little submarine.

Air was knocked out of human lungs by the shock, so that the gasps of men catching their breath mingled with the inferno of sound. The curved, steel sides of the boat seemed to jump inwards, and, as suddenly, spring back again like a concertina. Fragments of insulating cork from the deckhead spattered downwards and speckled men's hair and the corticene deck. Silently they stood there, each man reacting in his own different way. The Outside E.R.A. picked his teeth. Elliott had removed his headphones. The crack of the explosions would have split his eardrums, but he was quick to replace the headset to continue with his listening watch.

Number One was quite expressionless, hands on hips, legs astride to feel sensitively the slant of the submarine's deck beneath him. His eyes were glued on the 'bubbles' of the planesmen. Slowly he stretched up his left hand and removed the clapper of the ship's bell that hung just above his head. "Just in case," he murmured, and a chuckle of relief passed through the Control Room.

Joe remained in his usual position, stooped and slouching, his head jutting forward, his arms hanging down. His piercing eyes were everywhere. He watched Number One, the planes, the helmsman, the panel and the Fruit Machine. He watched everything that could give him information and a large grin creased his leathery face as the hubbub subsided.

"You'll have to do better than that!" he taunted the enemy.

Tension relaxed as the others watched this imperturbable man. The duel was becoming personal — the wits of the Captain of the submarine against the Senior Officer of the skilful destroyers who were weaving above.

"Port fifteen, half ahead starboard," Joe ordered as he peered at the telegraphsman.

"Half ahead starboard, sir," and the telegraphsman's hand moved upwards to swing the brass handle.

"No! Use the telephone, Keating! D'you want to shout our position away from the rooftops?" Joe snapped.

"Sorry, sir."

Keating's eyes, old eyes in a young face, did not meet those of his Captain. If he had rung the telegraph, the clang of the bell in the Motor Room and Engine Room would have betrayed their position to the lurking destroyers only eighty feet above them. Now the destroyers lay stopped and listening … listening … listening for the faintest clue.

"That's all right, Keating, but don't forget again," Joe said, surprisingly kindly.

All knew that Keating was young and inexperienced and they appreciated Joe's leniency on this occasion. They also realised that his alertness had prolonged their existence.

Keating passed the orders aft by phone.

"Course oh-three-oh, sir," the helmsman reported.

"Very good. Steer oh-three-oh. Slow ahead together" — and once again Joe watched Keating pass the order.

"It's funny, isn't it?" drawled Joe to Number One. "It's odd how the Wops always think that we're deeper than we really are. Eighty feet is a good depth. The Wops wouldn't believe it if we told them, because, after all, they've only got just over the length of a cricket pitch above us! They think we're deep. They always do."

"Long may they continue to do so!" Number One said with a grim smile.

"'ere, 'ere!" Saunders murmured by the panel.

Joe smiled. He had a good team.

Benson looked at the clock and whistled beneath his breath. Twelve-thirty? It couldn't be!

But he looked again.

I'll be old before I know it, at this rate! he thought.

Elliott was carrying out his usual sweep and shaking his black head. "Nothing to report, sir. All quiet."

"Good! Perhaps we've given them the—"

But Joe's words were cut short by a dull clang which rang from the after-ends. Joe's eyes blazed. "Who did that?" he crackled. "Ring up the Engine Room and find out." Almost as if the telephone would bite him, Keating gingerly picked up the instrument. "Who did that?" he asked hesitatingly.

The earpiece crackled.

"Chief speaking. Give the Captain my compliments and apologies. Leading Seaman Flint dropped a wheel spanner on to the plating."

But before Keating could hang up the receiver Joe had wrenched it from his hands.

"Chief, I'll have your intestines for a necktie if you allow that to happen again! Sorry? It's too late to be sorry. We're not up against a third-rate team. This is the First Eleven!" and Joe savagely hung up.

But it was too late, the damage had been done … Tick-tick … tick-tick … tick-tick … the impulses were already swamping them again.

"Green one-one-oh, sir, destroyers in contact! Another destroyer right ahead, and another, red nine-oh. Running in to attack!"

"Thank you, Elliott."

Once again Joe's anger passed, and he bent his full concentration to the immediate battle about to be joined.

"Port ten, stop port!"

This time he would run to meet the attacker and stop engines just before the final run-in.

"Number One, I reckon that the charges were 'Over' on that first counter-attack, don't you?"

"Yes, sir, certain of it."

"Good. We'll throw him off if we can. I may go astern at the last moment."

"Aye, aye, sir," Number One nodded.

As the submarine twisted to port, the destroyer, which was astern, handed her target on to the ship that had been ahead of the submarine.

"New destroyer now in contact, sir. Green nine-oh."

"Blast! But I suppose it can't be helped! Steady on three-three-oh."

"Steady on three-three-oh, sir."

There was little time now to brace oneself for the shock for already the destroyer which lay ahead was speeding up for her run-in.

"Destroyer attacking right ahead!" Elliott reported in a steady voice.

"Very good."

"Changing transmission intervals, sir! All round H.E.! Range five hundred yards!"

Elliott removed his headphones because the roar and clatter was now all about them.

"Stop both, port ten," Joe ordered crisply. "Half astern together!"

A split second out in his timing now might mean disaster and this was a trick that he used rarely. It was not easy to trim a stopped submarine.

Smack! ... smack! Smack! ... Click! ... click-click-click!

"Stand by!" Joe yelled.

"I wish I had no imagination," the new Sub-Lieutenant, Benson, whispered to himself. Already he knew that depth-charge after depth-charge was tumbling down to meet them. Each man's imagination played hell, and each man tried to force the awful picture from his mind.

Then, in an instantaneous moment of time, the little submarine seemed to burst asunder in an ear-splitting cataclysm, a very holocaust of hell itself.

Joe staggered as the deck shivered beneath his feet. Number One reeled against the steel ladder and clutched at a rung. Lights flickered and went out. Broken glass shivered and splattered to the deck.

Again the boat jerked. Again she was squeezed in a giant's hand, so that her puny sides leapt inwards before springing outwards once more. But this time, the emergency lights did not flick on. The boat was in pitch darkness, except for the luminosity of the gauges.

Men's bodies crashed to the deck, and at the same instant the boat heaved and started to tilt with a terrifying bow-down angle that sickened human stomachs. Steeper and steeper the angle became. Keating slithered across the deck and his hand shot out instinctively. He felt a sharp pain as his fingers grasped the lip of the after periscope well. Then his fingers closed and his body swung round across the greasy deck.

"Torches!" the Captain's voice crackled through the din.

"Here we are, sir!" Number One shouted, an unusual occurrence for him. A pencil of light pierced the darkness.

There was utter confusion. The Coxswain had been thrown from his stool and was crawling on all fours, scrambling, struggling to get back to his vital after-planes. He dragged himself upwards and wrenched at the wheel.

"After-planes jammed at hard-a-dive, sir!" He raised his voice to Joe and an understanding look, an imperceptible glance, passed between them.

"All right, Coxswain," Joe replied, and then continued quietly, "I'll take her now, Number One."

"Aye, aye, sir."

Then Joe's crisp orders sizzled through the confusion.

"Ring up the after-ends and go to after-planes in hand."

"Aye, aye, sir." Keating's ashen face mouthed the reply, his mouth working like a miniature bellows. He hauled himself to the telephone.

"All compartments make your reports," Joe snapped.

The for'd telephone operator was hanging on for dear life, as the deck slipped from beneath his feet.

"I can't hold her, sir!" Number One reported. "All pumps are sucking."

By now the boat was completely out of control and plunging to her death … one hundred and fifty feet … one hundred and seventy feet … two hundred and ten feet, as the gauge pointers jumped round the dials.

Joe's eyes flashed round the Control Room. Under the skilful fingers of Elliott, an emergency lamp had flicked on to cast a pale light on the scene.

"Check telemotor pressure," Joe barked at the Outside E.R.A.

But Saunders, the Outside E.R.A., had folded up in a heap by the for'd bulkhead door. He was trying to climb uphill towards his panel, and was hauling himself along, heave by agonisingly slow heave. As he reached his panel, he glanced at the telemotor pressure-gauge.

"Pressure's gone, sir," he said, white-faced. A fracture in the pressure line would seal their fate at this moment.

"Hell!" Joe cursed. "Check the pump!"

"God, in Thy mercy, save us!" was the unsaid prayer on every man's lips, for a hideous end was now inevitable.

CHAPTER 14

The Admiralty Regrets to Report …

"Have you been up there yet?" shouted Antonio to his olive-skinned companion bicycling slowly behind him. Luigi felt in no mood to pass idle chatter at this early hour of the morning. Already the sun was peeping around the hills, warming the grey dust on the roads. He had been fishing until two this morning and he did not agree with his younger companion: Antonio was too young and energetic, but he would soon learn! It was annoying to be forced out to sea again so early — there were no fish there anyway!

"No, I have not, Antonio. Why should I bicycle all that way uphill to look at those cocky Germans guarding a few Englishmen? Why can't Italians guard them? Are we not good enough, *hein?*" And he spat derisively in the dust.

"The Germans are very efficient, my friend, and don't they know it?" Antonio replied with a shrug of his broad shoulders. "We happy-go-lucky Italians cannot compete with them."

"Bah! They have caused this war and spoilt my fishing. It's all these so-called sailors in our so-called Marine who smother our so-called *Mare Nostrum* with their useless depth charges! They've driven away the fish — all the fish," he continued, mumbling away to himself.

"But they got that Inglisi submarine, anyway," retorted Antonio, a note of annoyance in his soft voice. "But let us not argue, my friend," he went on, "we ought to have a good day's fishing today — the mullet are out."

His steady eye instinctively swept the blue horizon which stretched far below him to the southward and then, with a squeal and a rasping noise, his old bicycle grinded to a halt.

"Look, Luigi!" he shouted, pointing seawards, one foot outstretched on the ground to maintain his balance.

Luigi swerved to his left and halted ahead of Antonio in the centre of the dusty road. Carefully and methodically, he clambered from his ancient steed, leaned on the saddle with one bent arm and gazed out to sea.

"Curse them! Antonio, what did I tell you? There will be no fish today."

He swore and his old eyes wrinkled at the corners as he half closed them to see the better.

Well out to sea and almost on the horizon, three light-grey destroyers slowly slid in a circling movement, high spouts of white water foaming from their stems as depth charges shattered the deeps. Even from the cliff road, they could hear the distant crack and rumble of the exploding patterns.

Antonio dreamily watched the spectacle; it had become almost a daily routine with the fishermen. The sun warmed his brown arms as he dismounted from his bicycle and slouched over the frame to see more comfortably. His dark, Latin eyes gazed distantly across the blue sea as his forebears had done throughout the centuries.

"You know, Luigi, I do not feel so good when I think of the men in those infernal submarines. It moves the pit of my stomach, making me feel ill. Even though they are Inglisi, I can't help feeling sorry for them while they're being hunted. Do you sometimes feel like that, Luigi?"

The older man paused and then once again he spat into the dust.

"No, Antonio, I do not. I do not love the Inglisi, but I do not hate them. I do not love the Germans, but I hate them. Both of them, curse them, spoil the fishing!" — and, spitting again, he continued, "Let us go, Antonio. The fishing will be no good again today."

He checked the length of rope which was coiled around his left shoulder.

"Let us sit in the sun on the quay and mend our nets," he went on, and deliberately mounted his bicycle without waiting for his companion to reply.

Antonio grunted and dragged his eyes from the sea.

"Wait, old friend! Let us not quarrel; there's only a mile to go and you can share my litre of vino," he said pleasantly, drawing abreast of the old man.

Luigi's eyes twinkled as he looked at his young friend.

"Thank you, Antonio, I should be very happy."

Then Antonio nearly fell off his bicycle as a wild figure stepped out from the group of grey olive trees which flanked the side of the road, ten yards ahead. The wild man was pointing the glistening blue barrel of a revolver at them, waving it from one to the other, and there was relentless determination in his white face.

"*Santa Maria!*" whispered Antonio, crossing himself as he jumped from the wobbling machine which fell skidding and clattering into the dust.

Three yards farther on, old Luigi brought his bicycle to a jerky halt and slowly dismounted, fear stopping his very speech as the gun flickered from side to side, signalling them to move into the olive grove. The wild man flicked his finger in a spiralling gesture, silently ordering them to turn round with their backs to him. He forced them quickly into the grove and they heard the click of the trigger as the gun was cocked. Both fishermen held their hands high above their heads. They dared not look back and Luigi sobbed quietly to himself, eyes closed, lips moving noiselessly as he recited his prayers.

They heard the clatter of ironwork and then the madman was beside them, shoving the bicycles into their hands. Black hair hung in matted strands around his face, and his fierce eyes burned fanatically. The fishermen crossed themselves again.

"The devil himself," Luigi whispered.

The gun jabbed Antonio's ribs.

"*Avanti!*"

The madman pointed towards the cliff which was now only thirty yards distant. The two men halted, rooted by fear to the ground on which they stood.

"*Avanti, avanti! Pronto, pronto!*"

The gun ground into Antonio's back, galvanising him into a trot, while Luigi followed close on his heels. Within two yards of the cliff, the pressure of the gun decreased and before they knew what was happening, the mad figure snatched their bicycles from them and hurled them over the edge.

A curious sensation slowly drummed through Peter's limp body and into his semi-conscious brain. Thump! Thump! Thump! Regularly and methodically he felt the soft blows pummelling his back and dimly he recalled strong hands rolling him over. A comforting glow began to warm his shuddering body which twitched spasmodically like a puppet on a string. Far, far away, he heard the low murmur of the surf, a sound he vaguely related to himself. A steady pressure of deft hands pressed and pumped his chest, slowly and certainly bringing him back to life. A trickle of salt water still glistened from the corner of his mouth, as another wave of nausea swept over him. His clutching hands groped at his stomach and, turning over on his side, his whole frame retched with spasms of sickness. Then the nausea passed, warmth crept through his belly and slowly his grey eyelids opened. The blueness that was his whole world filtered into his bloodshot eyes. For what seemed an eternity, with the blessed relief of an exhausted body, he lay still, drawing deeply into his reviving flesh the comfort and warmth of the sun. His eyes were unseeing and his lids blinked as a shadow passed across them.

"Come on, sir, c'mon! Everything's all right, sir," a familiar voice spoke hoarsely, a voice he had known somewhere, sometime, eternities ago. He looked round him, his head moving slowly from side to side.

"Bill," Peter whispered.

"Yes, sir. It's me, sir."

To his left Peter faintly heard another quiet voice.

"Don't talk, Peter boy. Can you hear me? Can you understand what I'm saying, Peter?" Harry's voice spoke slowly.

Barely moving, the weary head nodded.

"Stay where you are, Peter. I'll be back in a few minutes. Stay where you are. Stay where you are, Peter, Bill will look after you. Do you understand, Peter?"

Peter's dry and cracked lips whispered inaudibly, hardly moving.

"Well done, Bill! I won't be away long," Harry's gentle voice said and then he was gone.

Peter sighed as he felt the comforting presence of Bill sitting beside him and soon the soft soughing of the breeze gently, caressingly drew his resilient spirit back to life, until into his consciousness there floated the homely mewing of sea terns wheeling above his head. The pervading warmth of the hot sun, reflecting off the flat rocks, flowed into his flesh to find every fold of his naked body.

I might be on Cornborough cliffs, he thought, and then suddenly remembered where he was.

He dragged himself upright, taking his weight on his outstretched arms, and looked around him. In front of him stretched the beach, the surge of the breaking surf, white on the dark, volcanic pebbles. A screen of black rocks shielded him from the wind on both sides to complete the three walls of his box-like world.

The sturdy figure of Bill Hawkins was by him.

"Thanks, Bill."

Bill's open face looked down at him and smiled and a rough hand grasped his shoulder.

Peter sighed in deep contentment, relishing the lifegiving warmth. On a flat rock behind him, he saw his sodden trousers stretched out to dry, steaming in the hot sun, and then he heard a warning clatter. He looked round to his left and saw two figures come stumbling across the pebbles towards him, prodded in the back by Harry who drove them before him like frightened sheep.

"The 'eavenly twins, sir!" Bill grinned, springing to his feet.

"Hullo, Peter! Feeling better?"

"Yes, thank you, Harry. Whom have we here?"

"Two uninvited guests!" His friend smiled as he motioned the two terrified fishermen to sit down beside Bill.

"Welcome to our ancestral hall, my boyos!" Bill bowed low, while Peter, quickly regaining his stubborn vitality, added "Allies of the Master Race!"

Harry stood above them and, uncocking the .45 he had taken from Peter, replaced it in the pocket of the sodden trousers that clung to his legs like clammy sheets.

"Best get changed, Bill; off with their clothes!"

In a brace of shakes, the protesting Italians stood in their primitive underclothes.

"Rope 'em up while I change, Bill."

Deftly, Bill uncoiled the Italians' rope and tied up the protesting men with their wrists firmly secured behind their backs and, in a minute, Harry stood before them, the image of an unshaven Italian fisherman, the dark blue woollen cord sweater enveloping him like a rugger jersey. Peter and Bill shared the remaining clothes.

"You have the jersey, sir. My vest's nearly dry," said Bill as he picked up his thick vest from the flat rock.

"Thank you, Bill."

When they had dressed, they turned out the Italians' pockets, and Harry announced the contents: "Cigarettes, sandwiches, matches, knives, a ball of string — any more in yours, Peter?" he asked as he slapped the last item down upon a flat stone.

"Only a wristwatch, but it's all very welcome," Peter grinned.

The Wops eyed them with murderous glances.

"I'm as hungry as a wolf, let's eat the food," spluttered Harry, already munching voraciously at the thick, black bread. "And give them a cigarette, Bill, they deserve it!"

Soon the comic figures of the semi-nude Italians, puffing away at their rancid black cigarettes, made them roar with laughter and joining in the joke, the Italians' eyes twinkled.

The food gave new life to the three friends and then, threatening their prisoners with everlasting hellfire if they tried to escape, they withdrew out of earshot, and, squatting down on the warm pebbles, puffed at the sour cigarettes while they laid their plans.

In the afternoon Harry reconnoitred towards the little white fishing village which trickled down to the water's edge like a cascade of pearls. The village lay half a mile away, behind a bluff headland which cut it off from Peter and Bill's restricted world on the isolated beach.

Meanwhile, these two, with the joy of being alive again, tugged contentedly at the foul tobacco and leaned against the cliff, while the two fishermen lay on the sun-kissed pebbles, clad only in their underclothes.

The sun was already reaching up to its zenith, while from seaward the distant 'crumps' of sporadic depth-charging still thumped in their ears, when Peter, handing Bill his revolver, said, "Take care of them, Bill."

Brandishing his Commando's knife before the eyes of his two prisoners, Peter, whose strength had welled back with the vigour of youth, clambered up the cliff and, with his back to the rocky face, spread-eagled himself to watch the grim battle being played out to seaward.

The glassy calmness stretched before him like a mirror. Five miles distant, the three enemy destroyers, like cats playing with a mouse, slowly closed in upon their tortured prey. Either they were driving *Rugged* in towards the beach, or Joe was deliberately trying to close the rendezvous position, so that he could be ready to take them off that night. Two destroyers lay stopped, their pale-grey outlines reflecting the dazzling sunlight which shimmered like a mirage upon the wavering horizon. A flurry of whiteness would kick up and foam from the stern of the third ship, and she would race in to the kill, directed by the other two. As she increased speed, the creaming wake built up astern of her and then, suddenly, fountains of white spray would leap skywards, splitting the depths. Quickly the wake would vanish, as the attacker turned to replace one of her consorts, who, in her turn, would dart in and deliver her load of destruction.

So the grim game went on, now bearing to seawards, now turning towards the land, but always, always drawing closer to the rendezvous. As each depth-charge exploded, Peter felt as if a knife were tearing at his vitals. Poor old *Rugged* was getting the 'heat' all right! The Trapani Team were not to be ignored. Fortunately the calm day favoured Joe, whose wits were pitched against the adversaries above him and Peter realised that he would have found a 'layer' in these conditions, and would, quite probably, be out of contact with the searching destroyers. He knew, too, that someone had only to allow a spanner to drop, and the clanging noise would as quickly be picked up by the prowling enemy.

Weaving, spiralling, turning, still the remorseless hunt continued. To Peter, a helpless onlooker, the dreadful phrase, "Hunt to exhaustion", recurred continuously in his harassed mind. Our own destroyers were extremely skilled at this horrible game of patient hunting — hunting, wearing down the enemy until he exhausted his air or battery power, or until his nerve broke, whichever was the earlier. Peter turned away. He could watch no longer.

Then he realised that the explosions had ceased, and that the destroyers were merely moving slowly, too slowly across the placid sea.

They've run out of depth charges, he thought and looked again to see the blinking of a signalling lantern, flashing to the north-westwards. He slowly turned to see three more grey shapes, white foam at their stems, with bow waves cleaving the blue stillness of the sea, come belting across his field of vision.

"Their reliefs, curse them," he murmured. "It's no use now, Joe — leave us, Joe, leave us, please."

Tears welled into Peter's eyes as he tried to peer at the cheap Italian wristwatch which showed two-thirty.

"She cannot live in this," he whispered.

He slowly clambered down the cliff to find Bill sitting cross-legged, the revolver across his knees. His eyes were worried as he looked up at Peter.

"How's it going, sir?" Bill asked anxiously.

"They're giving her all they've got, Bill."

"Gawd help them, then."

Bill peered seawards, then his blazing eyes returned to the two Italians and his fingers itched on the trigger of the revolver. Peter put a hand on his shoulder.

"Better give me the gun, Bill."

It was past four when Harry rejoined them with a large pannier of fish which he slopped down at their feet.

"Fish for tea, let's get a fire going, Bill," he grunted. Peter dragged his eyes away from the distant battle.

"They're still at it, Harry. Look! They've driven her well out now," he said hopelessly, as his arm swept towards the hazy horizon line.

"Yes, but Joe's no fool, Peter. He obviously knows what he is doing, and realises that he can't rendezvous with us now. Apart from the fact that he will be hunted most of the night, he's got to get in a charge on main engines and that means surfacing. He can't come in here for us, as they are bound to send out inshore patrols tonight. It would be suicide for *Rugged*."

But Peter knew in his heart that this was all make-believe, and that the game was already over.

Bill was silent, intent on fanning into life a small fire which was well hidden by the rocks. Their two prisoners crouched around it and enjoyed the honour of being allowed to gut and cook the fish on pointed sticks.

"Ummmm, good," mumbled Harry contentedly, as the fresh food filled his aching stomach. "That's better, isn't it, Peter?"

"Yes," he replied as again his pointed finger swept along the horizon to the blurs on the skyline. "But what are you so devilish pleased about? Don't you realise that there goes our last chance of escape?"

Bill looked at Harry anxiously.

"Oh no, it doesn't, my boyos, not by a long chalk!" laughed Harry. "Come here, both of you, and I'll tell you what I've discovered."

CHAPTER 15

The Abyss

The submarine was now quite unmanageable. The faster she plunged, the steeper the bow-down angle became, for she was now standing on her ends. The after-planes were forcing her down … down … down … 240 feet … 280 feet … 300 feet … when the pointers came up against the stops. She was now well past her safe and tested diving depth.

The phone from the after-ends crackled. Keating's agonised voice spoke.

"After-planes in hand, sir. After-ends reports much water coming in through the stern glands."

"Very good."

"Telemotor pump switch has been knocked off, sir!" shouted Saunders, the Outside E.R.A., at the top of his voice, and with one sweep of his right hand, he lunged at the switch handle.

Every man in the Control Room stood motionless, listening for the sweet sound of an electric motor whining into life. This was a moment of eternity. Hardly audible, a gentle whine whispered, then shrilled and shrieked into life as the pump-starter gave of its life-giving power. Slowly the pointer of the telemotor pressure gauge started to climb round its dial.

"I mustn't blow main ballast," Joe cried aloud. "They'll only see our bubbles when we are forced to vent."

The strained faces watching him now in this critical moment showed various stages of animal fear.

"Pressure's on, sir!" Saunders yelled exuberantly.

But wasn't it all too late, that fraction of a second too late? Surely they must be crushed now and fold up like a smashed eggshell? This was a moment when the stalwart shipbuilders' skill was put to the test. One faulty rivet and she was gone…

"Planes are free, sir!" the Coxswain shouted gleefully as he wrenched the wheel round to hard-a-rise, the gleaming spokes glinting as they spun.

But the pointers on the depth gauges were still off the dial, when the phone from the fore-end shrieked.

Number One jumped and tore it from its holder.

"Control Room?"

"Water coming in through the pump space, sir!"

"Very good, hold on!"

"All right, Number One," Joe acknowledged quietly.

So this was it! Nothing could save them now, for the seawater would seep into the batteries, and the chlorine gas which would be generated would creep through the boat like a miasma to choke them to death.

There was a gleam in Joe's dark eyes.

"You swine!" he hissed at the ruthless enemy above.

Unnoticed, without anyone being aware of it, the bow-down angle had lessened — or had it really? Yes! Yes! Already men were beginning to stand upright as the little boat began to take on a bow-up angle. A fierce, glorious bow-up angle; away, away from the black, hungry depths!

"Thank God!" Sub-Lieutenant Benson whispered, as she started her mad career upwards. Tears of relief were on many a man's face and the old Coxswain unashamedly crossed himself.

"May I pump, sir? I still can't hold her," asked Number One.

"Yes, if you have to," Joe snapped, for although the noise would give them away, there was nothing else for it.

Suddenly the pointer on the depth gauges came to life. 300 feet … 280 feet … 250 feet…

The phones buzzed again. Both leaks had slowed to a trickle.

"Take over, Number One," said Joe quietly as he scratched his head, "and don't speed up. I'm afraid they won that round!"

The lights came on again as the electricians repaired the fuses, and a scene of indescribable chaos met the gaze of all in the compartment. *Rugged* had held tight and was still alive and slowly she was brought under control as each man righted what he could. The pointers settled at eighty feet once more, and an audible sigh rustled round the Control Room.

"I reckon that pattern was definitely short," Joe laughed before giving his orders to Elliott. "All-round sweep, please."

"Aye, aye, sir," replied Elliott automatically, sitting himself down once again at his stool by his set.

Tick-tick … tick-tick-tick … Joe's heart sank.

"Destroyer in contact, sir. Green eight-oh."

"To hell with them! Port ten."

"Port ten, sir."

Joe padded through the Control Room in his sandalled feet. He spoke aloud. "Well, men, the gunnery experts reckon that if they have one *over* and one *short*, the third one will be a *straddle*, and that would be that! But *Rugged*'s not beaten yet." He was trying to infuse confidence, but for the first time in his experience of this game he was afraid, and there was no answering smile from his men around him.

"…the third must be a *straddle*" was in everyone's mind, "… the third pattern *must* be a straddle."

"Destroyer attacking, sir!" Elliott cried.

"Oh God!" Benson whispered as he looked at the clock. It had stopped at two-thirty exactly.

CHAPTER 16

The Owl and the Pussy Cat …

As dusk fell, the evening breeze softly sighed its offshore way, gently flecking the darkening seas. To the westward, a typically dramatic sunset painted the sky a burnished bronze. Bill kicked out the last embers of the flickering fire, while Harry and Peter bound each prisoner, now breeched in English trousers, to widely spaced rocks. Gagged and firmly tied, they offered no resistance as the three Britons thumped them reassuringly on their shoulders.

"*Grazias*," grinned Harry. "*Mucho grazias!*"

The greasy-haired Italians nodded, and the fugitives, dressed roughly as Italian fishermen, slipped quietly into the twilight.

"There it is, men!" Harry whispered.

Crouched behind the low breakwater which curved out into the darkening sea like a scythe-blade, Harry pointed towards a little harbour which was fast taking its night's rest. An occasional shaft of yellow light flashed carelessly from some open cottage door and they could just see the little fishing boats bobbing at their moorings in the groundswell.

"We'll take that one, far out by the entrance. There's a dinghy drawn up on the beach there, just below us on the breakwater," Harry whispered.

Peter nodded, slipping cartridges into the chambers of his .45.

"You got the knife, Bill?" Harry asked.

"Me comforter!" he whispered and slapped his hip.

"All set to go?" Harry asked them quietly.

"All set," Peter whispered.

The smell of appetising cooking wafted from the cottages and blue-grey plumes of smoke, blown by the evening breeze, trailed horizontally from the little chimneys.

"They're having supper now, I reckon," Peter said. "Come on, let's go, Harry."

The nearest hovel was thirty yards away from the inshore extremity of the breakwater, while the other cottages nestled shoulder to shoulder against each other around the little harbour.

Three dark shadows slipped across the cobbled breakwater and disappeared and then, in the blackness of the shadow below the stone wall, Peter, Harry and Bill crouched and listened anxiously, before starting for the small dinghy which was run up on the beach above high-water mark. They laid hold of each side of the gunwales and lifted the dinghy down to the water's edge, to avoid the scrunching noise of keel over rock, and then Harry jumped noiselessly into the stern. Peter and Bill waded in, shoved the boat out stern first, and vaulted lightly over the bows.

No oars!

Harry yanked at the bottom boards, which came away suddenly in his hands, causing him to fall back on to Peter for support. His feet caught the after-thwart and the clatter rattled noisily across the water.

Using the boards, they spun the boat round and paddled out into the harbour, keeping as close as possible to the breakwater. The small fishing boat was only ten yards distant now, lobbing to the swell which gently rippled in through the harbour entrance. Peter fended off, and his hands greedily grasped the side of the boat. Taking the boards with them, Harry went over the stern, while Peter and Bill slipped over the bows. Peter let go the mooring and dropped the glass mooring buoy gently into the water.

"All gone!" he whispered to Harry who was reaching for the tiller.

A cottage door flung open and a white light shimmered across the water. A black figure stood waving, silhouetted against the amber light, and a deep voice hailed them across the harbour.

"Antonio! Luigi!"

The three fugitives held their breath.

"Leave it to me," hissed Harold.

"Luigi! Antonio!" A note of urgency and interrogation was in the summons.

Harry stood up and waved his hand excitedly.

"Antonio!" The hailing figure started to walk towards them down the breakwater.

Peter swallowed, while a groan rumbled from Bill. So near and yet so far! Were they thus to be discovered at the last moment?

Harry waved again and, applying his hands to his mouth, shouted an unintelligible mumble shorewards, his voice rising and falling in the best Arkwright Italian, and ending with "*Santa Maria!*"

The figure ashore stopped in its tracks. For a long moment their fate seemed to hang in the balance or, rather, in the hands of the lone figure on the jetty. Peter hardly dared to breathe, and Harry sat down again in the stern, simulating an urgent interest in the tiller. Then, "Stand by, men," he whispered, while Peter loosened the revolver at his hip. They did not watch the man, in case some telepathic message was transmitted to complete a circuit of suspicion, but Bill looked up to see him start towards the open door of his cottage. Then he stopped and scratched his head, turned about again and, with hands deep in his trousers, shuffled down the jetty towards the point where they had stolen the dinghy.

"Go and get him, both of you. I'll reeve a slip-rope for a quick getaway," Harry whispered as he flattened himself on the bottom boards. "There's nothing else for it — he's too suspicious."

They let go the dinghy and, crooning the "Ave Maria" unmelodiously, Peter and Bill started paddling towards the shore.

"Oh-hez, Antonio!" the dark figure loomed above them on the breakwater.

"Oh-hez!" grumbled Peter's deep voice from the stern, and then he started to whistle.

"Stand-by to fall overboard, Bill," Peter whispered under his breath.

Bill grunted.

Five yards from the beach — four, three yards…

"Now!" hissed Peter.

Bill stood up in the bows, ready to leap ashore, head lowered. Then, pretending to stumble, he overbalanced backwards into the water.

Splash! The noise slapped the harbour.

"*Santa Maria!*" moaned the pretended Antonio excitedly, as he flailed his arms wildly in the air and went under for the first time.

"*Santa Maria!*" he screeched as he came up for air.

The body in the darkness threshed the water in a flurry of foam as Peter leaped over the dinghy, nearly capsizing it. The dark figure on the jetty galvanised into activity, clattered down the steps and rushed for the boat, wading to its prow. As he laid hold of the gunwales, a blond head emerged dripping from the water and then a straight left shot from an enormous pair of shoulders, with the whole weight of a powerful body behind it, took the Italian squarely between the eyes. Peter caught the man as he slumped backwards and Bill took the limp body and dumped it into the dinghy.

Peter leaped over the bows and shoved the boat back into the water again, while Bill repeated his horrible attempt at the "Ave Maria". With the unconscious man between them on the bottom boards, they once more regained their fishing boat and as they bumped alongside, the inert body shook itself. Terrified eyes gleamed from a swarthy face as the Italian looked straight down the barrel of Peter's .45 revolver.

"*Pronto! Pronto!*" Peter hissed at the Italian and, like a scalded cat, the man leaped into the sailing boat and landed with a clatter on the bottom boards. Harry secured the dinghy astern, Bill slipped the painter, and the small craft slowly drew out towards the entrance of the breakwater. As they rounded its extremity, their last glimpse of the harbour was a finger of light dancing across the black water from the open door.

Once outside the harbour, Harry slipped the dinghy and pushed it downwind with all his might.

Blackness enveloped them. Meeting a short swell as they reached the open sea, the little boat plumped and wallowed, the boom and rigging slatting clumsily.

The Italian soon realised that his task was to assist in setting sail, and, with encouragement from Harry's revolver, the large spread of the mainsail soon unfurled above them. Harry then put the tiller hard down and the little craft heaved as the mainsail filled, heeling her to port, gunwales under. While they scrambled to starboard to right her, she gathered way, running before the wind, away, away, away from the black enemy shore, like a whippet loosed from the traps.

Peter bent on the foresail, and, with a whoop of joy, hoisted it skywards. The yawing immediately came under control, and the little boat creamed her happy way downwind, every second putting more water between them and the sinister island of Sicily.

The night wore on with deadly monotony. Peter sat in the eyes of the boat in an attempt at keeping a lookout, while Harry lay crouched in the sternsheets at the tiller. On top of the fishing nets, which lay cumbrously at the bottom of the boat, their unbidden guest lay prone, in an attempt at sleep. Occasionally, he rubbed the bruise on his forehead while Bill, who was crouched near him, grinned and rubbed his knuckles in silent glee, with a happy look of contentment on his face.

"One o'clock, Peter!" shouted Harry. "At four knots I reckon we've put a good twenty miles astern of us at this rate, don't you?"

"Hope so, Harry. We can't see Sicily any more. As long as the wind doesn't shift and we don't run into any destroyer patrols, we'll be all right!"

"I'm trying to steer about south-east. I think that's about right for Malta, don't you?"

"I reckon so," Peter replied, looking anxiously upwards at the night sky. We ought to be able to see Etna in the morning, if the weather doesn't deteriorate."

The Pole Star, by which Harry was laying his course, lay on their port quarter heaving and curvetting above them when visible, for low drifting clouds were scudding across the sky, often blanketing the stars. A slight haze seemed to drop on the horizon, portending dirty weather ahead.

"Thank Heaven we've got a breeze, but I hope it doesn't freshen much more," Harry shouted above the wind.

But by three o'clock the weather had worsened so much that the boat yawed perilously and was in danger of broaching-to, creaming round beam-on into the wind.

"We'll broach-to if we're not careful!" Harry yelled. "Down mainsail, and I'll come up into the wind."

With the boat pitching and plugging into the seas, it was no easy matter getting the canvas off her. The Italian was terrified at the way in which the little boat was being driven, and fear added greatly to his efforts at assistance.

At last the mainsail was gathered in, the boom lashed, and the terrifying way taken off her. Running now under her foresail only, she steered sweetly and rode the seas without shipping them.

Daylight crept palely across the surging seas, turning the inky blackness into the welcome cold-grey of a humid Mediterranean dawn. Fatigue and cold seeped into the very marrow of their bones as, crouched below the gunwales, they surged and bucketed southwards. "She's a grand old lady, Peter!" Harry shouted above the whine in the slapping rigging. "If the wind doesn't veer, we might make Malta by tomorrow."

It was a dim hope, but to each came the remembrance of that courageous man, St. Paul, who, so many years previously, had battled his way more than once through a Mediterranean gale. Unbeknown to each other, they kept the thought to themselves, a secret comfort in adversity.

Daylight stole upon them, giving hope to what had been a cheerless night. Nothing seemed quite so bad, once dawn had broken. The Mediterranean is a lady of fickle moods, and by ten o'clock the raging wind had died away, to leave them wallowing in a long swell on a flat-calm sea.

"This is worse than a full gale, Harry," grinned Peter from a stubbly face.

Now there remained only a long, undulating swell to remind them of the night's ordeal. The sun crept up the heavens, beating strongly down on the glassy sea, and reflecting its burning rays directly upon the exhausted men in the motionless boat. Even with all sail once again set, she wallowed on the mirror-like surface, with no way upon her, boom slatting idly from side to side. To the northward, they could just see the snowy whiteness of Mount Etna, showing above the line of billowy clouds which swept like galleons across the invisible island. Peter thought how ethereal the snowy crest seemed, poised unsupported above the squabbling earth. His eyes slowly swept the horizon, until his gaze riveted upon a black speck. His arm shot out to port.

"Aircraft on the horizon!"

Bill emerged from the nets on the bottom boards.

The small black dot slowly enlarged and grew into the recognisable silhouette of a ponderous Cant 52, the reconnaissance aircraft of the Italian Navy.

"Get the nets out, pronto!" ordered Harry, drawing his revolver from his pocket and waving it at the Italian fisherman. Remorselessly the droning aircraft lumbered on towards them, dived, and pulled out immediately above the fishing boat, its flaps shuddering only fifty feet over them.

Four lazy fishermen were tending their nets which dragged out astern. The skipper of the fishing boat slowly got to his feet in the stern, turned and waved a greeting to the pilot who, grinning, returned the welcome. The roar of its engines passed overhead. The aircraft banked, turned landwards and resumed its lumbering patrol until it disappeared from view.

"Phew!" whistled Peter.

"That was a near one," Bill grinned at the Italian who shrugged his shoulders and spat over the side. But the aircraft's suspicions had not been lulled and half an hour later they saw the white crosstrees of an Italian destroyer's mast showing above the shimmering horizon line. The shape grew and enlarged into a bridge as the white bow wave of the destroyer came fully into view and charged down upon them. The Italian fisherman's face was creased into a triumphant grin, as Bill moved up alongside him.

Harry clicked the hammer of his revolver and laid the gun on the thwart behind him, tapping it for the attention of their prisoner. The destroyer swung round beam-on to them showing her gleaming side as she came foaming to a stop, her propellers thrashing up a boiling wake as she went astern. Sailors lounged about the deck, grinning and waving as they leaned against the guard rails. Bill looked at their prisoner and fixed him with a determined gaze. Then Harry waved to the destroyer, while the prisoner sat rigidly upon his thwart.

"Wave, you rotten Wop!" Bill dug his elbow into the Italian's stomach.

"*Pronto!*" hissed Harry, slowly edging towards the gun. "*Pronto!*"

Slowly the Italian lifted his hand and waved it. The swell from the destroyer's wash hit them and tossed the little boat almost on its beam-ends. An Italian curse instinctively leaped from the fisherman's lips, as he clung bitterly to the rigging for support. The oath rang across the water.

The white-clad officer on the bridge peered at them through his binoculars, Harry and Peter idly pulling at the ropes of the net. The suspense was unbearable. Peter felt his nerves reaching breaking point and it was all that he could do not to shout out a stream of abuse. Harry shrugged his shoulders and spread his arms wide, slowly shaking his head and indicating that they had no fish.

For a moment there was silence across the water. A shrill voice crackled from a loudhailer which was trained directly upon them from the bridge. Silence from the fishing boat.

Harry stiffened and glared fixedly at their prisoner who had edged towards the concealed revolver. Impatiently, the loudhailer crackled again. The sailors along the rail broke into good-natured laughter.

It was now or never. As Peter pulled listlessly at the ropes, he noticed that his fingers were trembling.

"Speak, Wop! Speak, pronto! Speak or I'll drill you dead and take you with us!" hissed Harry. There was no mistaking his intentions, as the Italian sat mesmerised by his captor's glaring eyes. With all his might, Peter willed the fisherman to save them, to save all four of them, for they would take the Italian with them once the shooting started.

The man stood up, transfixed in fear, his face twitching, a deathly white. Harry sat down, his hand sliding towards the revolver. The Italian watched from the corners of his petrified eyes, his mind considering his chances.

Bill loosened the knife in its scabbard.

And then the Italian's mouth jerked open. It worked spasmodically, hanging loosely, while saliva dribbled from the twitching corners. The officers on the bridge seemed suspicious. They stiffened in concentration, and picked up their binoculars once more.

"*Pronto! Pronto!*" hissed Harry, a dangerous gleam now smouldering in his bloodshot eyes.

A high-pitched gabble spat from the fisherman's mouth, quite unintelligible to them and the destroyer alike.

"Marsala, Marsala. Say we come from Marsala!"

The Italian became intelligible. He shouted once again, the word "Marsala" sounding like music in Peter's ears.

Harry waved and went on with his fishing. The Italian sat down trembling across the thwart, hands hanging limply at his sides. Bill spat delightedly over the side, and wiped the back of his hand across his mouth in the best Italian fashion, meanwhile glaring defiantly at the hostile destroyer.

"This is it!" Harry whispered to Peter.

The figures on the bridge waved towards Sicily and shouted instructions to the fishing boat, obviously giving them orders to return nearer to the island, and Harry stood up and waved in assent, at the same time starting to draw in his nets. As soon as the watching officers saw this, they seemed satisfied.

Slowly, lethargically, the white figures on the bridge straightened, turned their backs, and sauntered towards the centre of the compass-platform. The distant tinkling of Engine Room telegraphs rang across the water. The screws turned the glistering sea, the sleek white enemy gathered way and slowly slid past them, a last perfunctory wave flickering from the bridge.

"A-a-ah," sighed Harry, and, turning to the weeping Italian, he patted him on the back. "*Grazias, Señor,*" he continued, not beyond mixing Spanish with his limited Italian vocabulary.

Soon the destroyer was hull-down, her creaming stem disappearing below the hazy horizon.

"Surely nothing more can happen now?" Peter asked anxiously, as he sprawled across the sternsheets alongside Harry, while they sat drawing at the last of the black tobacco.

"Please God, no!" Harry replied, as he stripped off his evil-smelling jersey to allow his sweating body the joy of the beating sun.

"Proper skylark, ain't it, sir?" Bill exclaimed.

Even the Italian joined in the laughter.

CHAPTER 17

"… Next of Kin have been informed"

The only sound in the dimly-lit Control Room of His Majesty's Submarine *Rugged* was the laboured breathing of men struggling for life in the foul air.

But Joe was not yet beaten.

"Cheer up, for Pete's sake, we're not through yet," he muttered, his haggard face gleaming again with defiance. "They may not be as good as our gunnery school, Number One: a *short* and an *over* may not necessarily mean a *straddle*. The Wops' depth-charge pattern drill-book may be different!"

"Hope so, sir," gasped Number One, forcing a grimace of a smile even at this eleventh hour, for *Rugged* was now cornered, with one destroyer right astern of her and one on either bow.

"Destroyer attacking, sir!" Elliott's voice repeated wearily. "Green eight-oh."

"Well, chaps, pray to God, if you've never done so before," Joe said quietly, and then suddenly his head jerked upwards.

"Stop starboard, starboard fifteen, half-ahead port," he snapped, a fierce gleam of battle once more on his gaunt face.

Slowly the boat started to swing.

Tick-tick … tick-tick … tick-tick-tick… from all around whispered the spine-chilling accompaniment.

"They're in contact all right."

"Yes, sir," answered Elliott, as he slowly removed his headphones. "Five hundred yards, sir!"

But there was no need to make further reports. The evil cacophony was all about them, over them, around them, above and below them.

The attacker was overhead in a thunderous whirlpool of noise. At this very moment, her knife-like stem must be cutting the water above the fore-ends; her stem, well down in the foaming wake, must now be just short of the conning tower. Now, now, now was the moment she would be loosing her depth charges…

Throughout the boat, time stood still. Men peered upwards, waiting for the end. Ears strained to hear Death's final salutation: the smack! — smack-smack! of the charges slapping the surface, then the click! — click-click! of the springing detonators.

The tumult now swamped everything. The inferno of sound was loud, too loud… Joe closed his eyes. He was tired and could do no more.

Men had slipped to their knees, praying, waiting, waiting for oblivion, some with their eyes tightly shut, some looking upwards…

The thunder above them was interminable, but no one noticed that the inferno of sound was decreasing. Now, surely now, devastation must split them apart, down here in the depths?

A whispering sigh passed through the Control Room, like an evening breeze caressing silver poplar leaves on a summer's evening.

Joe slowly raised his head. "Well, I'll be…" he whispered, but then he galvanised into action.

"They've made a bloomer somewhere, Number One! Come on, let's not give them another chance! Slow ahead together, steer one-four-oh!"

But this time the searching hunter did not regain contact. The last attacking destroyer had been perfectly poised for the final kill and as she ran over the stricken submarine her Captain gave the order to let go her last pattern of depth charges, but the seaman on the traps had bungled his drill. The depth charges never left their traps and by the time the man had corrected himself, it was too late.

Instead, the destroyer thrashed ahead, amid furious recriminations from her two consorts, to circle for another try. Because of the mistake, they had allowed the trapped submarine precious minutes in which to make good her escape. Confusion reigned on the surface and *Rugged* seized her opportunity to slip through the net. The hunters did not realise that their quarry had escaped, however, for they continued hunting until they were relieved by a fresh team with more depth charges from Trapani.

Slowly but surely, *Rugged* sidled out of danger, away from the deadly hunters, but, alas! also away from the Spella rocks rendezvous.

"Issue an extra rum ration with supper, Number One."

"Aye, aye, sir."

The weary *Rugged* waited impatiently for the blessed mantle of darkness to fall, so that she could surface to recharge her batteries and replenish with fresh air.

Some ten miles offshore, and only five miles from the scene of the hunt, she surfaced without incident and set course for Malta, but in the minute Ward Room it was a sad circle that gathered for supper. There was little conversation although there was much to say. Their survival was balanced by the loss of three good friends.

"What a devilish thing is war, isn't it?" Joe confided to Number One when they were left alone. Seldom did these moments occur, and Easton was always surprised when they did.

"Yes, damnable! To save your own skin you sacrifice your friends."

"We tried, though!" Joe murmured, "but I wish I hadn't failed them."

"You did your best."

"That's not enough."

The moment was over.

The rest of the passage was uneventful except for a passing destroyer that steamed hull-down in the afternoon of the next day. She was steering westwards and seemed to be in a hurry, because her white wake showed clearly. By dawn, *Rugged* was off Fifla, but, as no minesweeper met her, she proceeded round to Lazaretto without escort. On the Lazaretto balcony stood a small knot of figures. They waved, caps circling in the air.

"Quite a reception committee!" Joe said quietly to Number One, as he conned *Rugged* through the boom and into the blue water of the harbour.

"Yes, sir, but we seem to have returned from the dead! Signal for you, sir" — and he handed a slip of paper to his Captain. The Signalman had been reading a winking light from the square signal station, high up in sun-bleached Valetta.

"From Captain, Tenth Submarine Flotilla," it read. "Congratulations on returning from the dead. I had just signalled Admiralty that you were missing."

"All's well that ends well, I suppose," replied Joe bitterly, as he gazed down upon the figure of Benson, his new Sub-Lieutenant, on the fore-casing.

The rust-blotched submarine circled inside the creek and came skilfully to her buoys abreast the Base.

CHAPTER 18

… To Fight Another Day

The night breeze failed them not. At dusk, as night once more drew a merciful curtain upon the sweltering bay, the sails of the little fishing boat flapped and filled. She shook herself and again gathered way. Once more her bows steadied on her homeward course. They slept fitfully, for hunger and thirst were now beginning to gnaw at their empty bellies. Peter and Harry took tricks on the tiller, while Bill kept a lookout. The Italian slept on the bottom boards, for they had discarded the nets to reduce weight.

With only an estimated forty miles between them and Malta and with the wind again conveniently on their starboard quarter, the small boat lifted her skirts and frolicked through the dark night.

But tonight there seemed no wickedness in the seas, no vicious battle to fight, no spite in the elements. Bowling along, they were awake at two in the morning, when the roar of an aircraft overhead shook them into alertness. Not one aircraft, but four! Four familiar shapes flying across their bows and disappearing on a course of east-south-east.

"Wimpeys! Dear old Wellingtons, back from a sortie!" shouted Harry hysterically.

"Ain't they lovely, sir?" Bill smiled in the darkness.

Harry laughed. "And they've even given us a course, Bill! They must be returning to base. You know what their base is, my boyos?" he sang out, bringing the boat round to her new course and following up the noise of the Wellingtons' fading engines.

"Malta — Malta — Malta, here we come," sang Peter, and even the Italian smiled, his teeth gleaming in the pale light of the stars.

At dawn, the diminutive island of Gozo, yellow and grey in the freshness of a new day, showed plainly to starboard.

"We'll sail right into Lazaretto with this leading wind, Peter," Harry yelled exultantly.

At two in the afternoon, a dirty little Sicilian fishing boat drifted listlessly off St. Paul's Bay, becalmed once again on the shimmering sea. The minesweeper which was sweeping the channel hove down upon it to investigate the lunatic occupants. Dark-skinned were the figures which waved, yelling and laughing as they danced ecstatically upon the thwarts.

"Madmen! These crazy lunatics seem to want us," observed the minesweeper's Captain as he peered through his binoculars. "Send the whaler's crew across, Number One, please."

The Ward Room of the Tenth Submarine Flotilla was in the centre of a large sandstone building on Lazaretto Island. It was a large, open hall with no doors, sparsely furnished with tables at the far end, and a primitive bar at the other. There were no carpets on the floor, and there were no chairs, but in the centre stood a battered billiard table, scene of many a 'bowls' game. Opposite the door was a huge, now empty, pigeon-holed letter-rack. When officers returned from patrol, this was their first port of call.

It was lunch-time and two small groups were chatting in separate corners of the mess. One group consisted of junior officers, *Rugged*'s new Sub-Lieutenant being the centre of the circle. The other was composed of the rotund figure of Captain 'S', Joe and two other Commanding Officers, just in from patrol.

Normally the hall was full of laughter and loud conversation, but today it was strangely quiet. Those who knew the ropes had only to glance at the letter-rack to know why. The pigeonholes now bore two empty nameplates.

"Tell me about it, Joe," Captain 'S' said kindly, when all the glasses had been filled.

There was a slight pause.

"Let's go outside, sir, if you don't mind. I'd rather tell you about it out there" — and his hand swept across the hall in a gesture of despair.

So the little group took itself outside to the veranda which bordered the creek and, when they had all seated themselves on the warm sandstone, Joe began his story. He talked quietly, with an occasional kind word from Captain 'S'. It was not easy and Joe's tired eyes focused themselves on the small minesweeper that was sliding through the boom. It was some time before he realised that the sweeper had not turned away to starboard to anchor in Sliema creek. Instead, she glided gently on towards Lazaretto.

"… and so, sir," he was saying, "I tried to close Spella rocks, but the heat was so intense—"

"Just a minute, Joe," 'S' interrupted, "what on earth is the sweeper doing so close? She doesn't come up here usually" — and he pointed to the grey minesweeper that now lay stopped in the aquamarine water, barely one hundred yards distant, and midway between Lazaretto Island and the Valetta battlements.

The khaki figure of the sweeper's Captain leaned over the bridge and his voice bellowed through a bell-shaped megaphone.

"Hullo, Lazaretto. I've got a surprise for you, and I'm doing you the honour of delivering the goods myself. I picked them up off St. Paul's Bay."

The little circle ashore had grown, and some twenty officers and men now crowded the balcony.

With pounding heart, Joe peered long at the sweeper. Then he heard a quiet cough behind him. It was Easton, his trusted First Lieutenant. There was complete silence from the little group, for no one dared to express an impossible hope.

As the whaler was lowered to the guard rails, the sheaves in the blocks on the falls sent their music squealing across the gap of water. Two wild and dishevelled figures then clambered over the rails, followed by another of slightly smaller build. They looked like grubby, Italian prisoners of war.

"More blasted Wops!" grumbled a disgusted voice from amongst the watching group ashore.

Joe was the first to recognize the three dirty 'Italians' who lifted their arms and began to shout hysterically, while the boat was being lowered to the water.

Joe's hand rose slowly for an instant, and then pandemonium broke loose. All the available sailors in the sweeper were crowding the guard rails and peering down at the whaler, as she shoved off from the ship's side. The sailors' voices broke into a bellow and they cheered until the reverberations echoed from the castle walls of Valetta, to be taken up again by the crowd now assembled on Lazaretto Island.

Little groups of Maltese, old men, women and jumping children had gathered on the Valetta side and were yelling themselves hoarse from the causeway. They danced up and down with joy, though they knew not why.

There was many a moist eye when the grey whaler bumped alongside and the dishevelled men jumped out of the sternsheets on to the sandstone steps of the island.

The first figure stood to attention and held out his hand to Captain 'S'.

"Reporting back, sir," the man said.

"Good to have you back, Harry," 'S' said huskily.

A second figure stood behind Lieutenant Arkwright, D.S.C., Royal Navy.

"Hullo, Sub!" Joe croaked, shaking Peter by the hand. "You've been a heck of a long time coming!"

Peter's eyes met those of his Captain.

"Sorry to be adrift, sir," he replied, smiling broadly, "but we wouldn't be here if it wasn't for Bill — sorry, sir, I mean Able Seaman Hawkins."

Bill blushed beneath his blond hair, shuffling his feet awkwardly in the background.

Arkwright turned about and dragged him before Captain 'S'. "Well done, Hawkins," 'S' smiled. "Well done!" He shook Bill warmly by the hand.

Bill was dumb, but his merry eyes twinkled. Captain 'S' threw his fatherly arms around them. He was laughing now, great gusts of laughter rolling across the Creek.

"How livid the Wops and Huns must be with each other," he chuckled. "Whose *Mare Nostrum* is it now?"

By the King's Order the names of Sub-Lieutenant Sinclair, Royal Navy, and of Able Seaman W. Hawkins, Royal Navy, were published in the London Gazette *on 11th June, 1942, as Mentioned in Dispatches for distinguished service in His Majesty's Submarines.*

— Extract from The National Press of 12th June, 1942.

GLOSSARY

ASDIC — The device by which submarines are detected. Submarines are also fitted with this device, when it is used as a hydrophone.

BEARING — The direction of an object.

BLOWERS — Machines with which to blow out the water in the tanks by using low-pressure air.

CORTICENE — A type of heavy linoleum used to cover the steel deck.

CRACK — To open a valve quickly, and to shut it again immediately.

E-BOAT — The fast enemy motor torpedo boat.

E.T.A. — Expected Time of Arrival.

FOCKE-WOLFE — German long-range reconnaissance aircraft.

FREE FLOOD — The open holes in the casing and tanks through which the water enters.

FRUIT MACHINE —A metal box into which all relevant attack data is fed, and from which the necessary information is extracted with which to carry out an attack.

GROUP DOWN — Low speed on the main electric motors, thus using up little electric power.

GROUP UP — High speed on the main electric motors, thus using up the battery power quickly.

H.E. — High Explosive.

H.E. — Hydrophone Effect, i.e. propeller noise.

HEAT — Slang for a submarine at the receiving end of a severe depth-charge attack.

H.P. — High Pressure.

HYDROPHONE — Underwater listening device.

JOLLY ROGER — Skull-and-crossbones flag, upon which emblems of sinkings are sewn. Flown to denote successes.

LAYER — A difference of temperature gradients in the ocean.

MAIN BALLAST KINGSTON — Water into the internal tanks amidships is allowed to enter through the Kingston Valves.

MAIN BALLAST TANKS — The tanks which give a submarine its buoyancy. All are fitted with main vents, numbers 1 and 6 being external, the remainder internal.

MESSERSCHMITT — Single-seater German fighter.

OLD MAN — Slang for Captain.

OUTSIDE E.R.A. — The Engine Room Artificer whose duty is at the panel in the Control Room, and who is therefore 'outside' the Engine Room.

PANEL — The conglomeration of valves, etc., all centralised at one position.

'Q' TANK — The emergency tank for quick diving. When flooded, the tank makes the submarine ten tons heavier than her normal dived trim. After diving, this extra water is blown out of 'Q' tank by high-pressure air. If this tank is required to be flooded when dived, its vent has merely to be opened, either into the submarine or outboard, and the sea will rush into 'Q' tank. In wartime, for obvious reasons, 'Q' tank is always kept flooded when the submarine is on the surface.

STICK — A salvo of aircraft bombs, falling in a straight line.

STICK — Slang for 'periscope'.

THIRD HAND — The Third Officer in a submarine.

U-BOAT — Enemy submarine.

URSULA SUIT — Waterproof overalls in general use, designed by the Commanding Officer of H.M. Submarine *Ursula*.

WIMPEY —Wellington medium bomber, British.

WOP — Slang for 'Italian'.

A NOTE TO THE READER

Dear Reader,
If you have enjoyed the novel enough to leave a review on **Amazon** and **Goodreads**, then we would be truly grateful.

Sapere Books is an exciting new publisher of brilliant fiction and popular history.

To find out more about our latest releases and our monthly bargain books visit our website: **saperebooks.com**